PRAISE FOR THE CHOSEN

The novels make me weep the same way Jerry's son's *The Chosen* does, which oughta keep tissue stocks rising. Don't say I didn't warn you.

Mark Lowry Singer, humorist

The novels bring the story of Jesus and his followers to life in a way never before seen. By imagining plausible back stories to well-known characters, Jerry allows us to see ourselves in them and bring our own frailties to Christ and draw closer to him. The streaming series and these novels may very well usher in a global revival of love for Christ and move us to love others as he loves us.

Terry Fator Singing ventriloquist/impressionist and winner of *America's Got Talent*

If you have ever wondered what it might have been like to have been a friend or family member of the twelve disciples of Jesus, *The Chosen* novels, written by Jerry Jenkins, will transport you into the minds of the early followers of Christ. You will be reminded of their humanity and might even see yourself as you seek to follow the One who still radically changes lives today.

Gary D. Chapman Author of *The Five Love Languages*

A fictional work that expands on Bible stories is successful when it drives you back into the Word of God. And Jerry Jenkins's novels paint a beautiful behind-the-scenes portrait of the first people whose lives were transformed by Jesus. The words chosen for poignant dialogues strike home in deep and powerful ways. Keep a tissue on hand; your heart will be moved.

Joni Eareckson Tada Joni and Friends International Disability Center

The stories of Jesus' life and ministry in the New Testament are some of the Bible's most encouraging and illuminating passages. Jerry Jenkins has once again provided a gripping story that will point readers back to the beauty of Christ as revealed in Scripture.

Jim Daly President and CEO of Focus on the Family

Well, Jerry Jenkins has done it again in *The Chosen* novel series. The depth of emotion he captures in those around Jesus only deepens our understanding of what Jesus goes through in this escalating, tension-filled period of his ministry. We were hooked on page one and left wanting more at the end. If you love watching *The Chosen*, this is a must read.

Al & Phil Robertson Authors & Co-hosts of The Unashamed Podcast

The Chosen novels connect me again to Jesus. And, oh, what a Savior he is!

Ernie Haase Grammy-nominated tenor and founder of Ernie Haase and Signature Sound

Writing with accuracy and immediacy, Jerry Jenkins immerses us in the greatest story ever told in a fresh and powerful way. Jenkins is a master of taking profound scenes and themes from the Bible and weaving them into captivating journeys, whether they are centered on the time of Jesus or the end times. *The Chosen* novels expand on the amazing TV series and will move readers through the unique retelling of the gospel story.

Travis Thrasher, bestselling author and publishing industry veteran

The only thing better than the film is the book, and the only thing better than the book is the film. Jerry B. Jenkins has taken the brilliant project of Dallas Jenkins—this look into the lives of those Jesus *chose* to be his followers, his friends, and his "family"—and gone a step (or more) deeper. Readers will be drawn as quickly into the pages as viewers were into the theatrical moments of *The Chosen* film project. I cannot say enough about both.

Eva Marie Everson, president, Word Weavers International, and bestselling author

The TV series brought me to tears, but Jerry's book showed me the Jesus I wanted to know. He draws the reader into the humanity of Jesus. The story captures authentic insight into his personality. His love, humor, wisdom, and compassion are revealed for every person he encountered. Through Jesus' interaction with the real-life characters, I too experienced the Savior who calls the lost, poor, needy, and forsaken into an authentic relationship.

DiAnn Mills, Christy Award winner and director, Blue Ridge Mountain Christian Writers Conference

Jerry Jenkins is a master storyteller who has captured the action, drama, and emotion of *The Chosen* TV series in written form. Far more than a mere synopsis, Jerry has shaped and developed the episodes into fast-paced novels. If you enjoyed the series, you will savor the stories again as Jerry brings each character to life. And if you haven't watched the series, these novels will make you want to start … just as soon as you've finished reading the books, of course!

Dr. Charlie Dyer, professor-at-large of Bible, host of *The Land and the Book* radio program

The Chosen series is Jesus in present tense. The story engages the heart and allows you to experience what people see and feel and taste. Get your feet dirty with them. It will transform *your* present tense.

Chris Fabry, bestselling author of *The War Room* and the *Left Behind: The Kids* series

What better way to bring the gospel to life than to explore the impact Jesus had upon those with whom he came into contact. And what better encouragement for those of us today who hunger for his life-changing presence. I heartily recommend both the TV series and the books for any who long to experience his transforming love more deeply.

Bill Myers, author of the bestselling novel *Eli*

For over 70 years I have heard the redemptive stories of the Bible told without the emotion and passion that would indicate real people actually experienced these events. Who drained the life blood from the hearts of these men and women? Jerry Jenkins's account is a refreshing transfusion that restores life to the people of the Bible and to its redemptive story. You will feel like you are there.

Ken Davis, award-winning author, speaker, and communication consultant

To a girl who cut her teeth on Bible stories, it's no easy task to transform all-too-familiar characters into an experience that is fresh and alive. That is precisely what Jerry Jenkins has done with these novels. From the first chapter, I was enamored. And by the second and third, I started to see the Jesus I've long loved with new eyes and a more open heart. These books offer the reader more than mere diversion. They offer the possibility of true transformation.

Michele Cushatt, author of *Relentless:The Unshakeable Presence of a God Who Never Leaves*

The story of Jesus has been told and re-told, but with this beautiful novelization, Jerry Jenkins brings unique and compelling perspectives to the biblical accounts of Jesus and his followers, echoing those in the acclaimed *The Chosen* TV series created by Dallas Jenkins. As someone who always thinks the book was better than the movie, I was delighted to discover a book and film series that are equally enthralling and even life changing.

Deborah Raney, author of *A Nest of Sparrows* and *A Vow to Cherish*

Any author who has written and sold as many books as Jerry Jenkins might be forgiven a tendency to lean on familiar structure while producing yet another manuscript. Fortunately, Jenkins is not just "any author." While the broad storyline of Jesus choosing his disciples will be familiar to some, it is the author's deft handling of the historical language and customs of the time that give his newest release a vibrancy rarely felt by readers of any novel. These novels have been crafted with wise and insightful context. These are the books Jerry Jenkins was born to write.

Andy Andrews, *New York Times* bestselling author of *The Traveler's Gift, The Noticer,* and *Just Jones*

The CHOSEN®

UPON THIS ROCK

NOVEL FOUR

JERRY B. JENKINS

BroadStreet
PUBLISHING

Upon This Rock

The primary source of Scripture quotations is *The Holy Bible, English Standard Version*. Copyright © 2001 by CrosswayBibles, a publishing ministry of Good News Publishers. Used by permission. All rights reserved.

Editors: Leilani Squires and Michelle Winger

"The Chosen" and the "School of Fish" designs are trademarks of The Chosen, LLC, and are used with permission.

9781424567713 (hardcover)
9781424567737 (softcover)
9781424567720 (eBook)

Library of Congress Cataloging-in-Publication Data can be found at www.loc.gov.

Printed in Malaysia

28 27 26 25 24   5 4 3 2 1

To Josh Lindstrom

Based on *The Chosen,* a multi-season TV show
created and directed by Dallas Jenkins
and written by Ryan M. Swanson,
Dallas Jenkins, and Tyler Thompson.

"There's little doubt *The Chosen* will become one of
the most well-known and celebrated pieces
of Christian media in history."
MOVIEGUIDE® Magazine

NOTE

The Chosen was created by lovers of and believers in the Bible and Jesus Christ. Our deepest desire is that you delve into the New Testament Gospels for yourself and discover Jesus.

Contents

*"…blessed is she who believed
that there would be
a fulfillment of what was spoken
to her from the Lord."*

LUKE 1:45

PART 1

The Dance of Death

Chapter 1

THE NAME

Nazareth

Young Mary still glows from the visitation. Had she heard this story rather than experienced it, she would not believe it in a million years. But the Lord Himself sends the angel Gabriel to her, a no one from nowhere, with a message so outlandish that at first it simply terrifies her.

But it is true. She, a virgin, is to bear the long-awaited Messiah, Son of the Most High God. She tells only her parents and her fiancé, who himself does not believe it until he is also visited in a dream. Almost as bizarre, the angel tells Mary that her mother's sister, her aged Aunt Elizabeth, will also bear a son. This Mary has to see.

Nearly ninety now, Elizabeth has been barren her whole life. Though women are forbidden to travel alone, and against Joseph's better judgment, Mary persuades her reluctant father to negotiate transport for her to the Judean hill country where Elizabeth resides with her husband Zechariah, a priest.

Mary is intrigued that even after paying the ragtag leader of a small caravan—consisting of a few meager animals—her father continues to talk earnestly with the man, no doubt impressing upon him how precious he considers this beloved cargo. At last her father helps her mount up and entrusts her small bag to the man. Mary is amused that the leader's wife, whom he calls Tzofi, doesn't even try to hide her curiosity.

"What was that all about?" Tzofi asks her husband.

He shrugs. "As long as people pay, we don't ask questions."

"It's just that—what business would someone, like her, from Nazareth, have—"

"He asked us to be discreet."

"Why?" Tzofi says. "And why choose us for passage?"

"As long as people pay, we don't—"

"Sometimes when a virgin gets sent away to stay with relatives for a while, it's because—she's not."

"Tzofi, don't be crude."

Including a night on the ground and a few brief rest stops, the ninety-mile trek takes nearly two days. Mary is largely ignored but strangely feels safe—despite that the road is widely considered dangerous. Besides the fact that Tzofi and her husband are armed and have clearly been leading caravans for a long time, Mary rests in the knowledge that God has a reason for protecting her.

The man brings the caravan to a stop, gazing at a collection of humble homes atop a rise. "Your stop, ma'am."

Retrieving her bag, Mary thanks the couple and adds, "May God go with you on the rest of your journey."

"God be with you," Tzofi says.

"On the rest of *your* journey," the man says, leering.

His meaning is not lost on Mary, but she doesn't care. Her spirits remain high, close as she is to seeing her beloved aunt and uncle. Taking a deep breath, she ascends the hill.

Elizabeth hums to herself in her kitchen, working around her plump belly while deftly slicing through a block of honeycomb. She's startled by someone calling out, "Elizabeth! Zechariah! Shalom!"

The old woman drops the knife and places a hand over her bump.

"I'm here! Elizabeth?!"

The old woman staggers backward, eyes wide.

Mary smiles and reaches to embrace her grinning uncle as he mince steps toward the door. He's still getting around fairly well for a man in his nineties.

"Zechariah!"

But he doesn't respond, seems agitated, fumbles for a chalkboard.

"Uncle?" she says, concerned.

He quickly writes a greeting.

"What?" she says. And here comes her aunt. "Oh, Elizabeth!"

They hug each other tight and Mary steps back, gesturing to the old woman's belly.

Elizabeth grabs her hand. "Zach can't talk right now. I'll explain later." Breathless, she leads Mary to the courtyard and they sit. Elizabeth closes her eyes and blurts, "Blessed are you among women, and blessed is the fruit of your womb."

"My-my womb? Wait, how did you kn—I suppose nothing should surprise me anymore. When my messenger told me about your news, I was so happy, knowing how long you've suffered. I want to hear all about it."

"Something better than that is happening," Elizabeth says, seeming to speak faster than she can think. "So humbling. Why is this granted to me that the mother of my Lord should come to me?"

"The mother of your Lord? Did a messenger tell you about me?"

"When I heard your voice, just the sound of your greeting, my baby leapt for joy. And blessed are you who believed there would be a fulfillment of what was spoken to you from Adonai."

"So a messenger *did* tell you."

"The messenger appeared to your uncle, and Zechariah said, 'I don't believe it.'"

Mary chuckles. "Can we slow down a moment? You're not in a condition to be losing your breath."

Elizabeth smiles and sighs. "The reason Zechariah could not speak with you is because he didn't believe the message from God about me."

"I wasn't sure at first either," Mary says.

"I feel bad he must go through this." She leans close and whispers, "But I admit, sometimes I don't mind the quiet." They laugh, and she continues, "But he wrote down for me what was said, and I've memorized every word. The baby's name will be John."

"Wait. Not Zechariah? Why John?"

"I don't know for certain, but perhaps because he will not be a priest like his father. Maybe he'll walk a different path for God. A bigger one, because Zach was also told that John will turn many of the children of Israel to the Lord their God, and he will go before him in the spirit and power of Elijah to turn the hearts of the fathers to the children and the disobedient to the wisdom of the just, to make ready for the Lord a people prepared." Elizabeth's voice becomes thick with emotion. "To prepare the way for…" She nods at Mary's womb, and Mary is overcome. "Oh!" Elizabeth adds, putting a hand on her own bulge. "There he goes again!" She grabs Mary's hand and presses it to her tummy. "Feel it?"

"Yes!"

"It's like he can't wait to get started."

Chapter 2

THE DANCE

Herod's Palace, Machaerus

A teenage dancer stands barefoot, sweating in a sunlight-bathed room with floor-to-ceiling arches that open to an outdoor promenade. Her teacher, a man in his thirties, leads her through a series of moves, alternately barking and cooing commands. She strikes a pose, a hand high above her head, fingers spread and taut.

The man reaches to gently close her hand. "More feminine, more purposeful. Flip the palm. Not flat. Cupped as if to catch the rain." He stares at her feet. "Too flat! Raise the heel. Higher! Up! Onto your toes."

She tries.

"The moment you feel yourself start to fall, bend and swivel so your left foot catches you. No! It cannot look like an accident. You must look in control even when you aren't! Again!"

A servant places a chair at the far end of the room. The dancer repeats the moves, faster, better. "Closer," her instructor calls out. "Still not all the way there."

An hour later

They're still there. The girl is getting it. Her choreographer draws with chalk a line on the floor. "This is the last place your feet hit before the final turns, understand?" He snaps his fingers. "And go!"

She rounds off a flip and twist that leave her about five feet from the chair. "Too short! Again!" He casually slides onto the chair, playing her royal audience. "Include the instruments this time. Be precise."

Musicians in the corner attack drums and cymbals, and he signals her again. This time she lands inches from his chair, freezes, and appears to struggle to control her breathing.

"That's my girl."

She looks relieved.

He guides her through a long, slow bow, urging her lower and lower, fingers up. "It's all in the fingers. Slower. Make him wait. Make it hurt." She raises her face, lashes heavy and flirtatious, finally giving him direct eye contact. "There! Now let's paint your face."

"Not yet!" comes a command from the doorway. "One more time," Queen Herodias says. "From the top. It must be perfect."

Chapter 3

THE RETURN

The Mission House, formerly Matthew's home, Capernaum
Since joining Jesus' growing band of followers, the Egyptian
Tamar can't deny the ups have outweighed the downs. After seeing
Jesus heal a leper, she and her friends lowered their paralytic mate
through the roof of a house in which Jesus was preaching, and
the rabbi himself told her that her faith was strong and beautiful.

Tamar had soon been welcomed by the disciples and the
two other women closest to Jesus—Mary of Magdala, who
told of the master having exorcised seven demons from her,
and Ramah, Thomas's beloved who had served as vintner at a
wedding in Cana where Jesus miraculously turned water into
wine. How long has it been since Tamar has seen the beautiful
youngster? Too long. Ramah had sojourned back to her father in
hopes of being there when Thomas asked the man for her hand
in marriage. Thomas had returned emptyhanded, and Ramah
stayed behind. How Tamar missed her, despite that they had
their differences.

Tamar and Ramah and Mary had found that familiarity had allowed a modicum of contempt to invade their camaraderie. Living and serving Jesus together in close proximity had unveiled misunderstandings, even petty jealousies Tamar knew were not honoring to their rabbi. So they had devoted themselves to reconciling. She and Mary had come to a warm meeting of the minds and seemed now on good footing together. Tamar knew the same would be true with Ramah because she found painful the young girl's absence. One does not miss rivals. One misses someone she cares about.

Tamar gathers her bag and paperwork while eavesdropping on the old, retired fisherman Zebedee and his two sons, James and John, whom Jesus nicknamed the Sons of Thunder. The love among these three men is palpable—though they squabble like schoolchildren. Zebedee is so obviously proud Jesus chose his boys to follow him that he can hardly contain himself. And now that he has given up his lifelong trade, even selling his boat, to dive into an entirely new pursuit, he appears giddy to be helping finance Jesus' ministry.

The three men are outside, and through the window Tamar watches them load onto a cart four large pithari jars full of Zebedee's newly pressed oil. Of course they're bickering, as it seems all men do. Tamar decides this must be their bizarre way of expressing their affection. She's also surprised at their choice of jars, as they are of Greek origin. Most of the disciples have little positive to say about the Greeks, but it seems everyone uses their jars for one purpose or another. Even the women have found that water stored in pithari jars evaporates in sweltering weather, somehow cooling a room.

Tamar can't help but smile as the men seem to have clear but differing ideas of how the jar packing should go. "These must not break," Zebedee says. "Understand?"

"Yes, Abba," James says.

"Our very first press," Zebedee continues, "sacred first fruits, holy to Adonai."

"But the way James has them situated," John says, "they won't make it to the synagogue in one piece."

A conveyance shambles to a stop outside, but the men don't appear to notice. It's a wine cart driven by a woman of about thirty who must be the vigneron. But next to her... Tamar drops everything and rushes outside. "Are my eyes lying?!" she says, beaming as she helps Ramah down and they embrace.

"Shalom! Shalom!" Ramah exults, grabbing her bag and paying the driver.

"It's so good to have you back!" Tamar says.

"I know!"

"I want to hear everything!"

The men remain oblivious and continue quarreling. "Every road is riddled with potholes," John says. "Where does all our tax money go?"

"You mean the shekel you owed last year?" his big brother says. "Look, there's straw between them to keep them from knocking against each other."

"Straw won't do us any good if they bounce out of the cart."

Zebedee sighs. "This is not happening."

"Strap them down," John says.

"Oh, okay," James says. "You've got rope then? I didn't think so. We're not fishermen anymore."

Ramah shakes her head. "So nothing's changed?"

"They've been at it since you left," Tamar says.

Zebedee finally notices. "Ah, Ramah!" he says. "You aren't doing anything. Come lend a hand."

"Ramah!" James says.

John says, "When did you get here?!"

The brothers hurry to her.

"I've been here a while, but you were—busy."

"Arguing like this is not good for the oil," their father says.

James shoots him a look. "What?"

"This will be used in sacrificial offerings as a pleasing aroma to Adonai, to anoint the high priest and his sons."

"Not if it's seeping into the cracks of the city's streets," John says.

James says, "So what are we supposed to do, carry them?"

"You'll trip!" Zebedee says.

"I'm not Andrew, Abba," James says. "My footing is solid."

The women wave them off with a smile and reenter the house.

Zebedee is exasperated but grateful to be working with his sons again. Even their arguing amuses him.

John says, "Your feet may be solid, but your hands are filthy."

James looks at his hands and quickly reaches to the ground. "Rope! Ha ha!" The brothers work together tying the jars in place. James turns to Zebedee. "Abba, the blessing. They're expecting us on the hour."

"Ah, of course. As best as I can remember—" He closes his eyes. "'Blessed are You, Lord our God, King of the universe, Who is good and bestows good. Let the favor of the Lord our God be upon us and establish the work of our hands upon us; yes, establish the work of our hands!'"

Zebedee releases a deep breath and smiles, opening his eyes to his sons regarding him with huge grins. "What? What are you looking at? Why are you smiling? Did I mess up the prayer?"

"It's nothing," James says. "It's just—"

"The Greeks," John says, "they put on plays—"

"We don't talk about that sort of filth!" Zebedee says.

"Yes, I know, I'm just saying that they break up the plays into acts. And you're starting a new act."

Zebedee studies him. "Tragedy or comedy?"

"I guess we're about to find out," James says, moving to the front of the cart.

The formerly blind Shula and the formerly lame Barnaby appear. "Sorry to interrupt," she says, "but we heard Ramah was back."

"How did you hear that?" John says.

Barnaby shrugs. "We hear everything. It's what we do."

"We also happen to know," Shula says, "that if she is back, Thomas would like to meet her in a forest clearing of the Terebinth Grove."

"He can't be alone with her," James says.

"Barnaby and I will chaperone."

Barnaby nods, raising his eyebrows. Shula yanks him toward the house.

Chapter 4

PRETENDING

Machaerus Palace

Joanna once reveled in her and her husband's exquisitely appointed quarters. She'd had what any woman would have dreamt of—marriage to a man in the upper echelon of King Herod Antipas's most trusted advisers, with an income to match. Chuza proved loyal to the royal even through the tough times—like now, when the crazy wilderness preacher and baptizer, the infamous John, called out the king for divorcing his wife and marrying his half-brother's divorced wife Herodias.

Herod had followed Chuza's advice and had John the Baptizer arrested, but he refused to execute the man because he actually enjoyed hearing him preach. Joanna found herself intrigued by the vagabond preacher and covertly visited him in the dungeon beneath the palace. When she discovered her own husband too was guilty of adultery, she demanded to know from John why he had not also exposed Chuza.

In her discussions with the Baptizer, Joanna became fascinated with the man he claimed was the long-prophesied

Messiah, Jesus of Nazareth. She traveled a long distance to hear him preach and became a clandestine follower, supporting his ministry and even sneaking in one of his disciples—Andrew, originally a disciple of the Baptizer—to see John. Meanwhile, she all but abandoned her duplicitous husband, creeping back to their quarters for necessities only when she was sure he was away. Now she returns temporarily, only to keep up appearances by attending the king's banquet scheduled for this evening.

She makes her way down a luxurious hallway and presses her ear to the door of their elaborate rooms. Hearing nothing, she peers in and enters. In the sumptuous boudoir, she opens a wardrobe where she riffles through a selection of elegant gowns. Vanity spurs her to look her best, but revenge nudges her toward something plainer, more sedate. No sense rewarding her wayward husband by letting him show her off.

She moves to the window at the sound of a cart pulling up. Servants unload a massive amphora of wine, a two-handled jar with a narrow neck. Others carry various lamps and torches. The door opens behind her. "Joanna?"

Her shoulders droop—the very man she doesn't want to see until she has to. "Chuza, I'm in here." She steps out, holding a gown. "What are you doing here? It's the middle of the day."

"A man has to explain what he's doing in his own quarters? What are *you* doing here?"

"A wife has to explain what she's doing in her own quarters?"

"I've been looking for you," he says. "But I didn't expect you in here. You haven't slept here in weeks."

"I wonder why *that* could be."

He looks ready to fire back but calmly says, "Listen, I'm not here to fight. I wanted to make sure you're fine for the banquet tonight."

"Why wouldn't I be?"

"And that's what you're wearing? It looks great."

"I'll consider something else then."

"Fine," he says. "Let's just be sure to have a good time, and—"

"And?"

"And nothing. Have a good time. Cooperate. Regardless how the evening goes, let's be sure to have a good time."

"Cooperate?" she says. "What's this about?"

"What do you mean? I just want us to have a good t—"

"You're not a good liar, Chuza."

"Neither are you. We know you've spoken privately with the Baptizer."

This gives her pause. "What does that have to do with anything? Wait, who sent you to talk with me?"

"I—no one—never mind. I just wanted my wife to—"

"Don't tell me to have a good time again. You haven't cared about that since you met Cassandra. Is Herod planning something with John?"

"No! No, he just finds him interesting. You know that."

"Yes, and I know it would be unwise for him to do anything rash when the people consider John a prophet. Herod should be cautious."

"I'm aware of your support for John. Just smile and pretend tonight. That's all I'm asking."

"Oh, I understand smiling and pretending, Chuza. I've had a lot of practice."

Chapter 5

LAUNDRY LESSONS

Shore of the Sea of Galilee

Simon, the former Zealot who has been nicknamed Zee by Jesus' disciples to differentiate him from Simon the former fisherman, is showing Judas how to wash clothes. "You've really never done this before?" he asks the once businessman.

"No. My business partner Hadad and I always had the laundry sent out."

Must have been nice, Zee thinks. Even the Zealots trained their men to take care of themselves. And he enjoys such tasks, not because they are fun in themselves, but because they remind him of the difference in his life since Jesus healed his brother. That obliterates any doubt or animosity toward spiritual matters. Nothing can change his mind about his new master's identity. He serves the Messiah, the Son of the living God.

Zee knows Judas shares his devotion to Jesus but wonders how he feels about now living like a pauper. "You have no savings left?" he asks him.

Judas shakes his head. "I had to divest my shares in the company in order to follow Jesus."

"A small price," Zee says, demonstrating the steps to do the wash. "And a wise choice."

"Well, sure," Judas says. "I mean, that's an understatement, but it turns out one wise choice only highlights how much practical wisdom I *don't* have—like how to wash clothes."

"Lucky for you, it's not that hard."

Zee motions for Judas to set his clothes into a large bucket and pours a few drops of a thick liquid from an alabaster bottle into the water.

"What is that?" Judas says.

"Some salts, oils extracted from plants, animal fat."

"Eew. Wish I hadn't asked."

Zee swirls the clothes in the bucket with a stick. "See, it's saturated. Then we take the clothes out and rinse them in the sea."

"You know," Judas says, mirroring Zee's every move, "if our funds weren't so low, we could hire people to do the wash, giving us more time to get to the real work and expand the ministry."

"And how would that look to people?"

"Like we're maximizing our time and resources to build the kingdom of the Messiah."

"You think the followers of Jesus are unwilling to perform mundane tasks?"

"You imagine a contingency for something unsaid," Judas says. "No one is examining Jesus' books. We should be out there spreading the word, gathering more followers."

"But, Judas, this is what the people we talk to do—laundry. If we appear lofty and too important for daily tasks, we will no longer be relatable." Zee takes a garment to a large white rock. "Now we ball it up and knead it hard against the rock." Judas tries it. "Harder," Zee adds. "It gets the water out and dislodges dirt from between the fibers."

As Judas scrubs, he says, "I'm not saying there couldn't be a perception problem. I'm just saying we could cross that bridge when we come to it. For now, we could do more if we had more funding."

"Well, there is Zebedee's olive oil business."

"Which hasn't brought in a shekel."

"Yet," Zee says, moving back to the sea where he dips the garment. "Judas, you are learned."

"Thank you."

"But you are not wise."

Judas stops and laughs. "Oh. Okay. Thanks for that. I liked the *learned* part."

"You have dedicated your life to a teacher, yes?"

Judas cocks his head. "He walks on water and controls the wind and waves, but sure, he's a teacher too."

"And yet you have overlooked his lessons to find faults in something you don't understand. There are lessons in everything he asks and shares."

"Fine. Where do I start?"

Zee knows Judas is asking about much more than the laundry but says, "Next, rinse away what's been scrubbed out. You're making the garment new again. Now my favorite part—" Holding one corner of the garment, Zee slams it on the rock over and over, like he's trying to beat it to death. "This is for those last most stubborn bits of what was there before. Ultimately this will help it dry faster too."

Judas tries but with less graceful swings and slams. "I always wondered how it is you never stink, even though you're exercising all the time. The sweat is no match for your strength."

"I have to do something with my strength," Zee says, "now that I don't need it anymore—or at least not in the way I thought I would."

"See?" Judas says. "You have it too."

"Have what?" Zee says, heading back to the water.

"You have an old way of being in the world, and you left it behind. Yet you can't really shake all of it, so you've adapted it."

"Third and final rinse. I'm not sure I follow."

"I left behind a way of life," Judas says. "And while I may be living radically differently than before, I just can't keep from seeing how we could do things faster and more efficiently."

"Did Jesus ask you to run his ministry more efficiently?"

"No, just to keep the purse."

"Then keep the purse."

"But Zee, all those people he fed in the Decapolis—they weren't all poor. They were just far from home with nothing to eat. If we had taken up a collection from just ten percent of the five thousand, just ten percent—a fraction of people's offerings of gratitude from those who could afford to give—we wouldn't be in such dire straits, waiting to do important work until revenue kicks in from Zebedee's olive oil."

They head for the trees to hang the garments. Zee says, "If Jesus wanted to take up an offering, he would have. You're asking why he didn't do it the way you'd have done it before you met him?"

"The old me would have sold those loaves."

Zee stares at him. "You should be asking to whom his charity was a lesson."

"I believe in his words and his lessons. They changed my life. But they're not where this ends. He's the Messiah, Zee."

"I know."

"Do you? Because if he is the Son of David and is to fulfill Isaiah's prophecy that 'the mountain of the Lord's house shall be established on the top of the mountains and shall be exalted above the hills; and all nations shall flow to it,' it's time for us to move faster. He won't become king by amassing no resources of power. It's unheard of."

Zee stops and looks Judas in the eye. "*He's* unheard of. Prophesied but never seen." He softens. "Your clothes are still dirty."

Judas laughs. "Come on, Zee. It's my first time. Plus, I'm not as strong as you."

"So put your ingenuity into it. Jesus asked us to get it done. There was a reason."

"You sure about that? I'm pretty sure clean clothes are their own virtue."

"It will become more clear," Zee says. "When I was new to this, I had some hard lessons to learn, believe me."

Judas sniffs a garment. "Animal fat? How? Wouldn't there be chunks?"

"Well," Zee says, "it's heated and melted and run through a sieve to separate the solids, sort of like the way you sift wheat, shaking it over a strainer to get rid of the impurities—separate the good grain from the bad."

Chapter 6

TASTE TEST

Capernaum Synagogue courtyard

Zebedee cannot remember feeling such tension since the births of both his sons. But now, here they are, with Tamar in tow, arriving with the pithari jars all still in one piece.

"Shalom!" the temple administrator calls out. It's Jairus, whose daughter Jesus raised from the dead not so long before. "You're right on the hour as agreed—a good sign already." The man impulsively embraces Zebedee's sons—no doubt because they were present at the raising of his daughter—but he quickly regains a sense of decorum and whispers, "Of course, I suppose I should expect nothing less from—*his* followers."

John shushes him as Rabbi Akiva appears at the door of the temple, chest puffed. "We haven't the time for pleasantries!"

Zebedee feels like a scolded child and approaches with reverence, the others following. "The woman will wait outside," the rabbi adds.

"But I helped make the—"

"Tamar," Zebedee says, "just for the transaction." He sees the pain in her face and is grateful when James offers to stay back with her and watch the cart.

Capernaum synagogue bet midrash
Zebedee can barely control himself as Jairus, Rabbi Akiva, and Yussif settle at a table set with oil lamps and small dishes. He catches Yussif's apparent look of support as the Pharisee seems to surreptitiously glance at him and John. He fights to not get ahead of himself, but he can't help imagining the honor of winning the synagogue's business and helping finance Jesus' ministry. He snaps to attention when Rabbi Akiva addresses him directly.

"First, can you confirm that this anointing oil was blended by the perfumer according to the formula laid out in the Book of Moses?"

"To the letter, Rabbi."

"Recite it, please."

Zebedee is so glad he took the time to memorize the formula. Now if he can only bring it all to mind under such pressure. He steals a peek at a scribe in the corner who has a scroll laid out on a podium and bears a yad pointer. "Of liquid myrrh 500 shekels," Zebedee begins, feeling his confidence grow, despite his racing pulse. "And of sweet-smelling cinnamon half as much, that is 250, and 250 of aromatic cane, and 500 of cassia, according to the shekel of the sanctuary. And a hint of olive oil."

The rabbi looks to the scribe who nods and says, "Word for word."

All three men at the table lift their oil lamps and hold the glass drams up to the flames.

"Extremely well-racked and purged," Yussif says.

"Clear," Jairus says. "Bright."

The rabbi curls his mouth and Zebedee fears the man is straining to find something to criticize. Meanwhile Jairus and Yussif taste the oil and look pleasantly surprised.

"It does stay on my fingers," the rabbi says.

Stays on his fingers?! "With all respect, Rabbi," Zebedee says, "we believe the viscosity is due to the correct amount of myrrh. The gum resin is expensive. It has binding qualities necessary for—"

"Yes," the rabbi says. "I know what myrrh is for." He wipes his fingers. "It's not what I'm used to. It's harder to wipe off. Jairus, why are we considering a new oil supplier anyway?"

Oh, no.

"Our current vendor," Jairus says, "travels a great distance from Judea and—"

"From the Gethsemane groves nearest the Holy City," the rabbi says. "There are none better."

"That may be true," Yussif says, "by way of proximity to Jerusalem."

"Nearest to the temple containing the Holy of Holies, man! The presence. Of. God. You think we should use a vendor farther away than that?"

"But, Rabbi, Rome has demarcated Judea as a separate province from Galilee."

"I would like to leave Rome out of this," the rabbi says.

Jairus says, "They imposed an import tax on goods from Judea."

The rabbi appears to consider this. "Better price and fair quality has its appeal. Still, oil from Gethsemane ..."

"In addition to the tariff," Yussif says, "we currently also pay for shipping and labor. Zebedee is local."

The rabbi turns to Zebedee. "You will never charge us a shipping fee?"

THE CHOSEN: UPON THIS ROCK

"Never, Rabbi. I will put it in writing."

Jairus says, "I believe this is higher quality for half the price, Rabbi Akiva. If you think the congregation can manage without the Gethsemane olives ..."

The rabbi falls silent.

"I don't know much about economics, Rabbi," Yussif says. "But by supporting a small local business, we help Capernaum."

The rabbi levels a gaze at him. "You may drop the façade, Yussif. You honestly think I don't know who your father is?"

Yussif pales, but the point is lost on Zebedee.

Jairus jumps in. "Yussif has a point. It's about responsible stewardship of the people's tithes and our time. As chief administrator of this synagogue, I consider the matter settled. Zebedee, congratulations on your fine work."

Zebedee shares a smile with him and feels he can breathe again.

Rabbi Akiva appears to want the last word, perhaps to save face. "I do not dispute your logic regarding the allocation of resources. But let the record state that I voiced reticence at the notion of abandoning the Gethsemane vendor. I want future generations to know that at least one person advocated for tradition and precedent over finances and practicality."

Jairus nods to the scribe. "Please reflect the rabbi's dissent in the record."

"So noted," the man says.

As the Pharisees rise, Jairus says, "Zebedee, please accompany me to my office to discuss a fee structure."

Chapter 7

INSULT UPON
INSULT

Machaerus Palace

Joanna is eager to visit John the Baptizer in the dungeon, so she disguises herself in a hooded cloak. She peeks into the hall where the opulent banquet will be held that evening. Vendors load tables with lavish flowers in ornate vases while others hang drapes. What a farce, all an effort by the king to advertise a flourishing, successful kingdom—despite that it's riddled with corruption.

A choreographer Joanna has seen before supervises a servant who stretches a line taut to a point where he kneels to chalk a mark. He suddenly rises and bows. "Queen Herodias! I believe we're ready."

"I'm sure you are," she says, "but we must make sure Salome is. Go lead her through it one more time."

He looks stricken. "If I may … we're pushing her too hard. We must let her rest before—"

"It must be perfect!" the queen says, hissing. "We must overwhelm him. I will do it with drink. You will do it with her performance."

"My queen, I know the Baptizer insulted you, but there are—"

"Insulted?!" she says, glaring. "Insulted. Do you believe my marriage to the king is wicked?"

"Of course not. I—"

"Do you believe I should return to that pauper Philip and the awful city he named after himself?"

"No, my queen."

"Why not? If the Baptizer's comments in front of the whole royal court were just an insult, as you put it, then why not endorse him? Perhaps I should just ignore his little insult and allow the entire region to publicly rebuke all my decisions!"

"I apologize, my queen. I will work with Salome right away."

The dungeon, moments later

In the bowels of the fortress, Joanna always goes where she pleases, pressing a palm with a coin here and there as necessary. Not today.

The guard who usually accommodates her plants himself in her way. "Sorry, no visitors today."

"Why?"

"A, uh, high-profile inmate is being transferred to a cell near ground level so we can be ready to take action at a moment's notice."

She knows that he knows that she knows exactly who he's talking about. "Take action?"

"Are you hard of hearing?"

Joanna produces a coin from a small satchel full of gold.

"That won't work today, I'm afraid," he says.

"What action at a moment's notice are you talking about? What's happening?"

He shrugs. "Can't be certain. But this sort of thing usually means the inmate is about to be freed—or executed."

"By whose orders?"

He shifts and swallows and avoids eye contact. Joanna opens his cloak and drops the entire satchel into his pocket.

He appears to scan the area and whispers, "Herodias."

Over his shoulder, three guards appear, escorting John the Baptist. He looks pale, sickly, more ragged than ever. Joanna pushes past her guard and rushes the group, shouting, "John! Something's happening!" The guards pull their swords. "There's a plot! They're going to kill you!"

"Woman, stop!" her guard yells, grabbing her.

"John!" But as the group approaches and passes Joanna, she can't believe how calm he looks. "What are you going to—"

He smiles. "The blind see, the lame walk. Lepers are cleansed. The poor have good news preached to them."

"No!" she cries. "No!"

As the guards pull John into another corridor and out of sight, he calls out, "The hearts of fathers are turned to the children, and the disobedient to the wisdom of the just! The way of the Lord is prepared!"

Is this confusing, exasperating man, knowingly, *willingly,* blithely striding toward his own death? Joanna wrenches free and scowls at the guard. Beyond him another soldier sharpens a double-headed axe on a spinning grinding wheel, sparks flying.

Chapter 8

THE IDEA

The Terebinth Grove

Thomas has loved Ramah since long before he ever even hinted at it to her. When he catered weddings and she represented her father's vineyards, he tried often to suggest they were an item, but she seemed oblivious. Was she really, or had she merely been coy? Once in a great while she shyly complimented him, just often enough to keep him from abject disappointment over seeming unable to freely express himself to her.

He could hardly remember when things changed and it became obvious that, even if she didn't share his level of affection, Ramah was at least clearly aware of his devotion to her. Despite that she often corrected him from a business or logistics stand-point and even tried to talk him down when he grew fatalistic and questioned everything, they gradually grew closer. From his perspective, she made clear that she had feelings for him.

That's when he labored to clarify his intentions. Right around the time they met Jesus at a wedding in Cana, Ramah seemed comfortable with their familiarity—though she appeared as careful as he to remain perfectly appropriate at all times. He wanted to pursue her so honorably that her father Kafni would approve. But when they left the business and their homes to follow Jesus, that proved a setback with Kafni.

Now here they sit, with their older friends Barnaby and Shula chaperoning from afar—watching them from an overlook to be certain they only talk and never touch one another. There is nothing Thomas would rather do than to have all this behind him. He wants her father's blessing so he can propose to her. But short of that, just this is bliss.

"Finally quiet enough to have a moment together," he says.

"Bless Barnaby and Shula," Ramah says.

"Before the Decapolis and everything that happened there, which to be honest—"

"I've heard you're still having a hard time accepting—"

"But I'm getting better, right? At accepting things I can't explain?"

"You are. You're not the same man you were in Cana."

"So, yeah, so there is actually somebody who is still the same man he's always been—"

"My father."

"Tell me, how did it go, talking to him after I left?"

She makes a face and shakes her head.

"That good, huh? He loves you very, very much. There's no denying that."

"No denying it."

"And he knew what I was going to ask him, actually before I did. He made that clear to me back in Samaria."

"Nothing gets past him."

"Kafni is a hard man, Ramah."

She stands and turns her back to Thomas. "I was hoping he'd understand. I thought he'd be able to—to let me grow up."

"He finds Jesus objectionable," Thomas says as Ramah begins to pace. "And he disagrees with our choice to leave the profession and follow Jesus." He pauses. "I truly love you, Ramah." She stops. He continues, "There's got to be some way to make this work."

Ramah turns and smiles at him. "I was hoping you'd say this."

"You were?"

"Of course! I have an idea."

"You do?"

"I've carefully researched every rabbinic tradition, every minor detail."

"You did?" he says, knowing he sounds repetitive.

"According to the Halakhah," she says, reciting, "'in the event of an absentee father or exceptionally uncommon circumstances'—which I believe our following Jesus constitutes, 'there is a special dispensation for validating a marriage. A male who is at least thirteen years old verbalizes the formula, "You are hereby consecrated to me according to the Law of Moses and Israel." Upon recital, the groom must give the bride some object of value. If she accepts it, she thus validates the kiddushin as a legal act and is designated as betrothed—consecrated to him alone.'"

Thomas stares. "So wait—that's it? That's all you have to—"

She holds up a finger. "'The formula must be spoken in the presence of two competent male witnesses, one representing the groom and one representing the bride.'"

"I will ask John to be my witness."

She nods. "And we both know there really is only one man who can represent me …"

And they say in unison, "Jesus."

"The only one who can give me away," she adds.

"We'll ask him."

"And then it's done."

"It will take some time to draw up the contracts. I assume they must be signed by an official rabbi to confirm the circumstances are indeed extenuating and unique?"

"Yes," she says.

"If only we knew where to find a rabbi who could do that," he says, and they both chuckle. "Can this really happen within our faith? It feels right, but is it? I suppose it wouldn't be the first unorthodox betrothal in our people's history. Esther married a Gentile king to save Israel. David did not wait for his father to pick a bride. Even Jesus told us about his parents' unconventional arrangement. He could be—"

"Thomas."

"Yes?"

"We don't compare to them, but we do have Jesus to ask. He can decide."

"Yes, of course. Well, one unconventional arrangement will *not* be ours."

"Hm?" she says.

"Ruth was a Gentile, and she snuck into Boaz's bedroom and proposed to him. We're not going that route. I'm asking *you*."

"Aah, I forgot that part. Well, we'll see how that goes."

Thomas decides there's no better time than the present. "Will you forever walk with me and read with me and rattle off endless rules and extenuating circumstances with me?"

"Yes!"

He takes her hand and immediately hears Shula cry out, "Ah, ah, ah!"

Thomas leaps to his feet, hands in the air. "It's all right! We're getting married!"

Chapter 9

THE CON

Machaerus Palace banquet hall, night

Herodias tingles with anticipation at the royal head table, sitting next to her husband, King Herod Antipas. She knows this man—at least his weaknesses—inside and out, especially after having seduced him and broken up two marriages. And she has seen how he looks at her daughter, his own niece. Well, he's going to get an eyeful tonight. If the entertainment pleases him, it has always been his custom to fulfill the fondest wish of the performer. He's even been known to bequeath an estate with a vineyard to a fortunate entertainer. All he need do this evening is grant her daughter Salome's one simple request.

The queen has little doubt how easy this will be, but she leaves nothing to chance. While Herod is distracted by someone on his other side, Herodias snags a passing waiter and taps the rim of the king's goblet. He refills it, but she whispers, "More," and he tops it to the brim.

Next she catches the eye of her daughter's choreographer, who has been quietly surveying the platform where Salome will perform. He nods.

How will this go down with the wife of her husband's confidant, Chuza? Where is Joanna anyway? Her seat is vacant. Word spread quickly of her brazenly breaching the dungeon and screaming at the guards and the despised Baptizer. It would serve Joanna right if she spent the night in a cell herself, but the king refuses to risk such an embarrassment to his aide. Chuza is obviously trying to cover for his wife, raucously entertaining those at his table, likely having invented an alibi for her absence. Herodias can only hope the woman will arrive in time for the inevitable payoff.

After dinner, with the king already tipsy and having plainly overeaten, Herodias stays put while he is laboriously ushered to an ostentatiously upholstered chair at the middle of a stage. While everyone will be able to watch, he, as usual, enjoys the best seat in the house. And while Herodias could insist on joining him, she's more than happy to remain where she is and wouldn't have it any other way. But Joanna's seat remains empty.

The banquet host announces, "Honorable guests, noblemen, generals, commanders, and leading men of Galilee, I present to you for the king's pleasure and in the venerable tradition a special offering by Salome, daughter of our most high Queen Herodias."

Salome begins her dance subtly, expressing herself almost solely with her hands. Herodias has another goblet of wine sent to the king, who stares at Salome while guzzling. Salome moves and pirouettes, and Herodias notices sweat on her husband's forehead. If anything can keep a stuffed and inebriated king awake, it will be this seductive dance.

The girl moves with the music, faster and faster, more and more enticingly. Soon she reaches a fever pitch of movement and intensity, twirling, swirling before the king. To end the dance, Salome races toward the faint line marked on the stage and leaps, rounding off with a spring that drives her hands to the floor, causing a splinter to pierce her finger. She lands inches from the king's chair and hides her hands behind her, though Herodias can see she's bleeding.

Herod sits slack jawed while the crowd rises to a standing ovation. He's clearly overwhelmed, panting, drunk. The girl transitions into an elaborate bow, slowly lifting her head till she meets his eyes. Plainly smitten, he growls, "Ask me for whatever you wish, and I will give it to you."

Salome appears barely able to speak after her effort but whispers, "Anything?"

"Up to half my kingdom," Herod says, causing the crowd to gasp.

She steps to him and whispers in his ear. Herodias knows by the look on his face that the request has been made. As her daughter stands, her finger bleeding behind her back, Herod's look morphs from titillated glee to deep despair.

Chapter 10

THE DEED

Zechariah's courtyard, 31 years prior
Fifteen friends and family gather outside as Elizabeth holds her baby. Her mute husband, the priest, stands beside her.

A rabbi says, "Blessed are You, Adonai our God, ruler of the universe, Who has sanctified us through Your *mitzvot* and has commanded us to bring our sons into the covenant of Abraham our father."

Those gathered, all but Zechariah, say in unison, "May this little one grow to be great!"

Machaerus Palace dungeon, execution chamber hallway, dawn
Guards flank John the Baptizer, his face covered by a black hood. His hands are bound behind him, his feet shackled.

Zechariah's courtyard, 31 years prior
The rabbi says, "God of all our ancestors, sustain this child. Let him be known among the people, and in these parts, as Zechariah, son of Zechariah and Elizabeth."

"No, Rabbi," Elizabeth says. "Per God's command, his name will be John."

Execution chamber

A heavy wooden door opens to a circular room with stone walls and arched windows facing east. John is hauled in and the hood yanked off his head. He faces the chopping block but betrays neither surprise nor fear.

Outside Capernaum

Jesus has been praying all night alone. He pokes the final embers of a fire, not to reignite it but to simply rearrange the coals. His heart is heavy.

Execution chamber

Guards place John's head on the block, his cheek on the stone. He notices they work casually as if preparing a meal. One polishes a gleaming platter.

"That is a nice plate," John says. "Silver?"

"Only the finest," the guard says. "Intended for a royal banquet, requested by King Herod himself."

John chuckles, then laughs aloud.

"Why are you laughing?" a guard says.

"It's funny. I've never been to a banquet. But I'm on my way to one."

"What do you mean?"

"Never mind. You wouldn't get it."

A guard with a quill and parchment says, "Are those your final words?"

John chuckles again.

The guard shrugs and murmurs as he writes, "'You wouldn't get it.'"

Rural Galilee
Joanna's carriage races north. She leans out and settles back inside. "Just a few more miles," she tells herself, and continues praying.

Zechariah's courtyard, 31 years prior
"Elizabeth," the rabbi says, "none of your relatives are called John." He turns to Zechariah. "What is this about? Is she doing this because of what happened to you?"

Outside Capernaum
Jesus hears someone behind him and turns.
"Jesus the Nazarene," Avner, one of his cousin's disciples, says.
Jesus rises. "Shalom! To what do I owe the—"
The look on Avner's face stops him. Pain.

Zechariah's courtyard, 31 years prior
Zechariah writes on his tablet, "His name is John." His eyes widen and he makes a guttural sound. "Ahh! Blessed are You—" he begins haltingly. Then, "Blessed are You, Lord our God, King of the universe."

Everyone reacts as Zechariah reaches for the baby and Elizabeth smiles and touches her husband's cheek as she hands John over.

Execution chamber
The executioner sets the platter on the floor below John's head, then takes his position as the guard with the parchment says, "John, son of Zechariah and Elizabeth of Judea, you are on this day, by order of his majesty King Herod Antipas …"

John hears but doesn't hear as he imagines a scene. In the golden rays of morning light he sees a lamb in a clearing, grazing, wiggling an ear. *Behold …*

He feels a tear on his cheek and cracks a smile. "Thank you," he whispers.

Rural Galilee
Joanna's carriage thunders toward Capernaum, horse hooves pounding the earth.

Execution chamber
The executioner hefts the heavy axe high and brings it down with all his might.

Outside Capernaum
Jesus rips his tunic at the neck and drops to his knees, slowly doubling over and pressing his forehead to the earth near the dying embers and ash.

Outside Simon's house, Capernaum
Simon emerges to find Matthew, Little James, Thaddeus, and Nathanael gathered. "What's the morning report?" he says.

"The ones with news aren't here yet," Nathanael says.

"Which may be a good indication," Matthew says. "Perhaps there are details to work out."

"Or," Nathanael says, "they got rejected yesterday and drank away their disappointment at The Hammer."

"Sleeping it off?" James says. "I hope not."

Thaddeus leaps to his feet. "There they are!"

Simon shouts, "What's this I see? That doesn't look like a man carrying an empty cart!"

Big James, John, and Thomas approach. James raises the cart to show it's light and empty. "We got the account!" John says. "They bought every last jar!"

"Hah!" Simon chortles, moving in to hug John. "Your old man comes through!"

"It was Adonai alone," James says.

John looks knowingly at Thomas. "Abba wasn't the only one trying to close a deal yesterday."

Thomas nods toward Mary Magdalene, Ramah, and Tamar approaching. "You can ask her," he says.

"Ah, yes," Nathanael says. "I'm curious about the little songbirds."

"Lovebirds, you mean," Little James says.

"What? It's songbirds. It's always songbirds."

Thaddeus shakes his head at James. "Let it go."

"Well," Simon says, "out with it. How'd it go?"

Thomas and Ramah look at each other with pursed smiles, and eventually Ramah nods.

They all cheer. Thaddeus hugs Thomas. Matthew shouts, "Mazel tov!"

Little James looks to the sky. "Blessed are You Who causes the couple to rejoice, one with another."

Mary looks overcome. "So it's really going to happen?!"

"Well," Thomas says, "there are a couple more steps we have to take care of. One of which, John, involves you."

"Absolutely!" John says. "Just don't ask me to sew the chuppah."

Matthew shakes Thomas's hand and catches himself. Over Thomas's shoulder, he sees Joanna's carriage at the far end of the street.

Zechariah's courtyard, 31 years prior

Zechariah holds baby John before him, staring into his face. With deep passion he recites, "'Blessed be the Lord God of Israel, for He has visited and redeemed His people and has raised up a horn of salvation for us in the house of His servant David.'"

Capernaum street
While everyone else is hugging and congratulating Thomas and Ramah, Matthew squints, watching Joanna in her hooded robe, apparently checking house numbers against a piece of paper.

Mary Magdalene notices Joanna, and joy drains from her face. Joanna has arrived at Andrew's door. She pounds and shouts his name, now attracting everyone's attention. They stop the rejoicing and stare, all seeming to fear what this means.

Zechariah's courtyard, 31 years prior
Zechariah continues his recitation: "'As He spoke by the mouth of His holy prophets of old, that we should be saved from our enemies and from the hands of all who hate us.'"

Andrew's house
"Andrew! Are you home?!"

He opens the door. "Joanna?"

Her lips quiver and he slowly comprehends. "No, no, no!"

Judas appears behind him and Andrew buries his face in the man's chest, sobbing.

"Are you Philip?" Joanna says.

"I'm Judas. Philip is away."

Andrew pulls back and tells Joanna, "I will tell Philip."

Zechariah's courtyard, 31 years prior
"'To show the mercy promised to our fathers and to remember His holy covenant, the oath that He swore to our father Abraham.'"

Capernaum street
Mary Magdalene comprehends what's going on at Andrew's and starts down the street toward them. Simon runs past her, clearly overcome with compassion for his brother. One by one the others join them. Simon kneels before Andrew and gathers him to his chest.

Mary and Tamar try to comfort Joanna, but she says, "I'm fine. It's not my—I'm not the one who—"

"We should have known this day would come," Andrew says. "We should have been prepared."

"We were," John says. He stares at the ground and mumbles, "He was sent to prepare the way, and he did. He was not the Messiah, but he came to bear witness that he would be here soon."

"We have to find Jesus and tell him," Andrew says.

"I'll go with you," Simon says.

Matthew, with his back to the group, says, "You don't have to."

Zechariah's courtyard, 31 years prior

"'To grant us that we, being delivered from the hand of our enemies, might serve Him without fear, in holiness and righteousness before Him all our days.'"

Capernaum street

Jesus trudges down the street wearing sackcloth and ashes. He stops before the rest of them, Avner a few paces behind.

Zechariah's courtyard, 31 years prior

"'And you, child, will be called the prophet of the Most High; for you will go before the Lord to prepare His ways, to give knowledge of salvation to His people in the forgiveness of their sins, because of the tender mercy of our God.

"'Whereby the sunrise shall visit us from on high to give light to those who sit in darkness and in the shadow of death, to guide our feet into the way of peace.'"

PART 2

Seventy Times Seven

Chapter 11

THE OPEN ROAD

The mission house study, early morning

The window is draped in dark cloth and the only light emits from a small oil lamp. Jesus, deeply distressed, has been sitting *shiva* for his cousin John. Now he lies dozing on a mat on the floor, dreaming.

He's alone in an open field under a brilliant sky. His beloved cousin approaches, wearing handcuffs. Jesus' heart breaks for him, but John is smiling. The handcuffs break apart and John raises one hand, gesturing as if to say, "Right this way ..."

The way is prepared.

Jesus rouses and sits up.

"Rabbi?" In the doorway it's Andrew in shabby dress, his shirt torn at the collar like Jesus'. He bears a cup of water and a small plate of pita bread. "I'll just leave this here."

"It's all right. Please come in." Jesus pats the floor next to him. "Sit with me."

As Andrew sets down the cup and plate and joins him, Jesus says, "How are you holding up?"

Andrew hesitates. "I-I'm not sure what to say. I thought it would be far worse. Apparently Simon thinks so too. He keeps checking on me every five minutes."

"Like how you continue to check on me?" Jesus says with a wry smile.

"You knew John longer than any of us. But then you're—"

"I'm what?"

"You know. You're the—"

"Then why would you need to check on me?"

Andrew chuckles and shrugs. "Okay, well, I'll just say you're a mystery."

Jesus tries a piece of bread and coughs. "Oh, wow."

"I know. Pretty stale."

Jesus sips water and sighs. "*Pretty* stale?"

They both laugh, but Andrew stops abruptly. "Can we be laughing?"

Jesus cocks his head. "Some of our biggest laughs come around the time of a funeral. Our hearts are so tender, our emotions at the surface. Laughter and tears become closer than ever. And believe me, I sat many a shiva with John. He could not hold a sullen mood for seven straight days."

Andrew nods and chuckles and catches himself again. "I feel guilty. I should be in shambles."

"There is no *should* in the matter of grief, friend. No right way to mourn. You experienced much of your grief when John was arrested. Falling to pieces again would not honor his memory any more than feeling nothing at all would."

Andrew appears to consider this.

"So, Andrew, you say I am a mystery."

Looking cornered, Andrew sputters, "Well, I-I mean, you—"

"Who did John say I was?"

"Um, the one?"

Jesus rises and moves to the window, whipping off the heavy drape and allowing harsh light to pour in.

"What are you doing!?" Andrew says.

"You've given me an idea," Jesus says. "Where do we traditionally sit shiva?"

"In the home of the deceased."

"And where was John's home?"

"The open road."

"Gather the others."

Chapter 12

NEWS

Yussif's home, morning

Having just risen, Yussif dons his kethneth, an undergarment that extends to his knees. "The words of the son of David: 'Vanity of vanities,' says the preacher. 'All is vanity.'"

Pulling on his simlah, a heavier garment, he continues, "'I have done everything that is done under the sun, and behold, all is vanity and striving after the wind …'"

Now his long-sleeved outer garment of lighter fabric. He attaches the tzitzit. "'… a time to seek, and a time to lose; a time to keep, and a time to cast away; a time to tear, and a time to sew; a time to be silent, and a time to speak …'"

Yussif ties around his arms the tefillin—phylacteries with leather straps. "'He who loves money will not be satisfied with money, nor he who loves wealth with his income.'"

He applies a boxy turban to his head and rummages in a drawer for a golden key that, once in his palm, brings him to a heavy stillness.

Yussif's synagogue office, minutes later
Yussif sits at his desk across from a citizen and listens intently.

"At first it was only during the drought," the man says. "But now it's all the time."

"Is there any anxiety you can point to that may cause this sleeplessness?"

"It's not a thought but a feeling of dread. As if there were a snake under the bed or a lion crouching just outside my door."

Yussif ponders this. "The anguish of our forefathers lives on in our bodies."

"What do you mean?" the citizen says.

"Egypt. The forty-year wandering. The exile in Babylon. All that pain and fear is passed down in our blood, our bones, our stories."

"I just want to be able to sleep! I can't change my blood. I can't change my Jewishness."

"No, but you can pray. You can visit me every day and we'll pray together." He bows his head. "'He who dwells in the shelter of the Most High will abide in the shadow of the Almighty—'"

They are interrupted when Jairus rushes in, a letter in hand. "Thank you for coming," Yussif tells the citizen.

"Thank you, Rabbi."

"I only wish I were a miracle worker."

"There is one I've heard about," the citizen says as Yussif leads him to the door.

"Give my best to Ila."

"I will."

"Shalom, shalom."

Back at his desk, Yussif says, "I've been meaning to ask you, how is life at home since, you know, after all of the—"

"You know I can't talk about it," Jairus says.

Yussif studies him. "Can you imagine your life if you had been assigned a different post?"

"I don't want to." He hands Yussif the letter. "News from Jerusalem this morning. Shmuel has been promoted to the Sanhedrin. Shammai is scheduled to address the assembly today."

"Then Nicodemus should be present."

"Apparently he has missed multiple sessions recently, and we never sent your letter. Do you suppose word of the sermon on the Korazim Plateau has reached Jerusalem?"

"I can't imagine how it would not have," Yussif says. "But the sermon may fade in comparison to the rumors about what happened in the Decapolis."

"It's more than a rumor. Read on."

Chapter 13

BUSTED

The Roman Authority, Capernaum

The Honorable Praetor of Galilee, Quintus sits rigidly at his desk, posing for a sculptor. *It's long past time that this should be done,* he decides. How much does a man have to accomplish before he's immortalized? Though he's raced up the ranks to become one of the youngest men in such a position, and his influence is felt throughout the Upper Galilee, it's been anything but easy.

Quintus has always been seen by his superiors as an overachiever, a moniker that amuses him. What is an overachiever but a man who has risen in his profession through his own intelligence, guile, and—if he says so himself—wit? He must deal with many contemporaries who've put a target on his back, most of whom have achieved their positions thanks to unbridled nepotism.

Quintus feels he has evolved from resentment over his father offering him no advantages, indeed having none to give, to where he now appreciates that the man forced him to pull himself up by his own sandal straps. No favoritism, no rubbing elbows with influential Romans, just a father who demanded excellence and accepted nothing less.

How Quintus inwardly rebelled at this in his formative years! He wanted to lash out, to vent his rage, express himself, even throttle his father. Yet one thing he knows for sure: he would have been served Hades for breakfast had he tried. So he merely buckled down and did all and more than his father expected of him. When he left home for military service, when a normal teenager was likely to act out and give free rein to his rebellion, he found himself under even harder taskmasters.

Quintus didn't at first recognize that his father and his maddening ways had prepared him for this—oh, no, it took a while. But when his stellar performance was soon rewarded with better and better assignments, he knew he had his father to thank. And yet he never thanked him. The man who never acknowledged his son's achievements would have ridiculed him for any sentiment, any hint of softness. And now he is gone. Does Quintus regret neglecting to express some modicum of gratitude? Not in the least.

Rather, as he has always done, he turns his wrath on his own underlings. He feels forced daily to establish his superiority, his position, his class. Others must be willing to flounder after reaching the limit of their competence on the wings of familial favors. He is a self-made man, and may it ever be so.

But that also means he can never coast, never rest on his laurels. The emperor is always watching. So is the governor. So is the Cohortes Urbana, the smarmy Atticus who loves to subtly threaten by emphasizing that he bears the authority of both Caesar and Pontius Pilate and also has their ears.

And speak of the devil, that's none other than Atticus's syrupy voice in the foyer, blustering his way past the praetor's secretary, despite Quintus's insistence on privacy this morning. Here he has set himself up for the ultimate insult from a man who loves to dole them out.

"You're sure this is my good side?" Quintus asks the sculptor.

The man hesitates. "*You* said it was …"

"Am I wrong?"

"It's a bust. Your likeness will be seen from every angle."

"I'm not paying you for art lessons."

When Atticus appears, Quintus's eyes narrow. *Here it comes.* Caesar's goon looks as if he's had a slur presented him on a silver platter for the taking. "Say it now so we can get it out of the way."

"Not today," Atticus says and turns to the sculptor. "Leave us."

"Wait!" Quintus whines. "I'm in the middle of—this."

"And normally I'd tell the man he's immortalizing the wrong end."

"There it is."

"But today I need your latest intelligence on Jesus of Nazareth."

"Military intelligence?" Quintus says. "Doesn't that strike you as oxymoronic?"

Atticus, clearly not in the mood for word play, lifts the bust from its pedestal and holds it precariously. The sculptor pales and Quintus squirms. "Atticus—"

"Quintus, tell me about Jesus."

Quintus points at the bust. "All right, all right, just …" The sculptor throws up his hands and leaves. "Um, no change. Jesus and I talked. You were there. We have an understanding—"

"No new information?"

"No," Quintus says, feeling as if he's being set up.

"The Jews have new information."

"Of course the Jews know about a Jew! I don't think you understand my role as a magistrate."

"It's happening right under your nose."

Oh, is it? "Debrief me, *Detective*. What's so important?"

Atticus gazes, appearing to envision some faraway place. "It feels like the beginning of something. Maybe a war." Quintus scoffs, regaining the Urbana's attention. "I'm not going to do your job, Praetor, and make life difficult for the people who follow Jesus. I'm not going to break up their gatherings or expel the pilgrims. Do you understand?"

Quintus squints at him. "Something's spooked you. I know my Jews better than you do. What's going on with you?"

Atticus sets down the bust with a thunk and turns dramatically toward Quintus. "Right now the only thing keeping you in Pilate's good graces are your revenues. Don't become infamous for overseeing the town where a revolution began."

Atticus storms out and Quintus tries to cover with a facetious, "Hail, Caesar!"

In fact, he's angry, offended, and—in truth—scared.

Chapter 14

SHIVA ON THE ROAD

The western bank of the Jordan

Heading in the direction of Caesarea Philippi, Jesus walks several paces ahead of all twelve disciples and Mary and Tamar. Ramah and Thomas bring up the rear.

Judas asks Zee if he thinks Jesus might be leading them toward the valley.

Zee shakes his head. "We're heading north."

"To the Waters of Merom!" Judas says.

"Merom?" Mary says.

"Where Joshua claimed his victory over the Canaanites," Zee says.

"Maybe," Judas says, "it's where big things are really going to start happening."

"Many big things have already happened," Matthew says.

Farther back in line, Nathanael says, "I'll bet we're going to Mount Hermon."

"I haven't seen snow in ages," Andrew says.

Thaddeus chimes in, "Isaiah: 'Though your sins are like scarlet …'"

And three others finish, "'…they shall be as white as snow.'"

"What would Mount Hermon have to do with Jesus' cousin?" Philip says. "We're still in shiva."

"Shiva is as much about the living as the deceased," Simon says.

At the back of the line, Ramah and Thomas talk privately. She asks, "Are you sure you heard Jesus correctly?"

"'We can talk along the way,' he said."

"But this time is about the Baptizer, not us."

"I'm just telling you what he said, Ramah. And he actually smiled when he said it."

"All right, well, let's go then."

Thomas notices that as they hurry toward the front, most of the others fall silent. But leave it to Nathanael to comment. "Go for it," he says. "It'll *probably* work."

"Aah, there you are," Jesus says when they reach him. "I was waiting. How was your visit with Kafni?" Thomas hesitates and Jesus adds, "Hmm. I suppose that if it went well, we would all know by now."

"But," Thomas says, "there is another way."

"The kiddushin?"

"You're familiar, of course."

"I am."

Thomas isn't sure what to say and is relieved when Ramah takes over. "Rabbi, I left my father to follow you. I endured— many harsh words from him for choosing to do so."

"As did I," Jesus says.

"You are the closest thing to a father I have now." Thomas is convinced Jesus is touched by this. Ramah continues, "John has agreed to stand as the witness for Thomas."

Jesus stops, causing everyone else to do the same. It's not lost on Thomas that the others press close, not even trying to hide that they're listening.

"As my spiritual father," Ramah says, "will you give me away?"

Thomas sees sorrow, compassion, even love, in Jesus' eyes as the rabbi looks away, perhaps to collect himself. "We don't mean to burden you," Thomas says. "Kafni's refusal to sanctify our union—well, fixing that is not what you came to do."

"No. No, Thomas, you are wrong." Jesus turns to the others. "Everyone, please gather around. People think they know what I've come here to do. Do you think that I have come to bring peace on earth? I have not. Not peace, but a sword."

"A sword?" Zee says.

"I mean divisions, Zee," Jesus says, "within households and beyond. When someone makes a choice to follow me, it may mean in one house there will be five divided, three against two and two against three."

"Why?" John says.

"We see with Ramah and her father. It is not my *intention* to divide families, but the cost of following me can mean people will be hated by those closest to them because of their unbelief."

Andrew says, "But isn't honoring father and mother one of the commandments?"

"Honoring your parents is one of the highest social and spiritual obligations. But it is not higher than following God. Whoever loves father or mother more than me is not worthy of me."

Thomas feels momentarily speechless. After a long silence, he says, "It is decided then?"

"You will sign the letter," Ramah says, "and stand as my witness?"

"Let's talk about the details after this trip and the completion of shiva," Jesus says.

"Of course," Thomas says, noticing Ramah beaming.

"And Thomas," Jesus adds, "to complete the legal act, aren't you required to give something of value to Ramah as mohar?"

"Oh, well," he says, glancing at her, "we've agreed she doesn't need—"

"Bad idea!" Simon says.

"What's a bad idea?" Thomas says.

"Not giving your wife a gift. Specifically taking her at her word when she says she doesn't want a gift. Take it from your married friend, these words do not mean what you think they mean. Let me explain something. Rabbi, do you still need him?"

"No, please give him a talking to. And all of us should keep moving."

Chapter 15

ELEVATED

The Jerusalem Temple, Hall of Priests

Finding himself in a position he once longed for—in fact more than once had prayed for—Shmuel cannot revel in it. Being awarded a seat on the Sanhedrin itself shakes him to his core, and he wonders whether he should even accept it. He cannot decline it, of course, without setting in motion more noise and controversy than he and his loved ones are prepared to endure. Who has ever turned down such an honor? But he knows this singular achievement resulted from his reporting on Jesus of Nazareth, which he now regrets.

The clerical tailor Moishe fusses with his new ceremonial garments and Shmuel's associate Yanni flits around as if it's his own big day. Under his breath, Shmuel says, "Blessed are You, Lord our God, King of the universe, Who has given us life, sustained us, and allowed us to arrive at this moment. One generation shall commend Your works to another and shall ..."

Meanwhile, Yanni is exulting to the tailor, "All the way from the harbor villages of the Upper Galilee—Capernaum! Can you believe that, Moishe?"

Shmuel peeks at Yanni, annoyed, and resumes praying silently. "'On the glorious splendor of Your majesty and on Your wondrous works I will—meditate …'" He stops and glares at Yanni who continues to revel in Shmuel's success.

"I'm telling you, Moishe, the day this kid arrived in the Holy City, he still smelled faintly of fish and naïveté."

The man seems oblivious to Shmuel's discomfort, grabs a bottle of expensive perfume, and spritzes the air. "Bergamot! Mm …" He spritzes again. "Jasmine and—balsam from the shores of the Dead Sea. Take my word, Moishe, you are working with the robes of a rabbi whose name will be remembered in history! You will tell your sons about this day."

Shmuel can take no more. "Is that all this is about for you, Yanni?! Being remembered? Special robes and costly fragrances?"

Yanni looks not the least taken aback. "If they are befitting …"

"Anyone could have alerted the elders. Moishe, please, step out." When the tailor is gone, Shmuel whispers, "I prayed with the man, Yanni."

"You what?"

"In the Decapolis, while you and the others were busy quizzing witnesses, I came upon the man himself. It was accidental."

"But you never told us—"

"He was not what I expected or whom I remembered from Capernaum. He seemed sincere—"

"Sincerity can be cunning."

"I did not detect the evil I expected."

"Only God can discern the heart of a man, Shmuel. It is not for you to say."

"Then why should I be given this post?"

"No one's giving you anything. You've earned your seat."

"How? I studied, I wrote reports, I met with leaders of feuding traditions, and what is there to show for it? How is our faith, our nation, improved in any way?"

Yanni softens. "You're overwhelmed. It's normal to be nervous. Lots of feelings—"

"Yes, I am overwhelmed by how empty this entire exercise is. By posturing and congratulating—"

"Shmuel. I promise, when you hear Shammai's address, everything will make sense."

The man just doesn't get it.

Chapter 16

THE GATES
OF HELL

On the road

As Jesus and the rest of the disciples reach a fork, Nathanael realizes his worst fear is about to become reality. Zee reads the sign. "Caesarea Philippi."

There Nathanael endured the worst failure of his architectural career, where that career came to a horrific end. He had trudged through the wilderness from there, ending up beneath a fig tree, incinerating his drawings and covering his head with the ashes, demanding to know whether God saw or cared. His intentions had been more than honorable; they had been divine, at least in his mind. He had plied his trade and done his work for God, yet it had all come to naught.

Yes, in the end it had turned into the experience of a lifetime, of anyone's lifetime. He was led to Jesus, who had miraculously seen *and* heard him under that fig tree in the middle of nowhere.

And now Nathanael follows and believes in the Son of the one true God.

But he certainly never wants to see Caesarea Philippi again. Nothing good happened there—only a disaster he hopes to remember no more. He turns and shakes his head at Philip, the friend who insisted he come and see and meet the man Philip knew as the Messiah.

"That may be where you lived," Philip says, "but you're not the same man I found passed out drunk at midday in a cheap flat."

Nathanael finds that not comforting in the least. "Thanks for the memory."

"Just trying to help."

As they approach the city, Nathanael passes a toppled decaying statue. Matthew cocks his head and stares. "The Canaanite god Baal," Thaddeus says. "He used to be worshipped here."

"Actually in many places," Little James says. "But especially here."

"Why?" Matthew says.

"The water," Thaddeus says. "They regarded Baal as the god of rain."

Nathanael remembers. "A spring pours out of a cave in the side of the rock face here. The fountainhead of the Jordan."

Little James nods. "To sound the depths of the spring, they let down a stone on a rope, but it never reached the bottom."

"The gates of hell," Philip says.

Nathanael ignores him and walks on.

As the group turns a corner, Nathanael takes in a full view of the Grotto of Pan and some Greek temples. Idols of various gods are carved into the rock with piles of rotten food offerings at their feet. Nathanael and the others hold their noses.

THE GATES OF HELL

"You see?" Jesus says. "Doesn't the thought of our kosher food taste better here?"

Big James grimaces, but John says, "He has a point."

They come upon a pen of goats where men exchange coins with the keeper who hands each an animal on a leash.

"Are those for sacrifice in their temple?" Matthew says.

Little James shakes his head. "They're used for something much worse."

Matthew cringes.

Chapter 17

THE DECREE

The Jerusalem Temple

Guilt. Dread. Shmuel feels it all as he enters the horse-shoe-shaped arc three rows deep that sits the Great Sanhedrin Pharisaical body of seventy-one members. There are lesser Sanhedrins consisting of twenty-three members headed by a high priest in every Jewish city, but this, this is the supreme tribunal. Shmuel has known since childhood that this august council has religious, civil, and criminal jurisdiction over the entire Judaistic nation.

For how many years has he imagined this day, this lofty ambition of any Pharisee. And nearly every time he even considered it, he prayed for humility, for the right motivation, knowing that one who seeks such a lofty role is probably not qualified to take it. Often he has persuaded himself that if and when it came to him, it would be because he *was* humble enough to commit to the dire responsibilities and weight of it.

But now here he is. The day has come. All about him, before and aft, stride imposing men, their egos cresting a wave of pomp and circumstance with which they had apparently grown most comfortable. He can't imagine ever feeling that way, especially given what has brought him here.

A clerk sits meticulously recording the attendance in a journal. Shmuel recognizes one empty seat, which will result in the great and honorable Nicodemus being marked absent due to a research trip. The other empty seat awaits Shmuel himself, and as he approaches it, the clerk announces, "We are pleased to welcome Shmuel bar Yosef of Capernaum to succeed Rabban Seled in the seventieth chair."

The others offer appropriate and warm applause, and Shmuel bows graciously before sitting despite his nerves and anxiety.

Once everyone is seated, the clerk continues, "Senior Judge and Av Bet Din Shammai!"

More applause as the man rises and moves to the main floor, executing a slow, theatrical, plainly calculated march and pausing—seemingly for effect—even after the clapping has ended. "We venture north to Capernaum for fresh fish, not to discover great minds."

Shmuel feels his cheeks flush as the others laugh.

Shammai moves on. "And yet, unlikely as it may seem, from this backwater village in the Upper Galilee has arisen an intellect so enterprising, probing, and formidable that we cannot but rejoice in our good fortune to have found Shmuel bar Yosef, whom we now welcome to the high council."

While many applaud, hisses and sounds of shock also puncture the air.

"Unless you've been living in a tomb for the last six months," Shammai says, "you know that Jesus of Nazareth, once the subject of mere speculation, curiosity, gossip, and hearsay, has, through Shmuel's diligent reporting and eyewitness accounts, emerged as the most damning and dangerous figure to have arisen in this nation since Ahab and Jezebel."

More cheers, applause, and animated opposition. Shmuel abhors the attention—all of it.

Shammai is not finished. "Jesus has not only shown contempt for the old laws and traditions of our faith, but he has also amassed a devoted following. He travels and mingles with tax collectors, sinners, degenerates, and even a member of the Fourth Philosophy, not to mention counting among his followers multiple women—one of whom is a Gentile from Ethiopia!"

Alarming as that must be to most of those gathered, it's the mention of the Fourth Philosophy that catches one's attention. "The Zealots?!" he cries out.

Shammai thunders ahead. "Not one but *two* of his followers are former disciples of the late blasphemer John the Baptizer."

Did he say late?! Shmuel had no idea.

"We have Shmuel to thank, in part, for revealing the Baptizer's whereabouts to Roman authorities."

Shmuel feels bad enough about his contribution to Jesus' reputation with the Sanhedrin, but to have his intelligence lead to the death of the wilderness preacher? It's almost more than he can bear. He fights an urge to run from the assembly as a Pharisee he knows leaps to his feet. "Why were we not consulted before cooperating with Rome and handing over one of our own to them?"

Shmuel remains horrified as Shammai responds, "Sympathetic to the Baptizer, are you, Shimon? To one who called us a brood of vipers, murderers of our own mothers?"

"Shammai!" comes a booming voice. "You've gone on too long."

A hush falls over the room as Caiaphas, the High Priest of Jerusalem, appears. His lavish adornments make even the

Sanhedrin members look plain. Shammai steps aside as the priest strolls to the center and appears to make eye contact with every Pharisee in the room. "The time to passively observe is long past," he says. "The acts and whereabouts of Jesus of Nazareth are to be reported to the council immediately. Senior leaders in every district should question and expose Jesus. Listen carefully to what he says and search for ways to entangle him in his own teaching. If we can corner him into exposing himself by his own words in ways the people can easily recognize as heresy, they will turn from him, and we can dilute his influence."

Shammai looks pleased.

Caiaphas continues, "As for what happens if he's trapped and is brought before us, even if we find him blasphemous, I encourage you to resist the urge to enact the justice of the Law of Moses. Stoning is not only messy business, but stoning a preacher of the people also risks chaos we cannot afford. We must find a way to convince Rome he is worth their attention and concern."

A burst of applause comes from members Shmuel knows to be in Shammai's camp.

Caiaphas thunders on. "As much as the occupation is an endless source of pain for our people, we must be sober in admitting that our colonizers are better at tracking and killing people than we have the resources or the energy to be. We. Must. Keep. Our houses of power. Separate.

"We cannot afford to be perceived as hoping for disorder of any kind whatsoever. Pilate, as young and in-over-his-head as he is, will not abide that, and we can't give him another reason to do something rash. Let Rome enforce its own manmade law, and if that works in our favor, so much the better. We will concentrate on defending *God's* law and the sacred traditions of our faith. Am I clear?"

Caiaphas dramatically dusts off his hands, which Shmuel interprets as an indication of both the demise of Jesus and the completion of his argument. "Write up the decree and have it presented to me for review by sundown. This meeting is adjourned."

"Caiaphas!" Shimon shouts. "This report is bloated and skewed with bias!"

Shammai smirks and others weigh in before the High Priest says, "I said we are finished here!"

Chapter 18

THE ROCK

Caesarea Philippi

Simon has felt an entirely new level of faith and devotion since Jesus walked on the water and then calmed a raging storm with a simple command. The former fisherman had reached the nadir of his frustration leading to that point, and while he was ashamed and humiliated when his faith wavered and Jesus had to save him from the sea, all that came from that night has made him a new man. He again views Jesus the way he did when first he met the rabbi and saw him miraculously produce a massive catch of fish.

Simon has never since doubted that Jesus is the long-awaited Messiah. But he's also found Jesus a frustrating conundrum. After Simon's reconciliation with Eden, the love of his life, and Jesus' promise never to leave him, he has renewed his commitment too. He's absolutely convinced that nothing will ever again shake his faith.

That does not, however, mean he always immediately understands what Jesus is up to. Like now, as they approach the dark foreboding maw in the side of a mountain from which water gushes. Matthew is obviously spooked and hides behind Philip. "Don't worry," Philip says, "it's not the actual entryway to hell."

But to Simon it might as well be.

Jesus sits on a rock by the river and smiles at the group. The rest look as stunned as Simon feels. "Rabbi," he says, "this place …"

Andrew says, "Respectfully, Rabbi, why did you bring us here? It's an abomination."

"Pretty strong word, Andrew," Jesus says.

"And during shiva?" Philip says.

"Should we avoid dark places out of fear," Jesus says, "or should we be light to them as Simon and Judas were on their mission? Do you think my cousin would be afraid of this cave? Do you think he would be so appalled by what happens in that temple over there that he couldn't stand to be in this place?"

Looking sheepish, one by one the others join Simon as they sit on the ground around Jesus. Simon notices the rabbi catch Matthew's eye and give him a faint nod, whereupon the former tax collector pulls out his tablet. Simon finds himself eager for whatever lesson this is going to be.

"Who do people say the Son of Man is?" Jesus begins.

They say a lot of things, Simon thinks, *but is this a trick question?* The others must fear the same, because no one appears to want to go first. Finally, John says, "Some say you are Elijah, one who preaches repentance."

"Others say Jeremiah," Andrew says, "because he was rejected by the leaders of his time."

Matthew is quickly scribbling.

Big James says, "Others say one of the prophets, those who spoke on God's behalf."

Simon is puzzled, even frustrated, when everyone falls silent again. "Okay, what are we going to have to do, cast lots? Nathanael, this is your moment. Be yourself. You always have something to s—"

"Some say John the Baptizer."

"Which obviously isn't true," Philip says.

"Okay," Jesus says, "that's everyone else. But what about you? Who do you say that I am?"

No one moves. No one answers. Simon has no doubt about what he thinks. He stares unflinchingly at the rabbi. "You are the Christ," he says at last, "the Son of the living God. Those statues of Baal and Pan and other idols we passed, they're dead and decaying. But we worship a living God, and you are His Son."

Jesus' eyes fill. "Blessed are you, Simon, son of Jonah. For flesh and blood have not revealed this to you, but my Father Who is in heaven. Your whole life you have been called Simon—*one who hears*—but as of today, your new name is Peter—*little rock*. And you are the leader of the larger rock, my apostles here proclaiming the truth of what Peter just said."

I'm the leader?!

"And it is *this* rock on which I will build my Church, and the gates of hell shall not prevail against it. This is a place of death, and I brought you here to tell you that death has no power to hold my redeemed people captive. Because I live, you also will live.

"In time I will give you the keys to the kingdom of heaven, and whatever you bind on earth will be bound in heaven, and whatever you loose on earth will be loosed in heaven. You have the authority to declare the truth to others that I am declaring to you, that the repentant have a place in the kingdom of heaven."

What is he saying?

"You have confessed that I am the Christ, and you will in time influence many others to make the same confession. I will explain more later, but for now you must all keep this quiet. I strictly charge you not to tell anyone."

Simon finds it hard to gauge the reactions of the others. Some appear proud, moved, some perhaps jealous, others confused.

"Rabbi," John says, "some already know you are the Messiah. Why do we need to keep this silent?"

"In some places, for some people, it was important they know and believe. Right now, if all our people of this region hear the Messiah has come, they will rise up in multitudes, preparing to join a military figure at war with Rome. I want people to follow me based on my true identity, just like Peter here, not based on their misguided understanding of the title I hold."

"Teacher," Judas says, "our people are ready to believe in you and fight with you. Why else would you bring us to this place of death if not to defeat it?"

"That will come in time. I brought you here to honor my cousin John by showing you what he was here to do. He was preparing the way for this, for me to build my Church, a Church that will never be stopped, even in a place like this. He was fearless of evil and obedient everywhere. And so you must be, even at the gates of hell."

He turns to Peter. "Are you ready to follow in his footsteps and mine? Even if it leads you to a place like this?"

Resolute, Peter nods.

"That is all," Jesus says, standing. "We should be going."

As the group begins to move on, Jesus stops to help Little James with one of his straps, but Peter remains transfixed—bewildered but also thrilled. His brother slaps him on the back and squeals in a whisper, "Peter, The Rock!"

Chapter 19

PRESCIENT

Outside the Jerusalem Temple, late afternoon

Shmuel stands with Yanni at the bottom of the steps leading from the synagogue, feeling for all the world as if deception radiates from his very visage. Colleagues and even rivals smile as they congratulate him upon reaching this pinnacle of his profession, and he is able to fake his gratitude for this kindness. In truth, every compliment stabs deeply.

Two scribes from the Sanhedrin descend the stairs and hand copies of the new decree to four horsemen. Yanni appears barely able to control himself. "They'll take the message to the whole of Israel—all because of you! *Your* work created this!"

"He's dead," Shmuel mutters.

"He will be," Yanni says, "once he makes a false move and runs afoul of Rome."

"No," Shmuel says. "I mean the Baptizer. Shammai said it. I'm the first who gave him over to the authorities."

"Because you are prescient! You have eyes to see consequences far in the future that others are too distracted to consider. And now the entire Sanhedrin knows of your talent."

Shmuel stares into the distance.

"Are you listening?" Yanni says.

"I'm list—yes, I am."

"You should be the one who brings Jesus before the Sanhedrin."

"Me?"

"You're from Capernaum. You know people who follow him. You've spoken with him twice. You should try to find him!"

Actually, I should. "You're right ..." But not for the reason Yanni implies.

"Shalooom!" Yanni says, waving before Shmuel's eyes. "Are you alive?"

"No—yes, I'm thinking. I'm—yes, I'm going to try to find him."

Chapter 20

MATTHEW'S CONUNDRUM

The disciples' camp

Matthew is at a loss. The rest of the disciples busy themselves preparing the site for the night, and he wants to contribute. He's not handy like the rest, but surely there's something he can do. The newly labeled Peter is scavenging for firewood while Zee, Thaddeus, and Philip busily assemble the women's tent. They fall silent as Peter passes. Is everyone wondering the same things Matthew is?

He joins the others around the fire where Thomas and Ramah slice apples and James and his brother John sit together.

"Anyone could have said what Simon, er, Peter said," John says.

"Then why didn't you?"

"Why didn't *you*?"

"I thought Jesus was asking a question as part of a teaching. Simon just spoke up first."

"I don't know that we're to call him Simon anymore," John says.

"Don't we? Jesus gave *us* a new name, but we still go by James and John."

"I said I don't know."

"What are we going to tell Ima?" James says.

"We're not going to tell her anything. She can't know! Why'd you have to bring up Ima?"

The brothers grow quiet as Peter arrives at the fire and sets down the wood. Everyone stares. "That should be enough for the night, no?"

"More than," Nathanael says.

"All right," Peter says, turning to leave.

Thomas stops him. "Apple?"

"Oh, uh, sure." He takes one slice as he departs. "Thank you."

"There's plenty," Thomas calls after him. "You can have—"

"If he wanted more," Ramah says, "he would have asked."

"You can say that again," Andrew says. "I'll take three."

As the plate of apple slices is passed around, James and John continue. "She's going to find out one way or another," James says. "She finds out everything."

Nathanael speaks up. "I don't get it. Is Simon, uh, Peter, the best disciple?"

"Did Jesus say *best*?" Judas asks.

"I wrote it all down," Matthew says. "The word *best* was not used."

"Does it matter?" Mary says.

"I haven't been here as long as some of you," Judas says, "but Peter does seem like the best, or at least in the top three or four."

To Matthew, John looks offended. "Who are the other three?!"

"By what measure," Judas says, "are we determining this ranking?"

"Who said anything about rank?" James says. "What is this, the military?"

Mary shakes her head, "The opposite, I believe Jesus indicated."

"I don't know," Andrew says. "It's clear Peter is to be a leader."

"Does that have to mean the rest of us are less important?" Thomas says.

"No one asked my opinion," Little James says, "but I think we should all get some sleep."

The women appear relieved to hear that, but John says, "I won't be getting any sleep tonight."

"Great," Andrew says. "You can take third watch. I was scheduled, but if you're going to be awake anyway …"

Matthew quietly steals several yards away to Jesus' tent. The flap is open, and he finds the rabbi inside pouring water into a bowl.

"Matthew! How is everyone? Settling in for the night?"

"I don't know if *settled* is the right word."

Jesus chuckles as he removes his sandals. "I love that about you, Matthew. Always looking for the right word." He puts his feet into the water. "What about you? Are you unsettled?"

"If now's not a good time, I can—"

"No, please. Sit down. I'm listening."

Hesitant, Matthew sits. "Today you seemed to—elevate Simon." Off Jesus' look he says, "I mean Peter. I guess I'm not sure I fully understand his new position and what it means."

Jesus smiles. "I'm not sure *he* fully understands what it means."

"He was quiet the rest of the day," Matthew says, "which, I must admit, for me is a welcome change."

"Aah."

"I don't think you heard most of it, but that long day when we were in Syria, Simon—Peter—screamed at me in front of the others across the fire, said that I spit on the Jewish faith and that he would never forget what I did to him and that he couldn't ever forgive me."

"Have you asked for forgiveness?"

"Why would I when he's already said he wouldn't forgive? It's pointless."

As Jesus dries his feet, he says, "You don't apologize to be forgiven. You apologize to repent. Forgiveness is a gift from the other person."

"I'm just finding it hard to accept that the person you would formally assign leadership to over a group with the keys to the kingdom of heaven would be someone so temperamental. I know the term is a metaphor, but he doesn't act like a rock."

"I make people what they aren't. You know that more than most."

"You obviously can choose whomever you want, and your ways often seem very different from other people's ways. But I have to confess it hurts. You don't know how cruel he has been to me. Or you do know and chose to elevate him anyway. That makes it even more painful. I—"

Jesus lays a hand on Matthew's shoulder. "You're right. There have been times when Peter has been overly harsh with you, and that has not pleased my Father in heaven or me."

"Then why—"

"I'm not saying this is always the consideration, but I would simply ask who harmed the other first?"

Matthew sighs. "I guess, in the abstract, by accepting the job from Rome—"

"No. No, not in the abstract. In fact."

Matthew swallows. "By turning my back on our people and then by spying on him for Quintus, and ..." He's finally getting it, opening a door he's kept locked, comprehending the gravity of his offense. " … even coming within hours of turning him over to Rome and ruining his family's life …"

"And you've never apologized for that?"

"I want to forget about that time, the way Mary wants to forget about her time. And I want to keep peace. Apologizing would only cause an argument. The group already has enough of those. They're having one right now."

"There is no peace when two of my followers hold resentment in their hearts toward one another." Jesus pauses and Matthew hears crickets and wind. "You know what you must do, Matthew."

Matthew looks out into the night. He does know.

"It's been a long day," Jesus says. "I'm going to sleep now." He rises and kisses Matthew on the top of his head. "Good night."

In the distance, Matthew sees Peter setting up a tent. Zee, Philip, and Thaddeus have finished their work. Philip calls to the women and tells them their tent is ready. Mary, Tamar, and Ramah come running, as if escaping the argument around the fire.

"Andrew!" Peter hollers. "Our tent is ready too!"

"On my way."

"I heard raised voices. Were you arguing about something?"

John looks trapped. "About—who's going to take third watch."

"Isn't it Andrew's turn?" Peter says.

"John's taking it for me," Andrew says.

Matthew can tell Peter isn't entirely buying this. "Very kind of you, John. Philip, where's your lean-to?"

"It's my night to keep the fire."

"Oh, right, but then where is Matthew going to sleep?"

Matthew, surprised to hear Peter looking out for him, briefly meets his gaze.

Thaddeus says, "Little James and I made extra space for him."

"Thank you, Thaddeus," Peter says. "And Zee, you'll sleep just outside the women's tent?"

"As always."

What's gotten into Simon now that he's known as Peter? Matthew tries to slip away to James and Thaddeus's tent unnoticed. No such luck.

"Matthew," Peter says, "you talked to Jesus? He's good?"

"Yes. He went to sleep." Matthew can't hide his discomfort and knows Peter notices.

"All right then," Peter says. "Good night." He lifts his voice and begins the Hashkiveinu: "Lie us down, Adonai our God, in peace …"

Soon Andrew joins in, then everyone, including the women. "And raise us up again, our Ruler, in life. Spread over us Your sukkah of peace, direct us with Your good counsel, and save us for Your own name's sake. Shield us—remove from us every enemy, pestilence, sword, famine, and sorrow. Remove all adversaries from before us and behind us and shelter us in the shadow of Your wings. For You are our guarding and saving God, yes, a gracious and compassionate God and King. Guard our going out and our coming in for life and peace, now and always."

Matthew lies down, eyes open, wide awake.

Chapter 21

THE APOLOGY

The road to Galilee, the next morning

A war rages in Peter's mind. He knows the others are disconcerted by his relative silence, because he seldom refrains from saying whatever he thinks. But he's wondering what to do with all this now that Jesus has bestowed upon him a name—and dare he acknowledge it?—an expanded role too. He's honored beyond words, but how does it make sense that he, the one who bitterly questioned the logic and actions of the Messiah himself, should be singled out just because he accurately identified who Jesus is?

In many ways, yes, Jesus is right that flesh and blood had not revealed this to him, but God in heaven did. Not that he specifically felt that at the time he answered Jesus' identity question, though Peter did wonder how it seemed to pour from him so easily and with such conviction. He believes it with all his heart, and as valuable as he wants to be in serving Jesus, his doubts and fears and questions should have disqualified him, shouldn't they?

The privilege of walking with Jesus and all his new friends never gets old, but it strikes Peter that he seems to be the only

97

one *not* jabbering now. All about him the others discuss what his new name and potential standing means for them. The brothers John and James are deep in conversation. John says, "By *rock*, maybe he meant the foundation of a building. But that's not what is seen most prominently."

"Nor is it the highest point," James says.

"Maybe we could ask Jesus if Simon is going to be the main rock upon which his Church is built."

Thaddeus says, "I'm pretty sure Jesus is the main rock."

"If Simon is going to be one of the main rocks," John says, "then could we be the flags flying from the tallest parapet?"

"What about parapets?" Nathanael says.

"Nothing," James says.

"I think I know," Thomas says, "and I don't like it."

"So now that there aren't two Simons anymore," Zee says, "can I have my name back?"

Several shout "No!" in unison.

The group comes upon a merchant pulling a wagon, heading the other way. "Carob?" he says. "Mulberries, pistachios?"

Jesus stops the group. "Pistachios would be wonderful this morning. Judas, do we have enough in the purse for fourteen servings?"

Judas looks dubious and pauses to check. "Probably only if they're in-shell."

"With shells is no problem at all," Jesus says. "Fourteen servings, please!"

Thaddeus and Nathanael are assigned to pass out the servings. When Nathanael gets to Peter and Andrew, he says, "And look at that. Divided equally down to the last nut."

"Skills!" Andrew says.

"These are salty," Nathanael says, "and will make us thirst. Simon is your canteen f—"

"Peter," Peter says, surprising even himself. "The name's Peter."

"Right," Nathanael says. "You do know it's going to take us all a little time to get used to Peter. We're only mortal."

"To answer your first question, yes, this canteen's full."

"All right," Nathanael says, raising a brow and moving away.

"So," Andrew whispers to Peter, "my brother is The Rock. Feels like I should walk a little straighter."

"In more ways than one," Peter says. "You're going to have to stop bottling up your panic to the point where it explodes at the most inconvenient time—"

"I think I handled John's death better than I would have, say, a year ago—"

Peter says, "And I'm going to have to start—well, I don't know where to start. He didn't give any details."

"He did," Andrew says. "But they were cryptic. Like in Hebrew school when Rabbi Mordecai would read that passage from Shemot where God met Moses at a lodging place and tried to kill him—"

"Strangest story ever," Peter says, laughing.

"—but then his wife circumcised their son and touched the foreskin to Moses's feet and said—"

"'Surely you are a bridegroom of blood to me!' And then Rabbi Mordecai just—"

"Moved right along!"

"No explanation, no nothing. Just on to the next passage, and we were all left sitting there, completely confused."

"But Jesus isn't Rabbi Mordecai," Andrew says.

"And we're not little boys, fidgeting and wanting to go play outside. This is real." As Andrew munches, Peter changes the subject. "I had a bad time when Eden lost the baby. I questioned him."

"But you had the faith to step out of the boat onto the water."

"For about a second! Then I sank! Nathanael's right. We're only mortal. If I mess up again, will he change his mind and give the title to someone else?"

"Don't think about that."

"But I do, Andrew! You didn't notice me tossing and turning all night?"

"I sleep like a dead person, Simon."

"Tsk tsk …"

"Sorry, Peter! Peter, Peter, Peter …"

Farther up the line, Matthew, walking with Tamar, is deep in thought. *Never a dull moment. Something new to ponder every day.*

"So how do you decide?" she says.

Having never been comfortable around women, except sometimes Mary, he's alarmed. "Decide what?"

"What to include. I noticed you didn't write down the merchant exchange."

"Oh. If it was important, I would know."

"How?"

"Well, if it isn't obvious, and often it is, there's this look Jesus gives me, and then I know. We have an understanding."

Tamar gazes at him as if he's something special, which Matthew finds most disconcerting. He has to concentrate on putting one foot in front of the other. What grown man has to think about merely walking?

"You must feel so honored to be his scribe."

"I suppose."

"Matthew, are you feeling well? You haven't eaten any of your pistachios."

"Oh, these? I'm—saving them for later."

Jesus turns and gives Matthew a subtle glance. Tamar leans close and whispers, "Was that the look? Are you supposed to write this conversation with me?!"

"No. I'm—supposed to do something else."

"Oh," she says, looking deflated.

"If you'll excuse me …"

Matthew trudges back to Peter and Andrew, dreading the encounter as if he's been called on the carpet. "Sh-shalom."

Andrew points to Matthew's handful of pistachios. "You gonna finish those?"

"Andrew, c-could I have a moment with your brother?"

"You have to submit a formal request to speak to The Rock. In writing."

Matthew doesn't know what to say.

"I'm joking!" Andrew says and Matthew finally notices the twinkle in his eye. "Of course you can. I wanna go watch James and John pout anyway."

"Good morning," Peter says, when Matthew falls in line with him.

"I'm sorry," Matthew blurts.

"I said, 'Good morning.'"

"No, I heard you. I said 'I'm sorry' for what I did to you. It's been over a year now, and I realize I've never actually apologized for my role in your plight with the tax debt and for colluding with Quintus to report your activity."

Peter suddenly stops and they face each other.

Matthew continues, "It's strange. After the sermon, the big one, I immediately went to my parents and apologized to them for my actions. I should have gone to you next. And now my feelings are worse. And they won't be better if I don't ask for your forgiveness, so that's what I'm doing now. Well, actually I'm just saying I'm sorry. Forgiveness is a gift you can give. Or not give."

Matthew holds his breath. Peter looks away, then directly back at Matthew. He shakes his head and leaves Matthew standing there, devastated.

Chapter 22

"IT'S TIME"

The Capernaum temple

Yussif uses a yad pointer to scan a scroll in his office when he's distracted by excited voices outside. He rushes to the entrance and finds Jairus already there. Outside, a horseman wearing a dark russet cape dismounts, hands the reins to a rabbinical student, and jogs toward the two Pharisees. "You are?" he says, scroll in hand.

"Jairus, chief administrator here."

"Urgent, from the Jerusalem Sanhedrin."

Yussif looks on as Jairus accepts the scroll and quickly scans it.

"The scribes require oral affirmation you received this edict," the horseman says.

"Confirmed."

"Noted. I'm off to the next village."

Rabbi Akiva appears at the door. "What's all the commotion?"

Jairus hands him the scroll and with a subtle nod beckons Yussif to follow him back inside.

When they're alone in Yussif's office, Jairus whispers, "By name! They named him specifically for the charge of blasphemy. Jesus of Nazareth. How could this have advanced through the council so quickly?"

"I think we both know," Yussif says, quickly gathering his things.

"I cannot imagine a positive outcome."

"Jairus," Yussif says solemnly. "It's time. I have to go to Jerusalem."

"Where you will do wh—"

"Something I swore I would never do. Will you expedite the paperwork?"

"I can. I will. May God go with you, Yussif."

Minutes later

Yussif bursts through his bedroom door and heads straight for his desk, where he opens a drawer and seizes a golden key. He flings back a corner of a rug to reveal a compartment hidden in the wood floor. He unlocks it and reaches for a velvet bag before returning everything to the way it was.

Chapter 23

COMPLETION TIMES COMPLETION

Peter and Eden's home

Late at night, Peter lies next to Eden staring at the ceiling. He's told her all about the recent days on the road, but he has avoided what's really bothering him. He cannot find peace until he gets this one thing right. He has more questions for Jesus and wishes the rabbi would accept his and Eden's invitation to stay with them. Others invited him too, but the master prefers solitude. That only makes sense after his having to deal with more than a dozen personalities all day every day. Peter also worries about Jesus camping alone in the forest. At least he informs them where he will be in case of an emergency, but short of that, they are to leave him alone.

It wouldn't be beyond Zee to camp within a stone's throw of Jesus to keep guard. But Jesus would know, wouldn't he? And the disciples' number one job is to obey their rabbi. If he wants to be alone, they leave him alone. Would he forgive Peter if he interrupted Jesus' reverie just for a few minutes? He needs this question answered.

Peter can tell from Eden's breathing that she's about to drift off. But she has a question too. "So, do I call you Peter also, or is that just him?"

"I think everyone. From now on. Forever."

"There are so many Simons in this world," she murmurs. "I've never heard of anyone named Peter." She pauses. Then, "But it suits you. One of a kind." She kisses him, sighs, and rolls onto her side. Within seconds he can tell she's asleep.

How he envies her ability to shut things down, apparently stop her mind, and enjoy real slumber. Meanwhile he's reliving that night at sea, the one Matthew's strange recitation reminded him of. He'd had to catch enough fish to stay out of debtor's prison, and the result was agonizing bupkis. Despite his experience, his prowess, his expertise, all Peter did all night was cast his nets and drag them back in without so much as a minnow. Believing he was alone, he had cried out like an animal, ranted at God, questioned his own heritage, and argued against everything his people had faced for centuries.

None of this is helping him sleep now. Yes, the next morning he met Jesus, who miraculously produced a bountiful catch that not only spared Peter from the Romans and Matthew and prison and losing everything, but also set him on an entirely new course. But for this moment, the highs of following Jesus are again not outweighing a certain low. Jesus preaches salvation, repentance, the kingdom, forgiveness, and reconciliation. And Peter is all-in on all but the last two.

Careful not to awaken Eden, he slips out of bed and into his sandals and quietly leaves the house. The moonlit night is warm as he exits Capernaum's gates and follows a forest trail. It appears Jesus' fire remains lit, so he can only hope the rabbi is still up. Desperate as he is for answers, he would not wake the master.

Oh, good! Peter finds Jesus praying before the flames and tiptoes near. He doesn't want to startle him, but neither does he want to interrupt. Jesus stops praying but keeps his eyes shut. Peter stops and takes a deep breath.

Jesus opens his eyes. "Peter. It's pretty late."

"I could say the same to you."

"I suppose you could."

"Something keeping you up?"

"I could ask the same of you."

Fine. Well, awkward as he has made it, Peter decides he's here and might as well get to the subject at hand. He plops down next to Jesus, exasperated. "What do I do when someone has sinned against me egregiously, repeatedly, and without repentance?"

Jesus gives him what appears to be a knowing look. "Can't imagine who that could be."

Okay, so they both know. Peter's going to just come out with it. He begins counting on his fingers. "The betrayal of our people by working for Rome was one thing, a sin against all of his and our heritage. Then he showed no mercy when Andrew begged for extra time on his tribute debt. Then he even charged an extra sixty percent on what was past due. Next he was going to let Rome seize our boat as collateral. Which would have taken away our ability to work and landed us both in jail. Meaning Eden would have starved. And he didn't even hesitate a moment when Quintus asked him to spy on me." Peter shows Jesus his fingers. "I'm up to seven and we haven't even gotten to the fact that he was fully ready to turn me in the morning that—"

"The morning that what?"

"You know."

"I do. He may have been ready to turn you in, but it didn't come to that. So, for the moment, let's leave it at seven. The number of completion."

"He sins against me seven times, and I'm supposed to forgive that?"

"No."

Peter perks up. Maybe he's onto something.

But Jesus continues, "Not seven. But seventy-seven times."

"I could stack 'em that high if I really broke down each offense and its consequences."

"You know I don't mean literally seventy-seven. Seventy *times* seven, completion times completion. Endless forgiveness. Without limit."

Peter shakes his head. "You gave me a new name and made a big proclamation, but I'm still the same man I was the day before that. I'm still human, and I can't do this. I can't. And no one would blame me."

"You mentioned the consequences of Matthew's actions," Jesus says. "Remember the circumstances they put you in?"

"That's all I think about! It's why I'm here right now."

"But after that. When the sun came up."

Peter will never forget that. The miraculous haul of fish. Falling to his knees in the sand before Jesus.

The rabbi sighs. "I know it's hard."

"Why does it have to be?"

"Man makes it harder when he leans on his own understanding."

Peter can't argue with that. He raises his head, wipes his face, stares at the fire. "I'll leave you alone now."

As he trudges away, Peter shakes his head at the hard truths Jesus always makes so plain. He grabs a branch in the path, breaks it over his thigh, and flings both pieces against a tree.

Chapter 24

COMPLICATED

The Roman Authority

Primi Gaius and his subordinate Julius have been called before Quintus yet again to answer for what the praetor refers to as the riff raff who have cobbled together a makeshift shantytown not far from the Capernaum city gates.

"You know why they're still here?" Quintus says. "I'll tell you. Because they're comfortable. You may not think so, because they're living in a tent city while you live in houses with roofs over your heads. But the fact of the matter is that if they had a problem sleeping on the ground in squalor, they would have left a long time ago."

Privately, this is what Gaius actually admires about these people. But naturally he's not allowed to voice this to his superior. "We can't affect what the pilgrims are willing to endure for even the faintest chance they'll get to hear more teaching from Jesus of Nazareth. They're intractable."

"Wrong! That's the problem with you, Gaius. You accept things as given. Use your imagination! One week from today,

I want every last one of them gone and someone else's problem entirely. Do you understand?"

"Yes, Dominus." He understands all right, but he doesn't have to like it.

"Now, get out."

On their way down the hall toward the exit, Julius says, "Where do we start, Primi?"

The question of the ages. He separates from Julius, saying, "I'll think of something."

Gaius slowly heads down the street where Matthew once lived, deep in thought.

"Gaius?"

It's Matthew, and Gaius knows he must look a sight with his shoulders slumped and a scowl on his face. He straightens and tries to sound chipper. "Good morning, Matthew."

The awkward little man seems to be studying him. "It does not look like a good morning for you. Are you unwell?"

The one time I want Matthew to be oblivious ... "It's just— work. I'm fine, Matthew."

"You have some talents, Gaius ..."

"Thank you."

"... but you are not an effective liar. It is clear you are not fine. Is your family in trouble?"

How is it that this quirky guy can sometimes be so insightful?! "What do you know about families?" And now it's obvious he has stung Matthew. He didn't deserve that. "Look," Gaius continues, "I'm glad you have people now. Home is complicated. I'm helpless."

"You are right. I don't know families very well. And I complicate everything."

"Don't say that."

"My teacher, he makes life very simple. Every morning when I wake up, my ideas and fears are jumbled. I feel overwhelmed with doubt and regret."

"Yes."

"If I can just pause for a moment and remember."

He has an answer? I can't wait. "What? Remember what?"

"That I have only one thing to do today. Follow him. The rest takes care of itself."

Oh, for a peace like that. But Gaius catches himself. He can't let on that he's intrigued. "I'm happy for you."

"You could come. To see him. He will preach a sermon soon. Maybe even tomorrow."

Oh, no. "I would not advise a public appearance. Not for a while."

"I do not decide when or where—"

"If you have any influence, use it. It's not safe. In fact, we should not be seen talking. Take care of yourself."

Matthew does not know what to make of this as he turns toward his former home, now the mission house. Several of the disciples—all but Peter, it seems—and Mary chat outside when Ramah and Tamar appear at the door and Ramah announces, "We need three men to help with pruning in the olive grove today."

Thaddeus and Andrew immediately volunteer, but just as Thomas is saying, "I'm in!" John says, "Thomas, wait." Ramah looks disappointed, but John adds, "Matthew, can you go?"

"I suppose."

John thanks Matthew and pulls Thomas aside. "You and I are going to market. Peter's right. You shouldn't take Ramah up on the scrap of clothing thing being your gift to her. I told Abba about it, and he agreed it might sound romantic, but in ten years she'll wish you had bought something."

"That's the problem," Thomas says. "I can't buy anything. We don't have any money."

James flings a cloth cover off a tray with a flourish and shouts, "Ima's famous cinnamon cakes!"

John pulls Thomas away. "We'll barter," he says. "Let's go."

"How much could we possibly get trading cakes?" Thomas says.

"You'll be surprised. They're just the starter. We'll work our way up."

Peter arrives at the mission house and sees all the activity. He stops. Can he really go through with this? Thomas and James and John are leaving, and Tamar is handing out harvesting tools to several others. Resolute, Peter looks to the sky, closes his eyes, and decides.

He walks through the midst of everyone else, and they all seem to stop and turn and watch him. Peter zeroes in on Matthew, who looks petrified. Several others part, allowing Peter full access to the former tax collector. He wraps Matthew in a huge embrace and feels the man go rigid, obviously wondering what in the world is going on.

At last Matthew softens in Peter's arms, though he can't move, his own arms bolted to his sides by the former fisherman. Everyone has frozen in place and all eyes are on these two. Peter says quietly, "I forgive you." Matthew's face creases with emotion, and he slowly returns Peter's hug. "It's all forgotten," Peter adds.

He pulls back and grips the back of Matthew's head, staring into his eyes. "To the ends of the earth, right?"

Matthew nods, clearly overcome.

Peter turns to the rest. "It's over."

PART 3

Woe

Chapter 25

GONE

Jerusalem, 980 B.C.

King David lies prostrate before an altar of incense in the courtyard of his royal palace in the night. For nearly a week he has worn goatshair sackcloth intended to scratch and irritate his skin and remind him of his sin. It's wholly unnecessary, as he agonizes beyond regret, despising himself and his weakness. He committed adultery with the wife of a trusted aide, then had him killed in battle. Despite a life of humility and stellar leadership, the man "after God's own heart" had reached the depths of depravity. Worse, he had been found out, and the prophet Nathan told him that, while he would not die, the beloved son of the disgraceful union will. He has for days beseeched the Lord for pardon.

"Have mercy on me, O God, according to Your steadfast love; according to Your abundant mercy blot out my transgressions. Wash me thoroughly from my iniquity and cleanse me from my sin! For I know my transgressions, and my sin is ever before me."

Despite that his face is in the dirt, and wishing he were deep in the ground, the aroma of food reaches him, as does the conversation of two elders of the house standing behind a pillar. "He has to eat something or he'll die," one says. "As if his grief were not enough."

"It's repentance," the other says. He lowers his voice. "For the manner in which the child was conceived."

"Three days, maybe four, I understand," the first says. "But six? Can a person live without food or water for six days?"

"If anyone can, it would be him. He probably went longer when he was on the run from Saul."

"He was a teenager! If the king dies on our watch, we'll be executed. This regime has slaughtered people for less. Come on."

Footsteps. A gentle touch. "Your majesty, please. Take some nourishment."

Ravenous as he is, nothing appeals less. "Is the child restored?" he manages.

The elders share a look. "Not yet," one says. "But the doctor says he is fighting, my lord."

"Leave me to my prayers."

"Batsheva needs you. The child needs you."

"I said leave. What is needed is my repentance."

David remains there all night, fitfully dozing on and off between long, repeated pleadings to God.

Sunrise brings David a modicum of hope. God's mercies are new every morning. But just when he's tempted to check on the child, Batsheva's anguished wail pierces the silence—and his soul. From behind the pillar, one asks the other, "What are the right words?"

"There are none."

The king rises and approaches the men. They fall silent. He stands straight, shoulders back. Unyielding, he gathers himself. "I'm ready," he says, pulling off the sackcloth and tossing it away.

The elders grab a bucket of water, a towel, and a silk violet tunic. David raises the bucket over his head and douses himself, quickly drying his hair and the rest of his body before donning the tunic.

That evening he avoids eye contact with Batsheva, who stands before a vanity seemingly unable to dress herself or even move. David changes clothes behind a screen.

"Why are we getting ready for a dinner I cannot eat?" she says. "How can you eat at a time like this?"

"While the child was alive, I fasted and wept."

"As you should now."

"Would that bring him back? I asked our God to be gracious and let the child live. The answer was no."

"Why?" she says. "Why are some prayers answered and not others?"

He steps out to face her. "I don't know. I've never known."

"And yet still you worship."

"I do. Through sorrow and joy. And sorrow again. That is the meaning of faith."

"But we can't get our son back!"

"No, but sooner or later we will both meet the same end. He will not return to us, but we will go to him."

This seems to somewhat reach her. "The separation is only for now, for a time."

David nods. "A time. It could be a long time; it could be tomorrow. This is the way of all things."

Chapter 26

PRAETOR ON THE RAMPAGE

The Roman Authority

Quintus has long enjoyed his role as Praetor of Galilee. Even with the usual detractors, the envious, and the political opponents, he's found it fun. *If it were easy,* he thinks, *anyone could do it.* Most delicious to him has been showing off his nimble mind with biting, condescending turns of phrase that seem to come to him just when he needs them.

But today is anything but enjoyable. He's poring over financial ledgers, eyes darting. Quintus has largely been able to stay above the partisan bureaucratic fray because, aside from personality differences, he's proven adept at making the numbers work. No one above or below him has been able to quarrel with his results. Capernaum, under him, has been profitable—sometimes extravagantly so.

Until now. Furiously sliding the bronze marbles about on his metal abacus, he can't make the totals work in his favor.

What's costing so much?! Quintus can't make the budget balance, let alone show any hint of a profit. The more he studies it, the more those marbles fly, the worse it looks, and the more furious he grows. This will not do! This will more than embarrass him if he doesn't turn things around, and fast. He's sure to lose much more than his reputation. He could find himself back on military patrol.

Finding no way to even camouflage the numbers, he slams a fist on his desk, rises, and sweeps the books and the abacus to the floor. He storms past his secretary, prompting the man to call after him. "Dominus?"

Quintus barrels down the outside stairs and into the village. He blusters past Gaius's underling Julius and a couple other soldiers, aware of their wide-eyed stares. Behind him, his secretary bursts out the door, shouting, "Dominus! Your helmet and sword! Don't venture out unarmed!" As he passes the three guards, the secretary says, "He just walked right out! Didn't say anything!"

The praetor notices the soldiers now have his helmet and sword and are following him, but he's obsessing over a toppled bucket left in the street. "Who left this here?! It's obstructing traffic! Filthy animals!" He kicks the bucket aside. "Smells like a sewer on a hot day!"

As citizens sneak behind carts and around corners, Julius catches him. "Dominus, your helmet." Quintus slaps it away. "At least carry your sword."

The praetor grabs his weapon and angrily sheathes it. And here comes Matthew's dog. "Look at this," he rages. "Unattended, unchained, spreading disease."

A crippled man lying against a wall hollers, "Dominus, can you help me?"

"Another dog," Quintus growls. "What is your address?"

"I don't have—"

"Of course you don't. Why are you here?"

"Messiah is here."

"Get out of my street."

"Dominus," Julius says, "he has nowhere to—"

"Get rid of the dog! Both of them!"

In the market, Quintus grabs a skin of wine as he passes a booth. The vintner shouts, "Hey!"

The praetor whirls and points in the man's face. "Are you up to date on your taxes? Tell me the truth. You know I can find out quickly, and if you lie …"

"I'm—"

"You're what?"

"Making payments."

Quintus holds up the wine. "This is one of your payments." He uncorks the vessel and takes a swig, moving on toward a woman selling beads from a blanket. "Why are you not selling from a booth? Do you have a permit?"

Gaius has been on patrol when Julius reaches him and briefs him on what's happening. "And he didn't say what he was looking for?"

"No, Primi. Wouldn't even take his helmet."

They round the corner to the market to find Quintus ordering a pair of young boys to scoop piles of dung from the street. "Hades and Styx," Gaius mutters.

"That one," Quintus says. "And that one. And this over here! Can't you smell it? I don't know how you people live like this."

Gaius rushes to him. "Dominus, is everything all right?"

"Look around you, Gaius! Nothing is all right!"

"If you have an order to give, Dominus, we will carry it out."

Quintus grabs Gaius and shoves him against a wall. "Rome assigned me this hellhole because they thought I couldn't hack it in one of the bigger cities. But they changed their tune when my tribute record posted among the highest in the region. Now my ledgers are in the red. I told you to make life difficult for the followers of Jesus."

"We've enforced curfews and implemented stricter—"

"Taxes were the only leg I had to stand on in the empire, and these vulgar pilgrims have cut it off."

"What can be done, Dominus?"

"'What can—' I'm done giving you ideas, Gaius. No more conversations. No more mentoring you. Results only. The tent city will shrink by ten cubits a day. Say it back to me, Primi. I gave you that title and I can strip it away."

"Ten cubits a day."

"Ten cubits a day what?"

"The tent city will shrink by that much."

"Or?"

"Or I'll be—"

"A centurion again. Maybe something even lower, depending on how I feel that day."

"Yes, Dominus."

"I am *not* going to lose my job or my future because I hastily promoted some Germanic tax collector escort."

Chapter 27

SCHEMING IMA

Zebedee and Salome's house

James stands outside the door with little brother John, whispering. "We must keep this Simon, Peter, and The Rock business from Ima. She has us on a pedestal, and—"

"Let's just get inside before they suspect something."

"She's going to want to know what's going on," James says.

"Distract her. Distract 'em both with news of the growth of the tent city."

James nods. "Let's act in a hurry. Ready?"

He bursts through the door with John right behind him, only to find his father and mother already seated at the dinner table. "Oh!" John says. "Hello."

Zebedee seems to study them with that maddening glint in his eyes. He always appears to know exactly what they're up to. "Are you being chased?" he says.

"It's madness out there," James says. "The pilgrims."

"Come, sit," his mother says.

As James loads his plate, his father says, "I was just telling your ima how quickly word has spread. The synagogues of Gennesaret and Bethsaida sent in orders for oil. Ramah said just yesterday that she got an inquiry from the rabbis at Cana! We're going to have to buy another olive grove just to keep up!"

James knows he should say something, but at least this news avoids what he and John are determined to keep from their mother. John nods and Zebedee narrows his eyes. James wonders how he and his brother can be so bad at this.

"Is there something in your ears?" Zebedee says.

"What?" James says.

"You're not listening."

"Yes we are," John says.

"We are," James adds.

"You're getting more orders for oil," John says.

"You sound overjoyed," Zebedee says.

"That's very good for you," James tries. "We're glad."

"What do you want us to do," John says, "jump up and down and dance?"

"Us? We? I thought you two were fighting. Now you're *us*?"

"It never came to blows," James says.

"You know what I mean."

"How do you want us to be?" John says. "You say it's a shame if we disagree. Now it's suspicious that we're unified?"

"I may be getting old," Zebedee says, "but my eyes are still good. I see you boys."

"See what?" John says.

"You're hiding something."

"We're not!" James says.

"No, we aren't," John says.

Zebedee squints. "I know Jesus is teaching you important things, but apparently how to keep a secret is not one of them."

"He's asked us to keep many things secret," John says. "And we have!"

That maddening twinkle is back. Zebedee says, "Here's some free advice. The next time someone accuses you of hiding something, don't be defensive and show that you are. Dead giveaway."

How does he do this? James wonders. He can tell John is fuming as his brother snatches the pitcher and tries to refill his wine goblet. Upside down it produces only a half cup. "Is there no more wine?" he says, slamming the pitcher down.

"What happened on the trip to Caesarea Philippi?" Salome says.

Uh-oh, James thinks. Their mother seems onto them too.

Now both parents are leaning toward them. James knows he and John are not going to be able to weasel out of this. While they're stalling for time, John heads for another skin of wine and uncorks it on his way back to the table. "Jesus gave Simon a new name. Who wants more wine?"

Zebedee and Salome trade glances. James says, "Peter. The Rock."

"Happy now?" John asks his parents.

"I'm not anything," Zebedee says. "Just confused maybe. Rock meaning hard, firm, stable? I'm not saying I would ever disagree with Jesus, but that doesn't really sound like Simon."

"Sure," John says.

"He said," James adds, "like a stone for the foundation of a house."

"So," their mother says, "what are your new names?" At their apparently agonized silence, she adds, "This is ridiculous! You've done more for Jesus than Simon. Fivefold!"

"Five?" John says.

"Those rows you planted in Samaria! The notes you're keeping of his words and deeds!"

"Matthew is recording too," John says.

But she's not finished. "Controlling the crowds at the sermon. Staying behind to wait for Simon when he was full of bitterness and doubt over what happened to Eden …"

"That's four," James says, wishing he could get on board with her argument.

"Leaving your jobs to follow him!" she says.

"Everyone did that," James says.

"Regardless, you boys deserve real standing and blessing."

"Salome," Zebedee says.

"This is important, Zeb! When people see Jesus, our boys should always be by his side, one on his right and one on his left."

"If that's what Jesus wants," Zebedee says, "then that's what will happen."

"That's not what he said on the Korazim Plateau," she says. "You don't remember? 'Ask and it will be given to you. Seek and you will find.'"

Zebedee joins to add to the quote, "'Knock and it will be opened to you.'"

How well James recalls that portion of the sermon. "'For everyone who asks receives, and the one who seeks finds, and to the one who knocks, it will be opened'!"

"We really can ask him anything?" John says.

His mother says, "What else could 'ask and it will be given to you' mean?"

Zebedee says, "I think he means when you are seeking first the kingdom of God."

"This *is* about the kingdom of God," she says. "Kingdoms need officers and authorities, people of influence. Sounds like Jesus has begun assigning titles and roles, starting with Simon.

Don't you boys want to have influence? Don't you want the blessing that comes from being closest to God? I don't want you to be last, or far from God, but if you don't ask for authority now, others will get in front of you. I have to explain this to you?"

"Ima is right," James says. "If we can ask anything, as long as we are seeking first the kingdom, so can everyone else."

"I don't know," John says. "The group is doing so well. The grieving for Jesus' cousin has been completed. Peter forgave Matthew for everything that happened between them …"

Zebedee looks surprised. "Simon *forgave* Matthew?"

"Peter, yes," John says. "Hugs and everything."

"That really does deserve a name change," Zebedee says.

"Don't change the subject," Salome says.

John says, "We don't want to cause a stir, Ima. What if it casts a shadow over Thomas and Ramah's engagement? I could never do that to Thomas."

That quiets everyone. James shoots John a stinging look. Zebedee sighs. Salome refills her wine goblet and takes a sip, leaning back. "If you're going to sit idly by and do nothing, maybe I'll ask Jesus myself."

"Ima!" James shouts. "Please do not!"

"Don't do that!" John says.

"Salome!" Zebedee says. "Really?"

James cannot imagine anything more humiliating. His mother shrugs as if it were just a suggestion.

Chapter 28

THE OBJECT
OF VALUE

The mission house

John shows up to check on the work of his father's olive oil business and finds Mary Magdalene, Tamar, and Ramah busy packing bottles. Judas is nearby, recording orders in a ledger. All John cares about is that Ramah is present. His plan should work. "Shalom, boker tov, my friends," he says.

Tamar looks up. "Shalom and good morning to you too."

"To what do we owe the pleasure?" Mary says.

"Important business," he says, looking back and beckoning Thomas in. He's bearing a large bag on his back.

"Ramah?" Thomas says. She looks caught off guard. "I was wondering if we could go for a short walk …"

"We're—very busy" she says. "So many orders …"

"Please?"

Ramah looks to Mary who winks at her. She rises and Thomas turns to the courtyard where the other disciples have mustered. "Nathanael? Whose turn is it?"

John knows he's looking for a chaperone and says, "Most of them are gone. I'll just do it."

"John," Nathanael says, "you're an unreliable chaperone."

"*Unreliable?!*"

"Overly permissive."

"So whose turn is it?" Thomas says.

"I don't know," Nathanael says. "We normally cast lots."

"Can you?"

"Well, I could," Nathanael says, "except I don't want to." He looks back. "Andrew!"

Shore of the Sea of Galilee

How Thomas longs for the day—in the not-too-distant future, he hopes—when he can enjoy time entirely alone with his beloved. Andrew trails him and Ramah at an appropriate distance.

"The arrangements for the Kiddushin are nearly all in place," Thomas tells her. "John has agreed to be the witness on my side, and Jesus has agreed to serve as witness on your side—as well as serving as the rabbi to sign the ketubah, which confirms a unique circumstance."

Ramah nods.

"There's one thing left," Thomas adds. "The object of value."

Ramah flinches. "I thought we agreed—"

"I know, I know. But I wanted to give you *something*. Actually, I knew what I wanted it to be way back when we just worked together. Before the wedding at Cana." He pulls a box out of his bag. "I traded my way up from a cinnamon loaf to a fish to a lantern to a bookshelf, barter after barter all the way up to this." He hands her the box. "A sundial."

She gasps. "Thomas! It's perfect!"

"For our future home," he says, so full of emotion and desire that he leans toward her, glancing at Andrew. The chaperone turns and begins a series of coughs that conveniently turn him away from his line of sight to them. He wipes his mouth and clears his throat. "Phew! Thought I was a goner."

"It's beautiful," Ramah says. "And you knew for years? Why a sundial?"

"Because whenever we worked together I was always losing track of time, which is not like me."

She laughs. "No, it's not."

"When we would talk on the road or after an event, time stopped for me. I couldn't tell if it had been ten minutes or an hour."

"I felt the same. But I held back those feelings because I had so little control over who my father would choose for me."

"You don't have to be afraid anymore. We'll be together till the end of time. And we'll have this to keep track of the hours in between."

"I don't know what to say."

Thomas remembers her saying the same thing to him after the miracle at the Cana wedding. "So don't," he says, parroting how she responded at the time.

A couple strolls past on the beach, the woman obviously late in pregnancy. "Actually, I do remember something I wanted to say. When all of this started to become real, after we spoke to Jesus on the way to Caesarea, I visited Eden to ask for any advice."

"But Sim—uh, Peter and I are very different people."

"You are," Ramah says. "But marriage is marriage, and you do follow the same rabbi. He has called you to a very special kind of life."

"Yes."

"I want us to learn from what happened to Simon and Eden with their baby. We must not lean on our own understanding. We must trust and not lose faith when things become hard. And we know they will. Let's do everything in our power to help each other with this, with remaining faithful. Beyond all our other vows, let's promise each other that."

Chapter 29

GROWING TENSION

The Capernaum temple

Jairus is on his way to Yussif's office with a tray of inkwells when he passes the bet midrash, where Rabbi Akiva, waving a parchment from the podium, addresses a quorum of students. Jairus stops out of sight to listen.

"This edict," the rabbi says, "prompted by reports of what was a most impassioned speech by Rabban Shammai to the Great Sanhedrin in Jerusalem, identifies Jesus of Nazareth, *by name,* as a heretic and blasphemer to be challenged and questioned, and if caught in blasphemy, to be taken for questioning before the High Council. He is known to be in or near Capernaum. I myself witnessed him in the town square performing sorcery and necromancy and publicly self-identifying as the Anointed One! He was rude and dismissive and every bit as dangerous as this edict warns. Every one of you is to be on high alert. Jerusalem thinks little of Capernaum, but we know more than any other place in Israel about this person of interest."

Jairus fears this is not going to end well—for Jesus, for himself, or for Yussif.

Peter's home

Eden hopes Jesus will be pleased as she and Mary of Magdala set several plates of food before him.

"Oh, I appreciate this," he says. "But I don't think I'm hungry enough to eat all of this."

Mary says, "Every time you preach, you're exhausted and immediately ask for food afterward. We figured we'd get ahead of it this time."

"Well, I'm more than happy to test your theory," he says, taking a piece of bread.

"Rabbi," Eden says, "why are you teaching today?"

"Circumstances demand it."

"What circumstances?"

"There is growing tension here. The pilgrims. The Pharisees. Even the Romans. I must ensure the people listen to the right voice. They are being led poorly."

Across the room, James huddles with his brother, determined to be on the same page and preclude their mother from interfering. "Do we literally just come right out and ask to sit at his right and left hand, John? Where did Ima even come up with that?"

"I think she was referring to how Batsheva sat at the right hand of King Solomon."

"Wasn't that when she was trying to get someone killed? Like David wrote, 'The Lord says to my Adonai, "Sit at my right hand until I make your enemies your footstool."'"

"We're not trying to kill anyone," John says.

"But what if that's what it reminds Jesus of?"

"Maybe we just ask for seats, but then they could be any seats."

"Like at the back of the synagogue," James says.

"We're overthinking this, James. Tonight Jesus will be feeling good about his sermon, and we'll ask him then. It'll be a conversation."

"Just not in front of anybody," James says.

"Absolutely not in front of anybody."

Peter senses Matthew's agitation as he looks out the window, appearing hyper-vigilant.

"What are you looking for, Matthew? A lion?"

Matthew looks thrown, and Peter reminds himself that the man takes everything literally. "Why would I be looking for a lion?"

"You just seem nervous."

"Not about a lion."

"Okay, fine."

"Peter, do you think this is a good idea? This sermon? When I invited Gaius, he seemed very alarmed that we were planning a public gathering of any kind."

Peter shakes his head. "Frankly, with all the heat coming from both Rome and the Pharisees, I think it's a terrible idea. But what can we do? He is who he is. We can't run from every conflict." He gently bumps Matthew's shoulder with his own. "Besides, I didn't think a lot of things Jesus did were good sense." He puts an arm around Matthew. "But those things have turned out too."

Chapter 30

MORE FUN

Capernaum

It's nearly time to preach, and Jesus wants everyone with him. He leads the disciples and the women into the city square where he spots Shula and Barnaby. "Shula!" he calls out.

She turns, beaming. "Master!"

"What is it?" he teases. "Weren't expecting to see me?"

She laughs and Barnaby cackles, "It'll never get old!"

But Shula quickly sobers. "It's just that …"

"What?" Jesus says.

She leans close and lowers her voice. "We heard there's been some sort of edict. From Jerusalem."

"Isn't that where they usually come from?" Jesus says.

Peter and John edge closer as Shula whispers, "About you, Rabbi."

"By name?" John says.

She nods. "If anyone catches you in blasphemy, they are to have you taken before the Sanhedrin."

"There's more," Barnaby says.

Shula nods. "Rabbi Akiva has said that any person who confesses Jesus as the Christ is to be put out of the synagogue."

"Who did you hear that from?" Peter says.

Zee presses in. "Has it been enforced?"

"It doesn't matter," Jesus says. "I will be direct with the Pharisees today. They've gone too far." He's suddenly distracted by a man holding a beggar's cup and slumped against a wall. He feels for the man. "How long has he been here?"

"That's Uzziah," Shula whispers. "We've been friends since my malady started, but he's been blind since birth."

Jesus becomes aware that others have noticed he's out and about and begin gathering. Peter motions for them to not interfere. "Big James," Jesus says, "draw some water from the well. Shula, introduce me to your friend."

She hesitates, looking troubled. "What are you—you can't—"

Barnaby says, "I know that look. He's going to do it anyway."

"Why not, Shula?" Jesus says.

"It's Shabbat."

"That'll make this even more fun."

Jesus notices that Rabbi Josiah, one of his staunchest critics, has joined the growing crowd.

Shula approaches the blind man. "Uzziah," she says, "this is Jesus, the teacher."

"The one who healed Shula!" Barnaby says. "And me!"

"He knows, Barnaby," she says.

Jesus kneels before the man. "Shabbat shalom, Uzziah."

A bystander says, "Rabbi, please answer this for us: who sinned, Uzziah or his parents, that caused him to be born blind?"

"You're a friend of his?" Jesus says.

"Yes, and we've wondered for years."

"It was not that this man sinned, or his parents, but that the works of God might be displayed in him." This has apparently caught the attention of everyone, the disciples included. "Listen carefully," Jesus tells his followers. "We must work the works of Him Who sent me while it is day. Night is coming when no one can work. And as long as I am in the world, I am the light of the world."

Matthew stops jotting and cocks his head. "We can't work at night?"

"It's a metaphor, Matthew. We have limited time on this earth. I have limited time. Let's not argue about the sins of the past. We have light to give."

Jesus spits on the ground and forms a mud paste causing gasps and grumbles from the crowd. "This might feel strange, Uzziah, but it'll be worth it. Hold still." He rubs the mud on the man's eyes as James sets a bucket of water down next to them. "Now wash."

Uzziah rinses his eyes and leaps to his feet, blinking, squinting, staring in the sunlight. As the crowd exults, Uzziah embraces Jesus, weeping. Jesus can feel the glare from Rabbi Josiah. Others arrive at the commotion. A poor pilgrim. Also Rivka, Mary Magdalene's former landlady. And Sol, the eunuch bartender from The Hammer.

"Sol!" Mary shouts. "Rivka! Shalom!"

"We heard Jesus was here," Rivka says.

"Rivka," Sol says, pointing, "look."

"Uzziah?" she says.

Sol nods. "Isn't this the man who used to sit and beg?"

"Of course it is!" she says. "Uzziah, what happened?"

The poor pilgrim says, "No, the man who used to sit and beg had blurry white eyes."

"That's because he was blind!" Barnaby says.

Uzziah thrusts his cup into the air. "This is what I used to ask for alms!"

Rabbi Josiah approaches Uzziah. "You! Come with me."

"Now?" Uzziah says.

"Yes, now. To the synagogue."

"I can't think of a better place!" the healed man says. He turns to Jesus. "Thank you, thank you! They want me at the synagogue."

"I'm sure they do," Jesus says. "Be sure to worship while you're there."

As the rabbi pulls Uzziah away, he hollers to Barnaby and Shula, "Tell my parents what happened and where I am!"

"Absolutely!" Barnaby says. "Right away!" He turns to Shula. "Where do they live?"

"How would I know?" she says. "I was blind the whole time I knew him."

"Let's go. We'll ask around."

"Do another miracle!" someone shouts, and the crowd cheers.

"That's not how this works," Jesus says. "But I do have much to share with you."

As the crowd settles in, the poor pilgrim runs through the street toward the tent city, against the current of people flowing toward the square. When he reaches his own shabby quarters, he gathers up his family. "He's preaching in the square! Come quickly!"

His wife lets out a little shriek and he shushes her. "Don't draw attention!"

But it's too late. As he and the family sneak out, word spreads throughout the camp and hundreds pour toward the square.

The Capernaum synagogue

Jairus has just stepped out of his office when Rabbi Josiah appears with a shabby looking man who keeps grabbing objects and holding them up to his eyes.

"Where's Rabbi Akiva?" Josiah says.

"What's so urgent?" Jairus says as Rabbi Akiva approaches.

"There you are!" Josiah says. "That teacher from Nazareth is in town, and he just healed this man of blindness."

"What do you mean?" Akiva says. "It's Shabbat."

"I know," Josiah says, and Jairus senses his glee.

Rabbi Akiva addresses Uzziah. "You were blind?"

"Was, yes."

"How did you receive your sight?"

"He put mud on my eyes, I washed, and I see."

"Sorcery and dark arts!"

"That's exactly what I thought," Josiah says.

Jairus speaks up. "We have not seen him perform sorcery."

"The man has violated Shabbat," Akiva says, "broken bread with Gentiles, and made false, heretical claims. He is *not* from God."

Jairus decides it's time to risk everything. "If he's such a sinner," he says, "how then can he do these signs?"

Josiah asks Uzziah, "What do you say about him?"

"He's obviously a prophet. Look what he did for me."

An older couple rush in. The woman hurries to him. "Uzziah? Are you—your eyes! Can you see me?"

"This is your son?" Akiva says. "And he was born blind? How can he see?!"

Uzziah's father says, "They told us the teacher from—" His wife gives him a look and he slows. "Well, we do know this is our son, and yes, he was born blind. But how he sees or who opened his eyes, we don't know. Have you asked him? He is of age."

Akiva turns to Uzziah. "If this is all true, give glory to Adonai. But this teacher from Nazareth is a sinner."

"Whether he is a sinner, I do not know. One thing I do know is that though I was blind, now I see."

"You need to tell me how he did this," Akiva says.

"I already told you and you wouldn't listen. All I know is, this man must be from God. He must be the Christ, or he couldn't have done this."

Akiva reddens. "You were born in utter sin and you preach at us in our own synagogue?! You know the edict: if anyone blasphemes by calling this sinner Christ, he is banned."

"No!" Uzziah's mother says. "Our son doesn't know what he's saying. Please, we just know—"

"Out!" Akiva shouts. He turns to Josiah. "We have to get to him right now."

Chapter 31

PANIC

Capernaum square

Gaius remembers fondly when his life was straightforward. He has long prided himself on being a man of discipline, rising in the ranks to become a Primi Ordine—among the top five soldiers in what is called the first cohort and paid thirty times the starting salary for a man in charge of a hundred legionnaires. He ranks above all other centurions except for two.

Gaius's underlings respect him, even if his superiors—especially Praetor Quintus and Caesar's own Cohortes Urbana Atticus—are often dismissive and belittling. The primi enjoys the new level of income, despite that things are still difficult at home and the influx of pilgrims desperate for even a glimpse of Jesus of Nazareth have drastically complicated his life.

Gaius can't deny what he's seen of the traveling prophet. What others call sorcery or tricks, he's seen with his own eyes. While he doesn't know what to make of it all, he finds himself strangely sympathetic to the residents of the new tent city. Sure, it's an eyesore, and he can only imagine the threat it poses to

Quintus. But the people seem sincere. They're not here to make trouble. They just want a glimpse, that connection. They want to hear the man, maybe witness a miracle of their own.

The problem is that when Jesus is sighted, or even rumored to be sighted, crowds appear. Quintus grows concerned—sometimes agitated, sometimes angry. He wants his primi to keep a lid on things. And that's where Gaius finds himself today. Word has swept through the city that the Nazarene not only showed up but also healed Uzziah. That blind man has been a fixture in Capernaum for as long as Gaius has been on the job. He is mostly harmless, except his crying out seems to rattle tourists. And he makes a practice of grabbing anyone he senses is close enough to touch, pleading for their help. The man is persistent.

Well, apparently he succeeded in getting help. It is going to be hard to persuade Uzziah that Jesus is anyone other than who he claims to be. Who else could give a blind man the ability to see? Word is, Uzziah has been hauled off to be interrogated at the synagogue, and Jesus is still here. Multitudes are gathering, the tent city emptying. Everybody seems eager and interested. Including Gaius. But he also dreads this. It is exactly what Quintus expects him—has ordered him—to preclude. His boss wants the pilgrims gone and their tents with them.

Gaius moves to where he can see Jesus. The man appears no more a threat than he had back when Gaius arrested him and hauled him before Quintus. But appearances can be deceiving. For some reason, the Jewish religious leaders view him with suspicion too. *How intimidating would that be,* Gaius wonders, *to have both Rome and the Pharisees consider you an enemy?*

Gaius wants no harm to come to the pilgrims, to his old friend Matthew the former tax collector, his new friends, or to Jesus himself. But with the preacher so boldly appearing in public and clearly about to address the crowds, Gaius fears what may result.

Rivka, whom Gaius recognizes as a woman of questionable repute from the Red Quarter, shouts, "Blessed is the womb that bore you!" Is it possible she has changed her ways and become a follower of the man too?

Jesus responds, "Blessed rather are those who hear the word of God and keep it. For whoever does the will of my Father in heaven is my brother and sister and mother."

What an interesting comment, Gaius decides. The man always speaks in parables and paradoxes.

A pilgrim with his family in tow hollers, "Some of us weren't here when you healed the blind man! Show us another sign!"

Oh, that's all I need, Gaius thinks. *I'll have to act or tell the praetor why I didn't.* He scans the crowd, discovering that Atticus has arrived—looking none too pleased—and also Rabbis Akiva and Josiah from the temple.

Jesus says, "I know you want more signs and wonders so you can believe for sure. And I have done them. But it is an evil generation that seeks a sign. And when all you seek are signs and wonders, no sign will be given to you except the sign of Jonah. For as Jonah became a sign to the people of Nineveh, so will the Son of Man be to this generation. The queen of the south will rise up at the judgment with the men of this generation and condemn them, for she came from the ends of the earth to hear the wisdom of Solomon, and behold, something greater than Solomon is here."

Oh, no, Gaius thinks.

Akiva looks outraged. "You would proclaim yourself greater than Solomon?!"

Rabbi Josiah adds, "What right would the Queen of Sheba have to judge us?"

Here we go, Gaius thinks.

"Aah," Jesus says, "Rabbi Akiva, you are back. Are you wanting to better understand my teaching?"

"Perhaps. You heard our questions."

"Let me make it more plain," Jesus says. "The men of Nineveh will rise up at the judgment with this generation and condemn it, for they repented under the preaching of Jonah. And behold, something greater than Jonah is here."

"The men of Nineveh were evil!" Rabbi Josiah says.

"Yes," says the disciple Gaius has heard the others refer to as Philip, "but even they will be qualified to judge this generation, because at least they repented!"

"Is anyone writing this down?" Akiva demands. Gaius's old friend Matthew raises his hand before another disciple lowers it. Akiva adds, "This must be recorded word for word so it can be held up in the Sanhedrin and exposed for the contemptible insolence even his followers espouse!"

"You've interrupted him enough!" a man shouts. Gaius can hardly believe his eyes. It's Sol, the bartender at The Hammer! "We want to hear more!"

"Aah, so it's infectious?" Rabbi Akiva rails. "Like a disease, this heretic's arrogance and insubordination spreads quickly to the susceptible minds of Capernaum's uneducated class!"

Oh great, Gaius thinks, *here comes Atticus.*

The Cohortes Urbana leans close and whispers, "Go tell Quintus what's happening and pass along a message directly from me: 'What you do next will determine your career.'"

Force the praetor to act? Not on your life. "I cannot leave this situation."

"You will get him that message, Gaius. If you serve him, you will."

Gaius is stuck. If he doesn't do what Atticus says, it will get back to the praetor anyway. He could lose much more than his rank. He could lose his life.

Atticus moves away and Gaius espies Julius. "Alert Quintus that there's a gathering, and let him know Atticus passes along this message: 'What you do next will determine your career.'"

Julius looks alarmed but says, "Yes, Primi."

"He is no heretic!" Sol shouts. "We just saw him perform a miracle!"

"Ah, yes," Rabbi Akiva says. "Nazarene, I just spoke with a man who claims you healed his blindness. Today." Jesus merely stares at the rabbi. "On Shabbat," Akiva adds.

"Is there a question coming?" Jesus says.

"I was told you put mud on his eyes. Where did you get mud, knowing you are not to mix healing concoctions on Shabbat?"

"It was easy. I just spit on the dirt."

"You touched his face with *filth*?"

"Cleanliness? That's what you're focused on?"

"You claim to be a rabbi, to be the Son of God, and don't honor purity laws, even on the most sacred day of the week?"

"You Pharisees," Jesus says, and Gaius is secretly pleased he's calling out the Pharisees and not Rome. "You cleanse the outside of the cup and of the dish, and then you eat and drink food that goes into a body full of greed and wickedness."

The crowd seems as shocked as Gaius is.

Jesus continues, "You fools! Did not he who made the outside make the inside also? But give as alms those things that are within, and behold, everything is clean for you."

"Are you saying," Akiva says, "that giving alms is more important than being ritually clean?"

"I'm saying that your obsession with what is clean or unclean goes further than God intended and does no good for anyone but yourselves."

This man has no fear! Gaius has never heard anyone, not even a Roman, speak to Jewish religious leaders this way.

"We tithe everything," Rabbi Akiva says, "down to the smallest plants in our gardens, so the poor can benefit."

"And to that I say woe to you Pharisees! You tithe mint and dill and cumin, carefully measuring the last speck, while neglecting what's actually important in the law: justice and mercy and faithfulness. You blind guides, straining out a gnat while swallowing a camel! Look at these people! What have you done to help them?"

"We have taught them how to observe God's perfect law, while you actively defy, break, and encourage others to deviate from it. All of you! This man is dangerous! He is leading you astray!"

Rivka yells, "His words bring hope and healing!"

"His words are blasphemous," Akiva says, "heretical, and rude."

Apparently Jesus has had enough. "I've been holding this in for a long time. Woe to you Pharisees! For you love the best seat in the synagogues and greetings in the marketplaces."

To Gaius, even the disciples look surprised.

"Take that back!" Akiva screeches. "Right now! Recant your insulting words!"

"Oh," Jesus says, "I am just getting started."

On the one hand, Gaius fears for everything in his life, on the other, he's beginning to really like this man.

A woman screams as she tumbles under a crush of pilgrims pressing closer to Jesus. "People are getting trampled!" one of the disciples shouts.

I must keep order, Gaius thinks, as the man he knows as Simon hollers, "Everyone stay peaceful!"

A soldier on horseback steadies his mare next to Gaius, who tells him to cut a path through the crowd. "It'll be easier to disperse by half." The primi grabs Matthew and pulls him close. "You need to get Jesus out of here. Tell Simon it's serious."

"Okay, okay," Matthew says, panic all over him, "but it's Peter now."

The Roman Authority

Quintus remains in agony over ledgers that don't lie. He's coasted a long time by making sure that the Capernaum economy remains robust. Tent City has jeopardized all of that, full of poverty-stricken pilgrims—most of them maimed or diseased, or they wouldn't be following the so-called miracle worker—who add virtually zero to local businesses. On top of that, they drain resources because shantytowns require extra manpower for patrols.

He looks up from his work to find Gaius's man Julius looking pained and timid. *What now?*

"Dominus?" the man says.

"I'm busy."

"The Pharisees have upset a gathering in the square." That gets the praetor's attention. "It started peacefully, but the people closed the market to protest the Pharisees."

Oh, for the love! Quintus leaps from his chair, grabs his sword, and dresses for action. "No! No! The market cannot be closed! Commerce is not to be halted for even an hour! Where is Gaius?"

"In the square, doing what he can to keep order. He sent me with a message for you from Cohortes Atticus."

Quintus freezes. *Oh, no!* "What message?"

"'What you do next will determine your career.'"

He sends a rank minion to me with a message like that?

The square

This is the time, Thomas thinks as he stands protecting Ramah, *where Simon really becomes Peter The Rock and takes over.*

"We're losing control!" Peter shouts. "James! Zee!"

But the two are trying to manage the crowd. Thomas touches Zee's shoulder and points at Peter who beckons them. "Both of you," he says, "we need to make a way out."

"How?" Thomas says.

"Zee," Peter says, "keep a perimeter around Jesus."

"That won't be easy," Zee says.

"Even an arm's length. Thomas, find a door, a gate, a shop we can pass through to an alley—anything to get Jesus out."

Thomas nods and turns to Ramah. "You should go."

"I'm staying with all of you."

"It's not safe," he says, but he can tell from her look that she's not leaving. He doesn't have time to argue. "Mary, will you stay with Ramah?"

She nods and Andrew approaches. "What do you need, Thomas?"

"Make a path for me?"

"I've got you." Andrew lowers his shoulder and pushes through the crowd.

Jesus is still preaching. "Beware the leaven of the Pharisees, which is hypocrisy. Nothing is covered up that will not be revealed or hidden that will not be known. Therefore, whatever you have said in the dark shall be heard in the light, and what you have whispered in private rooms shall be proclaimed on the housetops."

Rabbi Akiva says, "How can you claim to be the Son of God and create this division against God's appointed leaders?"

Thomas finds an entrance to an alley and gives a thumbs up to Andrew. Now they have to somehow get back to Peter through a crowd that seems to have doubled in minutes.

Across the square, Gaius has decided this is not going to end well, but neither is he going to stop it. He's finished doing the bidding of Rome against this innocent man. No surprise, Atticus has found him again. "You have not moved a cubit, Gaius. What are you waiting for?"

"I passed your message along. We're just waiting for—"

"For what? You are in command, Primi!" He's now nose to nose with Gaius. "Has the preacher gotten to you?" So Atticus has seen through him. So be it. But it appears some realization has come over the Urbana. He laughs and says, "Perhaps you *want* Quintus to take the fall for another riot. Yes, that's it. I was wrong about you."

Could this be a reprieve? Gaius says, "If I did, what would you do with me?"

Atticus scoffs. "Rome doesn't penalize ambition, Primi. But you are taking a huge gamble. One of you won't survive this."

That's certain, Gaius thinks, taking in the pandemonium.

Chapter 32

UNSPEAKABLE

The Capernaum square

Quintus arrives in all his finery, ready to do battle. Of course Jesus of Nazareth is at the center of all of this, and it will stop now, whatever that takes.

Jesus is speaking, the Pharisees are shouting, Jesus' disciples and followers and the pilgrims are all trying to drown out the religious leaders. What a mess! And where's his primi?

Quintus shoves through the crowd and finds him. Gaius is just standing there, ramrod straight, observing. Doing nothing! "Arrest Jesus," the praetor says.

"No, Dominus."

Was I not clear, or have I misheard? This man's life is on the line! "Arrest Jesus of Nazareth, Gaius."

"No."

"Arrest Jesus or you will hang!"

"I won't."

"Guards!" Quintus bellows, and soldiers arrive from the perimeter. "Arrest this man for dereliction." As a soldier places

Gaius in irons, Quintus points at Jesus and says, "The rest of you, arrest that man! Now!"

Peter quickly assesses the situation and rushes to Jesus, whom Zee has already begun pulling away. "Master, it's time," Peter says. "We have to go."

As they begin to move, the crowd protests his exit and, it seems, the advancement of the guards.

Thomas points Peter to the escape route and quickly looks for Ramah. He calls for her while Rabbis Akiva and Josiah indignantly protest the guards making physical contact with them.

Quintus roars, "Everyone out of this square! That man is under arrest! Move away!"

But nothing changes. His voice is drowned out as the people scream when mounted centurions move into the crowd. Thomas watches Thaddeus rounding up the disciples, pushing Matthew toward Philip who grabs him. They follow Jesus, trailed by Judas and Nathanael. Thomas stays behind, searching.

"Hurry!" Thaddeus yells.

Andrew says, "Where's Mary?"

She's supposed to be with Ramah! "Where's Ramah?!"

Anarchy reigns as Thaddeus runs to help Mary pulling an elderly woman from the ground. He takes Mary's hand and tells her they have to leave. "But Ramah!" she says. When she reaches for her, Quintus seizes Thaddeus.

"You! Where did Jesus go?"

But Quintus is bowled over by the crush of pilgrims fleeing the soldiers. He whips out his sword as he lands at Thomas's feet—who ignores him, barely realizing that by standing his ground to search for his beloved, he's protecting the praetor from being flattened by the crowd.

"Where is he?" Quintus demands of Thomas now. "Answer me!"

Thomas pays him no mind. "Ramah!?"

Quintus struggles to his feet, where he's bumped again and separated from Thomas.

"Thomas!"

He'd recognize her voice anywhere, but he can't see her. He follows the sound while Quintus continues to rage, "Where is *he*?" But Thomas has tunnel vision. He's not answering anyone or going anywhere without Ramah. And there she is!

Thomas grabs her. "Come on! Let's find the others."

Quintus is incensed. *Who does this man think he is, ignoring me?* He brandishes his weapon, determined to run through this disciple. He barrels toward him with a mighty thrust as he hears Atticus calling for him. At the last instant the uncooperative man turns his companion toward the edge of the crowd, and Quintus misses him with his sword.

Thomas is confused. Ramah started with him step for step, but now she's still. He turns and sees a strange look on her face. Shock? Horror? She slowly looks down and he follows her gaze. Blood pools on her stomach, the tip of a blade at its center. "My love?" she says.

As she slowly slips from his arms to the ground, Thomas is face to face with the praetor, who still grips the hilt of the sword that has run her through. Quintus is ashen as he removes the weapon from her body and is nearly tackled by Atticus.

Thomas thunders "Ramah!" as Thaddeus and Mary hurry to him. Mary drops to her knees, trying to stanch the blood.

Thomas pulls off his tunic and presses it to Ramah's stomach. "Help!" Mary cries out. "Somebody help! We need a doctor!"

James, taking it all in, charges toward Quintus, intercepted by his brother John. Quintus doesn't seem to even flinch as Atticus drags him away, the sword falling from his hand.

In the alley

Jesus has been led to safety by Peter and Zee when he finds himself filled with despair. Something has gone wrong.

"Zee," Peter says, "get him back to the house without anyone seeing! I'll wait for the others!"

But Jesus resolutely turns back to the square. He pushes past those fleeing in terror when he sees Ramah lying limp between Thomas and Mary. Magdalene is calling for help. Thomas cradles Ramah in his lap.

"Ramah, hold on. Hold on. You're fine, you're fine. Ramah!"

"Remember what I told you by the sea," she says, her voice raspy.

"It's not over," he says through tears. "It's not that time—" She reaches for his face. "Don't go, Ramah. Don't. Please. I can't—"

"Stay with Jesus," she says, struggling for breath. "That's all I—"

"Ramah?"

But she's gone.

The others arrive and Thomas sees Jesus. He leaps to his feet. "Heal her. Fix this."

"Thomas—"

"You're here now, Rabbi. Please. This is a mistake."

"Thomas, I'm so sorry."

"Rabbi, you don't need to let this happen. Just take it back. Take it back. She might not be dead yet. You can heal, right?"

"It is not her time, Thomas. I love you. I'm so sorry."

Peter grips Thomas's shoulder as the man gasps. He falls to a knee and folds himself over his love. "No," he moans.

PART 4

Crushed

Chapter 33

SOMBER PROCESSION

The Roman Authority

Gaius is convinced his life is over. A Roman soldier simply does not counter a direct command from his superior, certainly not that of the Praetor of Galilee himself. He prays only that he might find a sliver of a chance to get word to his wife and sons of why he is being executed. If only they can see in Jesus of Nazareth and his followers what Gaius has seen.

The problem is that he doesn't know to whom he is praying. The one true God of the Jews, as Simon—or now Peter—has told him of? Or to Jesus himself, whom Gaius has come to believe is the Messiah the Jews had for eons longed for? Can one pray to Jesus? Gaius's haltering, stammering attempts include beseeching both God and Jesus.

So is this the answer to that prayer? He has been delivered, shackled and sandwiched between two guards, to the reception area outside the very office of the man he defied. The praetor's secretary looks shocked beyond comprehension and the man clearly avoids eye contact with Gaius. *Am I to be hanged here without even a pretense of a trial?* Regardless, he has no defense that would move Roman officials.

From the office booms the formal sonorous voice of the official Tribunis Militum. "Quintus Benedictus Dio, having sworn the sacramentum to Caesar, the Senate, and the people of Rome to lawfully fulfill the conditions of service as Praetor of Galilee on pain of punishment and found guilty of the murder of a citizen under your charge, you are hereby reduced in rank—"

Gaius recoils. *The dreaded gradus deiectio! What happened? Who did he murder?*

"—and relegated to lesser service—"

The milita dismutation!

"—to be determined at tribunal."

Gaius recognizes Corhortes Urbana Atticus's voice, as he orders Quintus to remove his armor and his insignia. The guards then escort the former praetor out, basically in his undergarments. Gaius has never seen the man ashen and silent, the smirk gone, eyes downcast.

His own guards nudge Gaius forward. "Your turn," one mumbles.

Quintus murders someone and is merely reduced in rank? Does that mean I might live?

In the office, Atticus nods at the guards and they remove Gaius's restraints. The Urbana hands Gaius Quintus's breastplate and insignia. "Congratulations, Praetor Gaius."

Reeling as Atticus points to the desk and directs him to stand behind it, all Gaius can think of is answering his wife's typical question when he gets home: "How was your day?"

That was one unique answer to prayer.

Capernaum outskirts

Peter has led Jesus and the others here, away from the tumult and beyond the eyes of pilgrims and soldiers. The ghastly silence is broken only by soft murmurs of comfort here and there. Mary rests her head on her knees as Tamar presses her cheek to Mary's shoulder. Thomas paces, apart from the others, eyes vacant.

Peter whispers to Jesus, "I want to do something. I want to help him."

"That's not how grief works," Jesus says.

"I'm failing."

"Failing at what?"

"Being—you know."

"I don't," Jesus says. "It's not a test."

"Being who I'm supposed to be now. How can I be a rock for someone in a moment like this?"

"Thomas doesn't need a rock right now."

"He needs firm footing!" Peter says. "Everything's just been pulled out from under him!"

"This is the way of all the earth. For now."

"Loss?!"

"You know the truth," Jesus says.

"I can't just tell him this is the way of all the earth!"

"Then maybe don't say anything at all. Would words from him have helped you after you found out about Eden and the baby?"

Hardly.

"You have experienced loss," Jesus adds. "That makes you more able to go to him now than being a rock."

Peter hesitates, then approaches Thomas, who is grinding a flower into the dirt with his foot. Peter won't speak unless Thomas does.

"What just happened?" Thomas says at last. "I don't even know what just happened."

"I'm so sorry."

"She's gone," Thomas says, gasping. "She's gone. She's gone. I just don't believe it. She's gone."

"I know," Peter says. "Just breathe."

"I can't! I'm gonna be sick."

Peter envelops Thomas and lowers him to the ground. "Here, lie back. What can I do?" Thomas shakes his head. "That's it, just breathe. It's okay to cry, but just breathe."

"No," Thomas says, sitting up. "It feels wrong to breathe when she isn't. I can't relax. I don't want to."

Across the way, Mary lifts her head. "What if we had kept our eyes on her?"

"Please don't ..." Tamar says.

"I was holding her hand, pulling her away—"

"She was murdered, Mary. You couldn't stop the evil in his heart."

Mary nods toward Jesus. "Could he have stopped it?"

"Ask him."

But Mary wouldn't do that in a million years.

Thomas wriggles away from Peter and gets to his feet, holding his side as if someone has punched him in the kidneys. He turns and runs, only to collide with Jesus. The rabbi just holds him tight until he stills and becomes a dead weight. The others approach and gather around them. John relieves Jesus of Thomas and takes him into his own arms.

Jesus addresses everyone. "We've been granted her body and have sent word to Tel-Dor in the Plains of Sharon that we will leave here in the morning to take her home."

That night

Peter stands with James and John, watching the others around a campfire share their memories of Ramah—except for Zee who guards her shrouded body on a cart nearby. Thomas sits a ways off, staring into the night.

"Someone should go sit with him," John says.

"He needs to be alone right now," Peter says.

"How can you be sure?"

"Believe me."

James looks conflicted. "What I'm about to say I can say only in the presence of you two. It's been rattling around in my head all day."

"Careful, James," Peter says, wondering where he's going with this.

"It's just this: why doesn't Jesus do what he did with Jairus's daughter?"

"I've been thinking the same thing!" John says. "A single word from him and we wouldn't be here."

"Boys," Peter says, "we vowed never to speak of what we saw in that house."

"To anyone else, sure," James says. "But we know what we saw. He brought that little girl back to—"

"I understand where you're coming from," Peter says. "I wrestled with exactly the same question about Eden. Why didn't he intervene? I resented him performing miracles for others."

"Seems reasonable to me," John says.

"But remember the words of Isaiah," Peter says. "'For My thoughts are not your thoughts, neither are your ways My ways,' declares the Lord." And the brothers join him to finish the recitation: "'For as the heavens are higher than the earth, so are My ways higher than your ways, and My thoughts than your thoughts.'"

"That doesn't make this easier," Big James says.

"Jesus had a reason for allowing what happened to Eden, which I didn't understand at the time. I may not fully in this lifetime, but I do know it made me desperate for him."

"Thomas wasn't inside Jairus's house," John says. "He doesn't know that Jesus can bring someone back from death."

"But he believes Jesus can do anything," James says, "and why shouldn't he believe that? Was Jairus's daughter more important than Ramah?"

"Or than your unborn child?" John says.

"Enough," Peter says. "We told Jesus we'd keep that a secret, and now more than ever it's clear why Thomas must *never* find out."

"What if Jesus does it again?" John says. "For someone else."

"It would destroy Thomas," James says.

"Let's take this one day at a time," Peter says. "We are his students, not his equals."

John says, "I never said we were eq—"

"I mean if we don't know the answer to something," Peter says, "we can let Jesus speak for himself. You'll write it down. Matthew will write it down. Time will reveal the wisdom hidden in these mysteries. But I trust a God who walks on water." He embraces the brothers one at a time and holds them tight. "Seems like we don't do that enough."

When Peter heads to join the others around the fire, John stays put with his brother. He's intrigued when James waxes nostalgic. "Back when we fished, remember how the older guys would sometimes call you James and me John?"

"They got it right half the time. And it wasn't just the old guys."

James nods. "People thought of us as the same because we were never apart. We fished together, went to The Hammer together, synagogue together, then we even followed Jesus together. But when you came back from your mission with Thomas, it felt like you were closer to him than to me. Like he was new and interesting, and I was old and boring."

"I never intended that," John says. "I'm sorry."

"But the bond is obvious. We're doing the biggest thing of our lives, of anyone's life, and you're doing it with him."

"We're doing it together," John says.

"But some have grown closer to others in the process."

"What do you want me to say, James?"

"I admit I was jealous of your friendship with Thomas. But none of that matters now. All that matters is that he is in pain, and he needs you."

"Me?"

"Who else, John? Even if you don't know what to say, your just being by his side would mean more to him than any of the rest of us."

On the road

The melancholy walk of more than fifty miles to Tel-Dor on the ocean the Romans called Our Sea, takes the grieving band eighteen hours over two days. Jesus is not in a hurry to face Ramah's father, but he far outpaces the others, walking with a purpose. Behind him, Zee leads the donkey pulling the cart that bears Ramah's body, which is wrapped in linen and spices in a box covered by a heavy drape.

Thomas strides next to it, accompanied mostly by Peter but sometimes also John, neither of whom speaks to him unless he initiates conversation. By the time the journey is nearly over, Peter quietly says, "Tel-Dor, Thomas. Just ahead."

Thomas stares at the ground. "This is only the beginning," he says. "I have no idea what I'm going to say to Kafni."

"You may not have to," Peter says, peering into the distance.

Chapter 34

THE CONFRONTATION

Outside Tel-Dor

The road ahead is blocked by at least thirty men. No surprise to Jesus, Zee steps forward and tells Thomas, "I'll talk to them."

Peter says, "You should probably hang back here, Thomas. We'll take care of it."

"No," Thomas says. "This is mine to do. I can't let you shield me from this." He lays a hand on the drape covering Ramah's body.

Zee says, "We'll just find out what they want and report back."

"It's all right, Zee," Jesus says. "I'll go with Thomas. We'll face them together."

As they approach with the cart, Kafni advances with five of the men. "Where is she? Where is my daughter?"

Thomas appears to try to speak. Kafni runs to the cart and unwraps the cloth around Ramah's face. He gasps and covers his mouth. The men with him take over the cart and one begins to lead the donkey away. Thomas lunges toward the cart.

"Thomas!" Kafni bawls. "Stop!" He faces the entire entourage. "Proceed no farther! You are forbidden to enter this town."

"Kafni," Jesus says, "we are in mourning as you are. We grieve, but we are not dangerous."

"Then why is my daughter dead? Dead!"

"I'm so sorry," Thomas says. "So sorry."

Kafni gets in his face. "You've already killed me, Thomas. And then you went and killed her. You did this!"

"I blame myself," Thomas says. "I'm sorry. I broke my promise to you."

"Thomas loved Ramah dearly, Kafni," Jesus says. "And she loved him."

"What are *your* words worth?" Kafni says. "You're a fraud and a devil! Deceptive sorcerer! The greatest disappointment of my life is that I didn't teach my daughter better. She had a brilliant mind until you cast a spell on her!"

Thomas stands straight, shoulders back. "Ramah was murdered by a Roman, Kafni! And you don't speak for her. She loved Jesus. She felt her calling was an honor. She wanted everyone to know that, including you."

Peter throws an arm around Thomas and leads him away. Zee and Big James flank Jesus, arms crossed. "Let's go," Jesus tells them.

Peter signals the others to depart also.

"I curse you and your followers," Kafni says.

James calls over his shoulder, "We grieve with you."

Kafni rants, "I will spread the word as far and wide as I can! As long as blood runs in my veins, I will move mountains to expose you, Jesus of Nazareth! I will make sure the world knows you're a liar and a murderer!"

Zee whirls. "You have made your feelings clear. We leave you in peace."

"You will see me again!" Kafni continues. "And when you do, it will be the last thing you s—"

Zee says, "No more."

As the rest of Kafni's men encircle the cart and lead it back toward the city, the man stands alone in the road.

Chapter 35

ANTICIPATION

Jerusalem, two months later

The disciples and Jesus' other followers have settled into a daily routine that—while often frantic and busy—also finds them still deeply sobered and grieving their loss. Zebedee, followed by Mary of Magdala and Tamar, drives a cart into the city to deliver olive oil. They pass graffiti scribbled in Aramaic. "Jesus is Messiah" it reads. Zebedee locks eyes with Mary, knowing she can decipher it too and will worry what it means for all of them. Jesus is trying to lie low. This won't help.

"What does it say?" Tamar says.

Four days and eighty miles later, Mary and Tamar find Judas at Andrew's home in Capernaum poring over his ledger. He doesn't appear happy, and the meager funds the women have brought from the sale in Jerusalem seem to trouble him even more.

Not long later, Jesus leads the disciples down a country road in the region of the Gerasenes. They're followed by a crowd, which has become the norm. Everyone, it seems, longs for the chance to be present when Jesus teaches, preaches, or heals. A man bursts from the mass and hurls himself at Jesus' feet, convulsing and writhing and pleading with guttural utterances no one appears to understand. Except Jesus, who immediately delivers and heals the man.

The next day, in the Capernaum market, Jesus is with Nathanael, Little James, and Thaddeus when the ever-present blind man grabs the rabbi's robe, as he does of anyone close enough to reach. "Are you the Messiah?"

Jesus kneels and touches the man's eyes. He stands and squeals, hugging Jesus and the other three, racing away and shouting the news of his healing.

Since the riot that cost Ramah her life, Jesus has become more overt and visible. Outside Capernaum he preaches to a crowd that includes Rabbi Akiva and a Pharisee who seems to pay close attention. Too close.

The Roman Authority

Praetor Gaius tries to get his mind around his new position, especially as Julius delivers a report of larger and larger crowds following Jesus of Nazareth. Gaius thanks him and can tell Julius expected more of a response or perhaps a specific order. "That will be all," he adds. Julius hesitates, then exits.

When he's certain Julius is out of the building, Gaius folds the parchment and sets it in the fireplace, watching it burn.

Peter's house

Most of the disciples have joined Jesus and lounge chatting on stools, the floor, rugs, and pillows. Eden sits eating at the counter, and Peter knows she will want to be free to serve when Zee and Judas arrive from the market.

Meanwhile, Peter stands in a corner with Thomas. "Sleeping any better?"

"Better than a couple of months ago, but still not great."

"It took me a couple of months too. Eden even longer. How are your prayers?"

Thomas shrugs. "It's hard to mean them sometimes."

"'When I remember God, I moan. When I meditate, my spirit faints. You hold my eyelids open.'" He pauses. "Have you thought about leaving even just for a short time to get away?"

"I just can't. It's too painful to be here, and yet there's no place I'd rather be."

Zee and Judas enter, and Judas sets down a basket. "Fresh fruit!"

"Finally!" Andrew shouts as the group advances on it.

"At least you're back to eating," Peter tells Thomas. "Come on."

Zee takes a bag to Eden. "And for you, garlic, onion, malva …"

"Perfect," she says.

While the rest help themselves to various fruits, Matthew appears to study a pomegranate. He leans over to Philip. "H-how do you eat a pomegranate?"

"You need a knife." He pulls his out and takes the pomegranate. "Start here at the top and cut off the head …"

Peter, his mouth full of apricot, says, "You can just cut it in half and pull the seeds out with your fingers."

"Cut a pomegranate in half?" Nathanael says. "Were you raised by wolves?"

"You might say that," Peter says.

"Peter," Andrew says, "they did their best."

"Did they?"

Eden looks up. "Don't start, you two."

Philip holds up the fruit with the top sliced off. "There's six sections. You're supposed to score through the white part and pull them apart, like slices of an orange."

"No one ever taught me that," Andrew says.

"Case in point," Peter says.

Nathanael says, "You've been wasting pomegranate seeds your whole life?"

"Am I on trial here?" Peter says.

Jesus and Eden share a wary look and he steps outside to find Little James and Thaddeus on the stoop. James is pulling mint leaves off sprigs, and Thaddeus is squeezing lemon juice into a bowl. Jesus sits between them and pats their backs.

"What are they going on about in there?" Thaddeus says.

"I don't know. Wanting to be right about something?"

"Or for someone else to have been getting it wrong their whole lives," James says.

"Yes!" Jesus says. "How did you know?"

"You're telling me you haven't noticed a pattern?"

They all chuckle and Jesus rests his head on James's shoulder. "Remember when it was just the three of us? Do you ever miss those days?"

"We did get to spend more time with you," Thaddeus says. "But to wish that others would not get that gift by joining us also—"

"Would be selfish," James says.

"Feels like a lifetime ago," Thaddeus says.

"A lifetime we can't go back to," Jesus says.

"Where *will* we go?" James says.

The question intrigues Jesus. "Why do you ask?"

"We can't stay in Capernaum forever."

"No," Jesus says. "We can't. Let no one underestimate your wisdom, James."

"It doesn't seem so much like wisdom to me, but more of a feeling—in my gut."

"A good feeling?" Jesus says.

"I can't describe it."

"Try."

"Well, lately—I don't even want to say it."

"I'll do it," Thaddeus says. "You've been saying things about when you're 'gone'—more frequently."

James jumps back in. "You told us you must suffer many things at the hands of the elders and chief priests. Those people aren't in Capernaum."

"They're not."

"So it means we'll be on the move soon."

"When did you say?" Jesus says with a twinkle.

"That word," Thaddeus says, "over and over again."

"It's true," Jesus says. "We will make our way south toward Jerusalem. The time has come. Things won't be simple anymore."

James and Thaddeus lean into Jesus from either side. Jesus is overcome with emotion.

"Sorry to interrupt," Peter says.

"It's all right," Jesus says, sniffling.

"Eden sent me to ask about the mint and lemon. She's ready to—"

"Here," James says.

"What happened?" Peter says. "Why are you all cr—"

They all fall silent as Roman soldiers approach the house. Jesus, James, and Thaddeus rise. One introduces himself as Julius and says, "Is the former publicanus Matthew at this residence?"

"Who's asking?" Peter says.

"Praetor Gaius."

Jesus nods at Thaddeus to go get Matthew.

"One moment, Julius," Peter says, then whispers to Jesus, "You think Gaius intends to bring Matthew back for tax collection?"

"I suppose we could ask."

"Let me go with Matthew. I can talk to Gaius."

Matthew appears at the door, trailed by Thaddeus, Andrew, and Zee.

"Publicanus!" Julius says.

"No one has called me that in a long time."

"Please come with us."

"It's all right, Matthew," Jesus says. "Peter will join you."

Matthew looks petrified but hesitantly proceeds.

Zee asks Jesus if he should follow. Jesus shakes his head.

Andrew whispers urgently, "Is he in trouble?"

"I don't think so," Jesus says. "Tell the others to gather their belongings and prepare for a journey."

Chapter 36

RED SKY

Capernaum street

As he and Matthew are hustled toward The Roman Authority, Peter is feeling more like his old self than the man Jesus has renamed. He and Matthew have reconciled and forgiven each other, but Peter's old frustrations resurface when the eccentric little man resorts to comforting himself with his ubiquitous handkerchief. "Stop fidgeting with that," Peter says.

"I'm sweating. Can I wipe my brow?"

"Just try to stop looking nervous."

"*You* look nervous."

There's that typical Matthew insight. Peter feels the need to clarify. "I'm curious. Not scared. Gaius isn't the same person who shouted after you when you left the tax booth."

"Maybe he's having trouble recruiting new collectors. The job pays well, but you lose everything else."

"You think he's looking for hiring tips?"

"Honestly, you would know better than me. You've spent more time with him lately."

"And beyond," Peter says.

"Beyond?"

"It's nothing."

"Why do people do that?" Matthew says.

"Do what?"

"When someone says something is nothing, it always means it's something. Very odd."

Peter says, "When they say it's nothing, what they usually mean is that it's nothing for you to worry about, or it's none of your business, or it's a bad time to talk about it."

"Then why wouldn't they just say that? It would eliminate a lot of confusion in this world."

"It would. It's just that …"

"It's just what?"

"Nothing," Peter says with a wink, and Matthew chuckles.

The Roman Authority

Peter is impressed by how quickly Gaius seems to have assumed the gravitas of his new role, rising regally as the two disciples are delivered to his office. He dismisses the guards and waits until they're gone before speaking. He smiles, tells them to sit, and thanks them for coming.

As if we had a choice, Peter thinks. "You couldn't send word what the nature of the summoning was?"

"Absolutely not."

Peter shares a look with Matthew, wondering where this is going. Gaius peeks at a piece of parchment on his desk and says, "Peter," emphasizing the T. "Am I pronouncing that right? Someone brought it to my attention."

"Close. It's a little softer. Peter."

"Peter," Gaius says carefully. "You're a seafaring man."

"Was."

"You still know how to tie knots. When the sky is red at dawn ..."

"We expect storms."

"When you look south to Jerusalem," Gaius says, "there is a very, very red sky this morning. The edict coming out of Judea from your religious leaders are serious. More threatening than before."

"How threatening?"

"The Pharisees here are watching your every move, trying to trap your rabbi in his words or actions. I am telling you—they want him gone."

"Gone?" Matthew says.

"Silenced. Censured. Worse. I don't know, you tell me: what's the precedent?"

Peter says, "Maybe the Baptizer?"

"The Pharisees didn't kill him!" Matthew says.

"But," Gaius says, "Herod is one of you, a client king. Galilee is his jurisdiction."

"Are you going to tell me how you knew my name was changed?"

"It's a long story," Gaius says, "but someone is watching us both very closely."

"Me and you?"

"Me, this whole town, and especially your group. Atticus Amelius Pulchur of the Cohortes Urbanae has taken a special interest in Jesus. He's monitoring activity in Capernaum."

"When we left the house," Peter says, "Jesus told my brother that everyone should prepare for a journey. Maybe that's why. He's no longer safe here."

"I'm to crush any religious extremism or fringe uprising swiftly and lethally," Gaius says. "If I don't, or if I even hesitate—"

"What, they'll fire you? I didn't expect you'd develop a taste for power so quickly."

"Worse," Gaius says, lowering his voice. "They might suspect that I believe in him."

"Ha!" Peter says, expecting Gaius to admit he's kidding. "Wait …"

"Jesus will be safe here," the praetor says, "I can assure you of that. But only if he keeps a low profile."

"That's not going to happen. A year ago, sure, he was forbidding people he healed from telling anyone about it. Now it can't be contained. Were you being serious?"

"I'm not telling you to stop his mission," Gaius says. "Just do it outside the city limits. That's all I'm asking. For his safety and yours. I need you to work with me on this."

Peter realizes something. Or does he? He must be sure. "Praetor. Do you believe in him?"

Gaius lets the silence hang a moment. "I'm not even sure what that means," he says.

"Why haven't you gone to see him," Matthew says, "if you're considering—?"

"I've seen enough. I've seen what he does for those who can be of no help to him whatsoever. I've heard him say things that both unscramble a lifetime of mystery and fill me with questions. The fact that I've seen him is why I am doing everything I can to—"

"Has your son gotten any better?" Peter says.

"What?"

"A while ago he was very ill. Did he get better?"

"Um—no."

"Son?" Matthew says. "Something is wrong with Marius?"

"So why haven't you brought him to Jesus?" Peter says.

Gaius shifts awkwardly. "Uh—"

"You say you've seen Jesus do things for people who can be of no help to him," Peter says. "So why wouldn't he do something for you, someone risking your life and career to protect him?"

"He doesn't need my protection. I just don't want his mission delayed by posturing and infighting."

"Some believe his mission is to overthrow Rome," Peter says.

"I'm sorry," Matthew says. "Why does Jesus need to see Marius?"

"Matthew, I made a mistake that resulted in a child not born of my wife."

"Doesn't that happen all the time with your people? I apologize, but at the risk of offending you even more, sometimes people are inclined to perceive judgment because they feel guilty."

"I feel guilty for betraying my wife."

"Do you feel repentant?" Peter says.

"For that, yes. And I love my son."

"And he's ill?" Matthew says.

"For a long time, yes."

"Then why have you not gone to see Jesus?" Matthew says.

"I know you've thought about this," Peter says. "You told your family about a Jewish doctor."

"Because I am not worthy!"

"Neither was I," Peter says.

"Neither was I," Matthew adds.

Gaius shakes his head. "You do not know the things I've done."

"That's exactly what I said," Peter says.

"I'm an outsider," Gaius says.

"One of his favorite kinds of people," Peter says.

"Someone who's not Jewish?"

Both Peter and Matthew say, "Yes," and Matthew adds, "Those dividing lines don't matter to him. It's part of why he's in so much trouble."

Peter decides it's time to force the issue. "Gaius, do you believe he's from God?"

Gaius's eyes dart between the two disciples. He draws a halting breath, closes his eyes, and bows his head. His shoulders heave.

"I know it must be intimidating," Peter says, trying to signal Matthew with his eyes to help him out.

"There, there, Dominus," Matthew says. "There's no need to be afraid."

Gaius looks up with a wide grin and tears streaming. "I do believe."

"You're happy crying?" Peter says.

"I know he can heal my son. Will you let me ask him?"

"I—uh—I suppose."

Gaius stands quickly and hurries around his desk, reaching for a hug from Matthew, who stiffens. He turns to Peter who says, "Okay, quick," and wonders what anyone else would think of the Praetor of Capernaum embracing Jews in his office.

"That's enough," Peter says. "We've haven't even gone to see him yet."

"Great point," Gaius says. "Why are we standing here? My son is as good as healed. Let's go."

Gaius leads the way out as Peter stands staring at Matthew. "Did he just convert?"

Chapter 37

THE ASKS

Zebedee's home

These boys, Salome thinks. Like their father, big, strong, gregarious, hard workers—men a mother can be proud of. She knows Jesus sees in them what she does and would be more than happy to honor them the way they deserve. All they need to do is ask! What's so hard about that? But they've found reason after reason to demur.

As she busies herself in the kitchen, their friend Andrew pokes his head in the front door. "James! John! Jesus says to gather your things for a journey."

"We'll be ready," James says.

"Where's the rendezvous?" John says.

"The usual. The well in the Southern Quarter." And Andrew runs off.

"Boys," Salome says. "This is the time."

"We'll see," John says. "We'll find the right time. We promise."

That's not good enough, so she fixes them with a look. "Listen. While it was the greatest day of my life when Jesus called you, I know being with the Messiah and doing his work has also been a weight. But I've also never seen the two of you closer than you've been these past six months. I never want it to end."

"It *has* been a quieter time," John says.

"John, you've always been the more careful one. But he has deep affection for you, and there's no harm in simply asking."

"We've talked about this," James says.

"I know," John says. "'Ask and it will be given you.' We will, Ima."

"On this journey?"

"Yes," John says.

"Let's go over it one more time," she says. "And don't forget about you sitting at his right and left hand in his glory so—"

"We know," John says.

"We've got it, Ima," James says.

"Good. What are you waiting for? Go get your things."

Outside

Peter leads Matthew and Gaius through the streets, looking to see who's watching. "We've done this before, Gaius. Don't you want to pretend we're your prisoners?"

"Those days are over," Gaius says. "Now I'm accompanying you, not the other way around."

"A praetor led through town by his own citizens?" Matthew says.

"Are you trying to talk me out of this?"

"Let's just keep going," Peter says. When his house comes into view, he tells Gaius, "Wait here. I'll make sure he's inside."

It appears Gaius can't stop grinning.

As Peter reaches the door, Matthew catches up to him. "I'm realizing we're bringing a Roman to see Jesus, who didn't give us permission or ask us to."

"I think by now we've both seen enough to know that this is what Jesus would want."

Inside, Peter finds everyone packed and ready to go. Matthew signals Gaius with a nod to come in. Everyone else appears stunned to silence. Zee looks particularly wary.

"Praetor Gaius," Jesus says, as the man drops to his knees before him.

Jesus' brows raise when Gaius says, "Lord …" then pauses before speaking quickly. "My servant boy lies paralyzed at home. He has been sick for so long, and now he suffers terribly, near death."

"Take me to him," Jesus says.

"Lord—"

"You call him *Lord*?" Nathanael blurts.

"—I'm not worthy to have you come into my home. And I know you wouldn't be comfortable, a Jew in a Roman's home. But you need only to say the word, and he will be healed."

"Not worthy?" Jesus says.

"The truth about the child is that he's actually my son. I'm ashamed and shouldn't even be asking you, but I am. And I know you can do it."

"Master," Peter says, "I never thought I would say this, but he is worthy to have you do this for him. He loves our people. He has helped us."

"I know."

"Don't trouble yourself," Gaius says. "You can heal him from a distance with only a word of command. I also have authority with men under me. If I say to one, 'Go,' he goes. And if I say to another, 'Come,' he comes. Anything you command in this world will happen. I know it. Even this."

Peter thinks Jesus looks genuinely surprised and impressed as he has Gaius rise. "Did you all hear this man?" Jesus says.

"Truly, I tell you, with no one in Israel have I found such faith. I was rejected in my own hometown, and I am threatened by the religious leaders of my own people. And yet this man, a Gentile, has more bold confidence in what he believes I can do than anyone I have yet encountered. Go, Gaius. It's been done for you as you have believed."

"Thank you," Gaius whispers, clearly overcome.

"Thank *you*," Jesus says. "Your kind of faith has brightened my day."

Outside

John and James have caught up with Andrew and approach Peter's house. John stops short at the Praetor of Capernaum striding briskly into the street. The other disciples and Jesus aren't far behind him, and they all look to be in good spirits.

As Gaius leaves, John and James push past Andrew. "What happened?" John says.

Peter says, "Gaius had faith that Jesus could heal his servant, without even coming to his house."

"We know he can do that," James says.

"But such faith from a Gentile?" John says.

"Exactly," Jesus says.

James leans into his brother. "Let's do it now, John," he whispers. "Let's ask him. It will change everything."

"Ask what?" Peter says.

"Rabbi?"

"Yes, James."

He clears his throat. "Remember when you said that we could ask for anything and it would be given us?"

"Knock," John adds, "and the door will be opened?"

"I don't remember," Jesus says. Then he laughs. "Come on. Of course."

John is spooked at first, then pretends to know Jesus is kidding. He can tell James feels the same. His brother says, "There's something we want to ask and for you to do."

"I'm eager to hear," Jesus says.

John takes over. "Would you grant for us to sit at your right hand, and your left, in your kingdom?"

Peter scowls as if the brothers have no shame.

Judas looks surprised but intrigued.

Andrew appears puzzled, as if he isn't sure he heard correctly.

Matthew whispers to Philip, "What does that mean?" Philip shushes him.

John is most interested in Jesus' response. The rabbi looks devastated. Maybe this was a mistake.

But James presses. "So ...?"

Jesus looks grieved, even angry.

Oh, no! John fears this is a failure.

Jesus storms off. "You don't know what you're asking," he says.

We need to clarify! John nods to James to join him and follow the rabbi.

Capernaum square

Gaius couldn't be happier and hardly believes his good fortune. On his way home—fully expecting to see his son entirely healed—he rushes about the market buying a skin of wine, a head of cabbage, a handful of red onions, and a sack of green grapes. He purchases a figurine of a lion and a toy horse with wheels for feet. He can't wait to see Livia and the boys.

Waterfront road

John leads his brother and the rest of the disciples, rushing to catch up with Jesus outside the gates of Capernaum. He has to make things right, but he's not sure what he's done to so upset the master. "Rabbi! What's wrong?"

Jesus whirls, serious as a viper's bite. "Are you able to drink the cup that I drink, or to be baptized with the baptism with which I am baptized?"

"We are able!" James says. "We're the Sons of Thunder—"

"We'll do anything for you!" John adds.

This is not working. Jesus looks hurt, deeply saddened. "You don't even know what that means," he says.

"Tell us," James says. "We'll do anything."

The disciples have pressed close. John especially feels the weight of having caused Jesus to become so agitated. *How can we fix this?*

Their rabbi speaks as gravely as he's ever heard him. "It means," Jesus says, "that when we go to Jerusalem, the Son of Man will be delivered over to the chief priests and the scribes, and they will condemn him to death and deliver him over to the Gentiles. And they will mock him and spit on him and flog him and kill him. And after three days he will rise."

Everyone but John seems shocked to silence. "What are you talking about?" he says.

Matthew says, "I thought the Son of Man was you."

"And you *will* drink the cup that I drink," Jesus says. "And be baptized with the baptism with which I am baptized. But you do not want that now. You are not ready for it."

John sees on James's face what he himself is thinking. *Yes, we are! Whatever Jesus is talking about, whatever happens, we're in!* But before he can assure Jesus of their undying devotion, the rabbi continues.

"To sit at my right hand and at my left is not mine to grant, but it is for those for whom it has been prepared by my Father."

Nathanael spits. "You have no business asking what you did!"

"No offense," James says, "but we were here before you."

Judas shakes his head. "How can you ask that in front of all of us?"

Peter says, "Ruling positions and high seats of honor?"

"Look who's talking," John says.

"I didn't ask!" Peter says. "He just gave it to me!"

"You don't even know what The Rock means," James says.

"Stop!" Jesus says. "All of you have been granted leadership and authority. All of you make up the foundation on which I'll build my church. But you're thinking like the Gentiles, whose rulers lord their authority over their inferiors. That is not how my kingdom works. I've told you this before, and you still don't get it. This *has* to change, because their way is not how it will be with you. Do you hear me?"

John and the others nod, but he's not exactly sure what he's heard.

Jesus continues, "Whoever would be great among you must be your servant, and whoever would be first among you must be your slave. Because even the Son of Man came not to be served but to serve, and to give his life as a ransom for many."

"A ransom for who?" Peter says.

"Who is being held hostage?" Zee says.

John is hurt that Jesus looks disgusted with them, as if they'll never understand. "Go," Jesus says. "All of you. Continue on the road to Jerusalem."

He's not going with us? John says, "What will you—"

"I'll catch up."

Zee says, "I can wait back with you and—"

"I said I'll catch up."

Gaius's house

The praetor, laden with his goods from the market, smirks at the wooden idol of Asclepius, the Roman god of healing placed outside his door. He snuffs out the votive candle at its feet.

"Gaius!" Livia calls from inside. She sounds frantic, but he knows better. As she bursts into view, she shouts, "You're not going to believe it!"

"I do believe it," he says, calm and smiling.

"Wait. What?"

He draws her into a compassionate, unreserved embrace. "I already know."

Marius comes around the corner, holding the hand of his fully healthy half-brother Ivo, both looking ecstatic. "Daddy, look!"

Gaius kneels and catches both boys in a bear hug. "Shalom," he says.

"What?" Ivo says.

"It's something my friends say. It means peace, wholeness. You're whole again."

Marius tries to say the word. Gaius repeats it, and Ivo joins in. "Sha-lom, sha-lom."

Just outside Capernaum

Finally alone, Jesus reels and resorts to a prayer of David. "'My sides are filled with burning, and there is no soundness in my flesh. I am feeble and crushed. I groan because of the tumult of my heart. O Lord, all my longing is before You. My sighing is not hidden from You. My heart throbs. My strength fails me, and the light of my eyes, it has also gone from me. My friends and companions stand aloof from my plague, and my nearest kin stand far off.'"

In the distance he spots Zebedee, with Tamar and Mary, emptying olives into a basket. At least they were not involved in the selfish craziness he just endured from the disciples. All are precious to him, but just now especially these three. He watches with a melancholy delight as they continue to work on his behalf.

In the distance
Mary of Magdala loves the labor, pedestrian though it may be. She's serving her master, her rabbi, her deliverer. Tamar hands her flat baskets filled with crushed olives. Mary stacks these atop the stone vat, while Zebedee empties more olives into the crushing system. "Zeb," Mary says, "we're ready for the top stone."

"Aah!" he says, ever gleeful. "I love this part."

Zebedee loads the top stone over the basket and adds the first stone weight onto the beam. As the weight presses onto the stacks of baskets, oil seeps through the wicker thatch and into the channel. "The first press," the old man says. "Sacred unto Adonai alone."

Just outside Capernaum
Jesus watches, rapt, short of breath as Zebedee pulls harder on the beam, forcing more oil out. Beads of sweat run down Jesus' forehead and he's reminded of his nightmare, foreshadowing his entering the Garden of Gethsemane. He shudders under the crushing weight of all he knows is to come, sooner than ever.

The new Praetor of Capernaum approaches with a look of deep gratitude but apparently unable to speak. He spontaneously hugs Jesus, providing the rabbi comfort just when he needs it most.

PART 5

Bitter

Chapter 38

BEYOND RUBIES

The road to Jerusalem

Peter feels little different than he had when he was known as Simon. As The Rock, he feels a little more responsibility perhaps—though he can't deny he has always felt in charge of the disciples, or that he should have been. Leadership has always been part of his nature. He's a doer and often feels he has the best ideas and everyone's best interests at heart. The others rarely saw it that way. He knows they viewed him as selfish, impulsive, ambitious. And maybe he was. Well, no maybe about it. He was.

Down deep his motives have been mostly pure, especially when it comes to Jesus. He finds himself defensive of the rabbi, even when he questioned the master's decisions. Peter has not doubted for a second that Jesus is the Messiah, not since the miracle of the fish that brought him to his knees showed him what a sinful man he was, and caused him to follow Jesus.

But now Jesus has thoroughly confounded him, praising his faith and knowledge of his rabbi's true identity, but also in effect making Peter the leader of the disciples in both name and in actuality. At the same time, Jesus made it clear that a true leader must be a humble servant. Humility does not come easily to Peter. In his flesh, he'd love to believe he deserves whatever honor Jesus has bestowed upon him. In his spirit, he knows the master has called him to a costly responsibility.

He feels that particularly now on this sojourn to the Holy City with the rest of the disciples and Tamar and Mary Magdalene, especially with Jesus absent for the moment. The bickering among the disciples over who should enjoy places of honor in the kingdom have so upset Jesus that it's as if he can't even stand to be around them for a while. Oh, he'll be back. He loves them and has made that clear. Everyone will feel better when Jesus returns. But for now, on the long walk south, Peter can tell that his compatriots have been sobered. Their conversations are subdued. Even out of sight of Jesus, it's as if they're all embarrassed.

Peter is glad to have Zee along for the safety of this entire entourage. The former Zealot would die before letting anything happen to any of them. Big James is a comforting presence as well, his size alone discouraging any who might assume the group is an easy mark. Peter keeps his eyes on the horizon as other travelers pass them heading north. Most don't even take their eyes from the road, but still Peter watches until they've passed. You never know …

And now he perks up as he leads the group over a rise and a man on horseback comes into view from the south. As he draws closer, it's clear he bears with him in the saddle a huge muslin-wrapped box. The rider wears expensive clothes, and the horse is bedecked with fringed blankets and a bejeweled bridle. To Peter's surprise, the man stops and calls out, "Galilean Jews! Twelve men and two women. I was told there may be as many as four women in your company."

So, whoever has sent this man is aware of Jesus' mother and of Ramah and are wondering where they are too. Peter glances at Thomas, who looks pierced anew at his loss.

"You are followers of Jesus the Nazarene?" the rider says.

"Who's asking?" Peter says.

"I have a package for Andrew and Simon, sons of Jonah."

"You didn't answer his question," Big James says.

"What's in the box?" Zee says.

"I'm the messenger, not the sender. I was given only delivery instructions. Whomever of you is Andrew, step forth."

Andrew raises a hand. "Me."

Peter wishes his brother was not so forthcoming and can tell that Zee and James feel the same. The horseman produces a small parchment and studies it, glancing from it to Peter and back. "Actually you match the description of Simon, down to the shortness of your garment."

"Tell us who sent you, and maybe we'll explain—"

But the messenger merely dismounts, unclasps the ropes securing the box, and sets it on the ground. Apparently satisfied, he leaps back into the saddle, reins his steed around, and gallops back to the south.

"Whoever sent this thinks I'm still Simon. Outdated information."

"And," Nathanael says, "they didn't know Ramah died."

"And why would they put your name first?" Peter says. "I'm older."

"Could it be from the Baptizer?" John says.

"Dead people don't send packages," Matthew says.

Andrew and Peter carefully remove the muslin to reveal an ornately gilded container.

"We could get a week's worth of rations for selling the box alone!" Judas says.

Andrew says, "John definitely couldn't have afforded anything like this."

"Remember the bag of gold someone left for us before we went to Samaria?" Little James says.

Big James snorts. "I also remember the sack of dead crows from a malcontent in Tel-Dor."

"People have sent letters asking for healing and signs in their towns," Mary says.

"Maybe it's from someone who *really* needs help," Thaddeus says.

"Trying to buy a miracle," Judas says.

"We did receive a gift of gratitude from Fatiyah, the Nabatean in the Decapolis after the feeding," Tamar says.

Peter is genuinely curious and not from jealousy. "Why was Andrew's name first?"

Big James says, "What if it's a rabid animal sent to attack and kill us?"

Peter rolls his eyes. Zee kneels, puts an ear close to the lid, then opens it an inch and sniffs. "Smells safe."

"Just open it," Thomas says.

Zee opens the box and gasps. "A ganavat hekdesh," he says.

"It's a treasure trove all right," Andrew says, snatching up a note from the top of a pile of expensive goods. "But it doesn't look like anything stolen from a temple. It's from Joanna! It says, 'For the uninterrupted continuation of the teachings and deeds of Jesus of Nazareth.'"

Over the *oohs* and *aahs* from everyone, Judas says, "We're going to need to split the work of selling these in order to liquidate quickly. It would take one person too long."

"So," Peter says, "split it up."

"Silver cooking blades," Judas says. "Zee?"

"I have someone for these," Zee says.

Judas lifts out a bundle of shimmering fabric. "Uh—"

"Silk from the Far East," Matthew says.

Judas tries to hand it to Matthew, but he flinches. "I don't think it's a good idea for me to—"

"But you know the value," Peter says. "You know how to get a good price for it."

"I thought we agreed Judas would handle the money," Matthew says.

"I am," Judas says. "Just bring me back whatever you can get for it."

"We trust you, Matthew," Peter says. "Implicitly."

Judas opens a box of gemstones and begins picking through them when Tamar pushes close. "Lapis lazuli!" she says. "Amethyst, carnelian, jasper—"

"Valuable?" John says.

"Beyond rubies," Judas says.

"Oh, they'll do well," Tamar says. "I promise you that."

"Big James," Peter says, "go with Tamar and Mary to the market and make sure no one bothers them."

"All that's left are the coins," Judas says.

"And the box itself," Nathanael says.

"You go on and sell the box, Nathanael," Peter says.

"I'll come with you," Thaddeus says.

"And the coins?" John says.

"Judas, take the money and add it to the purse," Peter says. "What are you all waiting for? Go, and let's make these gifts from Joanna go a long way."

Chapter 39

FRACAS

The Jerusalem Sanhedrin

Because of his da'aga, a deep concern over what was to become of Jesus of Nazareth, Shmuel silently quotes part of a psalm of David as he enters the vast room containing the august body to which he has been promoted. "'Cast your burden on the Lord, and He will sustain you; He will never permit the righteous to be moved.'" But is he righteous? It was, after all, his work in exposing both Jesus and John the Baptizer, informing his superiors where to find them, that landed him his membership among the elite.

Though this continues to weigh on Shmuel, he can't deny that the debates and discussions of the Sanhedrin have proven as invigorating and fascinating as he always believed they would. Today is a case in point. He has been assigned to moderate a debate between an elegantly dressed Sadducee named Gedera and a very portly Pharisee, Zebadiah. With his underling Yanni discreetly behind him and at his beck and call, Shmuel steps before three podiums: two for Zebadiah who has a scroll open on each, and one for Gedera and his own scroll.

A crowd forms around them, allowing Shmuel to put his own worries in abeyance so he can hold court for what he knows will be a most intriguing discussion. "You, Rabbi Gedera," he begins, "being of Saducean persuasion, contend there is no resurrection of the dead."

Gedera nods. "The holy law of Adonai makes no mention of an afterlife."

"It's right there in the Songs of David," Zebadiah says.

"David is not Torah."

"According to the *Doe of the Dawn*—"

"'My God, my God, why have you forsaken me?'" Shmuel says.

"Yes," Zebadiah says, scanning a scroll with his yad, "but further down, near the end, 'All the prosperous of the earth eat and worship; before him shall bow all who go down to the dust.'"

"I am so tired of this line of reasoning," Gedera says.

Zebadiah switches podiums and scrolls. "And then here in the Prophet Daniel, 'And many of those who sleep in the dust of the earth shall awake, some to eternal life, and some to shame and everlasting contempt.'"

From behind Shmuel, Yanni pipes up. "I don't know how anyone could refute that."

"Metaphorical language," Gedera says. "It's about Israel's national resurrection from being muddled amid the dust of the Gentiles."

The crowd groans and someone calls out, "Midrashic acrobatics!"

Another yells, "Halakhic contortions!"

Gedera raises his voice. "*Awakening* refers to the coming of Messiah, when Jews who love God's Law will arise from their spiritual slumber, and those who reject the Messiah will be put to shame and contempt."

"Rabbi Gedera," Zebadiah says, "how do you interpret the words *eternal life, hayei olam*?"

"God's immutable Law is eternal," the Sadducee says. "A life committed to studying Torah is a life centered on matters of eternal importance. That's hayei olam."

Shmuel says, "How does the Sadducees' rejection of an afterlife lead to more faithful adherence to Torah in practical terms?"

"Practicality is our entire agenda," Gedera says. "I would direct your attention to the words of the Fifth Book of Torah: 'You shall therefore be careful to do the commandment and the statutes and the rules that I command you today.' God's will is that we carry out His decrees, here, today, not in some imagined next world. The Pharisees' hyper-literal reading of the Prophet Daniel is both dangerous and distracting."

The crowd sounds scandalized as Gedera continues. "If all your work is only to receive a reward in the afterlife, it makes you blind to the realities of the one you're living in right now!"

"How would you respond," Shmuel says, "to the accusation that the Sadducees' wealth and social status make your interpretations all too convenient?"

"Your class is so comfortable in this life," Zebadiah says, "why should you care about a next one? Ordinary Jews live lives of such discomfort that the hope of a better life in the resurrection is what they have to cling to."

"And you, Rabbi Zebadiah," Gedera says, "haven't been missing meals lately, have you?"

The crowd erupts, some shouting, "Niveh zeh!" and others, "Dirty trick! Unfair!"

Shmuel says, "Rabbi Gedera, you are to assess his interpretation, not his appearance."

"Hypocrites!" Gedera hollers. "Both of you accused me of letting my supposed affluence distort my interpretation!"

"We bring our bodies to the study of Torah," Zebadiah says, "do we not? We cannot escape them."

"You seem to want to," Gedera says.

Shmuel looks to the crowd, which has devolved into a shouting match, and spots Yussif. He signals Yanni to take over moderating and heads toward his Capernaum brother. "What are you doing here? This way. Come, come, tell me." He leads Yussif into the hallway for privacy and grips him by the shoulders. "I saw your name on the attendance and thought it was a mistake!"

"So did I, honestly," Yussif says.

"You finally did it, leaned into your abba's wealth and connections. I never thought I'd see the day."

"Well, it's here."

"You could have used your inheritance years ago," Shmuel says.

"To do what? I knew nothing but scholarship. I had to minister to our people first."

"Setting aside my own jealousy of your wealth, I imagine your abba was upset."

"Yes, but his recent contribution indicates he's gotten over it." Yussif nods to the tumult. "That was something in there."

"Do you think the Sadducees have a valid point?"

"The only thing I agreed with him on is that you ought not to have brought his fortunes into the argument. Let the interpretation stand on its own merits."

"Sensitive about money, are we, Yussif?"

"We both used whatever means necessary to lay hold of our seats. You used bureaucratic triangulation. I used my abba.

What matters now is that we're both here. And the only question that remains is what we will do with our new positions."

"Fair point," Shmuel says. "Although I thought I did know what I came here to do. Lately, I'm not so sure."

"What has changed?"

Shmuel knows it's way too soon, and dangerous, to get into that. "Let me show you around …"

Chapter 40

HELMET HAIR

The road to Jerusalem

Peter is encouraged by the pace and that Jesus caught up with them several days ago. They had taken the direct hundred-mile route along the Jordan River Valley, ascending the Judean mountains. Their slowest member, Little James, had gamely kept up.

At breakfast around the campfire, Peter notices that Jesus has gone off privately to pray, his usual practice. "We'll reach the Holy City by nightfall," Peter tells the others.

John nods. "Well before that if we keep a steady pace."

Nathanael asks if they should plan to set up camp in the same spot they had for the Feast of Tabernacles.

"It's not a holiday," Big James says, "and a camp would draw attention. People are on the lookout for the master."

"What then?" Andrew says. "An inn?"

"Same problem," Peter says. "There are eyes everywhere, and inns document visitors."

"After Joanna's gift," Judas says, "we do have enough to stay at an inn, or perhaps several inns to spread us out and not invite suspicion. We could disguise Jesus and maybe use fake names."

"Fake names?" John says. "And violate the eighth commandment?"

"Ninth," Matthew says.

"He's right, John," Peter says. "Lying is the ninth."

"The order doesn't matter," John says. "Lying is lying."

"It doesn't matter," Big James says. "Zee, you have a brother in Jerusalem."

"I do. Jesse."

John says, "Last time I saw him, he was homeless."

"That could have changed," Zee says. "He certainly has. But I doubt his lodging would accommodate us all."

Nathanael says, "Does anyone have a rich uncle in the Upper City or something?"

"Judas says we have enough to stay under a roof," Peter says. "If we can just find a way to keep Rabbi's identity a secret—"

"And hide his presence from Jerusalem …" John says.

"Has anyone tried to contact Nicodemus?" Andrew says.

"We don't know his heart," John says, "or his intentions."

"When I spoke with him, John," Mary says, "he had an open heart."

"Good morning, my friends!"

They all turn and Peter, especially, is relieved to see Jesus. "Master, where would you like to stay tonight?"

"The property of my friend Lazarus!"

"I thought he lived in Bethany," John says.

"Correct. Instead of going directly to Jerusalem tonight, we'll stay over with Lazarus and his sisters. I want to see my ima. Just saying that out loud makes me even more eager. Let's get to the road quickly!"

Not long later, as they approach a fork in the road, Peter is startled by eight Roman legionnaires and their leader, a Decanus—normally a leader of ten. He shouts to his troops, "Halt! Jewish citizens!"

"Everyone remain calm," Jesus says.

"Disarm yourselves and put down your bags," the Decanus says. "You're carrying ours now."

"*What?!*" Tamar says.

As the armed disciples remove their weapons, Matthew tells her, "Under Roman law, a soldier can force a Jew to carry his things."

"At random?" she says, sounding incredulous.

"There is a limit. One mile and no farther."

"Master," Peter whispers, "this is humiliating."

"We will comply," Jesus says. "With dignity."

The soldiers load the disciples down with tents, furcas—four-foot-long T-shaped poles with leather bags strapped to the crossbar—, bronze cooking pots, canteens, flasks, food rations, swords, and shields.

A soldier says to John, "What must it be like, walking around all day with no metal weighing down your head?" He pulls off his helmet and runs a hand through his sweaty hair. "Whew! Ever had helmet hair?" He plops his helmet on John's head. "There!"

The rest of the soldiers laugh and do the same, forcing their helmets on the disciples' heads, jeering and mocking.

Peter grits his teeth as even Jesus gets one from the Decanus. Only Matthew, Judas, Thaddeus, and Andrew are spared the embarrassment. A soldier shoves a bag of tent poles at Mary. "You too," he says.

Matthew reaches for the bag, despite all he's already carrying. "I'll take that."

"I'm not made of straw," Mary says. "I can carry it."

"Mary, please," he says, and takes the burden anyway.

"Hurry along, rats!" the Decanus says, instructing the Jews to leave all their stuff at the crossroad. Peter wonders the odds of whether any of it will still be there when they return.

"Rats with nice hats," another says.

One pours water over his head and shakes his hair out. Peter is struck by how normal these men look without their helmets and gear. Just guys in red tunics.

"Master," Judas says, reaching for Jesus' helmet. "Let me take that. It is not right that you should—"

"It is no more unsuitable on my head than any of yours," Jesus says.

"We both know that's not true."

"Thank you for your concern, Judas."

The Jerusalem Temple

Shmuel strolls the outer rim of the Sanhedrin seating area with Yussif as various groups kvetch and confer. "In the months since I last saw you in Capernaum, Yussif, how have you grown in wisdom and stature—other than coming to your senses that you can leverage your family's wealth?"

"Will you stop with that?"

"Fine. But I can see you're not the same impressionable young man I knew in Galilee, always struggling with your tallit."

"I have become more committed, discerning, and observant, Shmuel. Who were the men we walked past at the entrance when we came back from the bet midrash?" Yussif turns to look back.

"I thought you said you were observant," Shmuel says.

"I meant in worship."

"Notice who *isn't* around here?" Yussif shoots him a look. Shmuel continues, "Okay, so you're observant. Now let's find out if you make observations." He nods toward a group of men at desks, copying literature on parchment, appearing to compare texts.

"Hmm. Lawyers of some kind?"

"Close," Shmuel says. "In here we call them scribes. But, yes, lawyers in the sense that they are chief authorities on the sacred Law of Moses, interpreters and arbiters of God's covenant with Israel."

"They're not dressed as nicely as most lawyers I know."

"They hold unpaid positions. They have second jobs to support what they do here free of charge."

"Why work for no compensation?"

"In hopes of finding favor with someone influential in here and securing a seat if one opens."

"'Whatever means necessary …'" Yussif says.

"Exactly," Shmuel says, nodding at a group of flamboyantly dressed Jews who stand out. "What about them?"

"Amethyst and topaz rings, popular in Greece," Yussif says. "Athenian blue headdresses. Hellenized Jews visiting from the Decapolis?"

"Hellenized, yes. But not visitors. Herodians."

"Of course."

"Supporters of King Herod Antipas, and by extension, Rome. They hope to secure greater political power at the expense of the rest of Israel. Morally compromised, selfish, misguided. The Zealots hate them."

"They hate us too," Yussif says.

"True," Shmuel says. "Everyone who isn't a Zealot. Even them," he adds, gesturing toward a dour-looking circle of whispering ultra-Orthodox Jews sporting curls on the sides of their heads.

"Payot!" Yussif says. "I haven't seen hair like that since I was a little kid."

"Following to the letter," Shmuel says, "'You shall not round off the hair on your temples or mar the edges of your beard.'"

"Devotees of the House of Shammai?"

Shmuel nods. "They're probably complaining about the Hillel acolytes right now."

"Hillel, the more lenient one."

"But both are equally committed to Torah. Shammai is more literal, while Hillel focuses on the broader principle. The latest dispute? Whether you should tell a bride on her wedding day that she is beautiful, even if it is not true."

"I'm guessing," Yussif says, "that Shammai says no, because it would be a lie."

"Correct. And Hillel maintains that a bride is always beautiful on her wedding day."

"A bigger story of God and His people," Yussif says.

"Be careful who you say that to around here," Shmuel says, laughing. "I have a feeling about you, Yussif. You weren't lying when you said you are observant, discerning."

Yussif seems to study him. "Shmuel, is something wrong?"

"Wrong? Throughout history men have called their age confusing or troubled. Our times are no different, I suppose. I can honestly say I'm glad you're here. You've done well."

"Thank you, Rabbi."

Throughout the assembly, factions debate, scribes scribble, and Sadducees drink wine. Gedera pounds a gavel and shouts, "Everyone! Attention, please! I have an entreaty!"

The road to Bethany

Peter has long taken pride in his stamina, and though he struggles under the load in the heat of the day, he's determined not to let it show to the Romans. Zee and Big James forge ahead too, but Peter can't say the same for the rest. Everyone seems to stagger and grow slower.

"It's not that I'm humiliated," Peter says, "which I am. It's that I'm so murderously angry that they're doing this to Jesus."

"I've done this plenty of times," Philip says. "That doesn't make it any easier."

A soldier pushes Thomas, and Peter can tell Judas is seething. Meanwhile, Jesus continues at a steady pace.

The Decanus grabs Tamar's wrist and raises her arm, asking his men, "So which one of you does this one belong to?"

She wrenches free and glowers at him as the soldiers yip and cackle.

Zee mutters, "I never could have imagined a moment like this—"

"He said submit," Peter says. "So we submit."

"—the painful irony of some of his teaching."

The Decanus crows to his men, "You know what the Jewish holy men who perform the circumcisions say?"

"What?" they call back in unison.

"'The pay's lousy, but you get to keep the tips.'"

Peter can tell the Sons of Thunder fight to keep from erupting.

A sign points toward a Roman outpost. A legionnaire tells the Decanus, "That's the one-mile marker."

The leaders says, "Aah, I'll bet you Jews have never been more grateful for enshrined Roman law."

A legionnaire adds, "We know it's been an honor for you."

"Stop here!" the Decanus says.

Everyone stops but Jesus, who keeps going as if he hasn't heard.

"I said stop!"

Jesus turns. "Your destination is that outpost another mile ahead, yes?"

"It is," a soldier says. "But we are permitted only one—"

"By *coercion*," Jesus says. "But there's no law against citizens assisting you the rest of the way of their own volition. Come, my friends."

The Decanus says, "But—"

"If anyone asks," Jesus says, "you can say we offered."

He continues and most of the disciples fall in after him. But Judas says, "Rabbi! What are we doing? Why would we—"

"Judas," Jesus says, "where did we meet?"

"At your sermon on the Korazim Plateau."

"Good. When you are troubled, think back to my message."

Judas falls back, but the Decanus seems embarrassed. He hurries to catch up to Jesus. "At least, uh, let us take the helmets back so, you know, there's not confusion at the outpost."

"If you like," Jesus says, and lets the man take his resplendent helmet back.

The others quickly follow suit, retrieving their own headwear.

Philip says, "'If anyone forces you to go one mile—'"

"—'go with him two miles,'" Andrew says.

Matthew stumbles, and Peter notices that instead of mocking him, the Romans rush to him and set him aright.

Chapter 41

YUSSIF'S CHOICE

The Jerusalem Sanhedrin

Yussif is intrigued by Sadducee Gedera's ability to command attention in the great assembly room. For all the years he dreamed of somehow landing an appointment to this esteemed body, he never expected anything like this—two articulate, bombastic leaders going head-to-head in front of all. He had assumed it customary for these elite members to calmly debate important biblical matters in a dignified way. He has trouble getting his mind around the fact that he is now a member, though he feels anything but elite or esteemed. If nothing else, this should be fascinating.

There isn't even time for him to see what Shmuel thinks of all this. The man appears as absorbed in the action as he does and seems to revel in the creative arguments coming from the podium. And so Yussif is content to hear where Gedera is going with all this.

"It brings me no pleasure," the Sadducee begins, "to direct your memories to a painful incident, but we have gained new insight that calls for revisiting …"

Is he really going here? Yussif wonders.

"We all still mourn when we recall that Governor Pontius Pilate did most barbarously appropriate funds from the temple treasury for construction of the Bier Aqueduct to bring water into Jerusalem."

Murmurs and hisses ripple through the room, and Yussif is impressed by Gedera's bravado. The man continues, "And worse yet, we still grieve the loss of those who resisted this provocation and were crushed, dismembered, disemboweled, and impaled on poles—made an example of so that none should defy Pilate's designs for this city—nor the means by which he deigns to carry them out."

Many shake their heads and express their sorrow. The portly Pharisee Zebadiah says, "Gedera, you do us harm by reviving this abominable anecdote! We are still trying to heal."

"It would be irresponsible," Gedera says, "to ignore the ways in which this cataclysmic bloodbath may now prove instructive."

"*Instructive?*" Zebadiah shouts.

"Credible intelligence has reached our ears that the event was a source of pain not only to us, but also to Pilate himself."

Zebadiah says, "The sniveling child has proven incapable of remorse!"

"Not when his job is threatened," Gedera says. "Emperor Tiberius was appalled both by Pilate's stealing from the temple funds, inexcusable even by Roman standards, and abundantly more so by the brutality with which he struck down our response."

"What are you saying?" Zebadiah asks.

"It would appear, however improbable, that we now want the same thing as Pilate."

What is he implying? Yussif thinks, and it's obvious from the tumult many others wonder the same.

"Peace," Gedera says. "Pilate wants peace. Or at least Caesar does."

Zebadiah speaks up again. "Emperor Tiberius Caesar Augustus is not fond of Pontius Pilate."

"Exactly," Gedera says. "Pilate's position as procurator of Judea is on the line. He was reprimanded and warned for sending troops to kill Galileans while they were offering sacrifices in our temple and was then given a second warning for the aqueduct massacre. He was already in over his head and too young for this position. And now he is officially on notice."

Zebadiah says, "Then let's make something happen so we can get rid of him."

Yussif can't determine if the hollered yeas or nays prevail.

"Shortsighted, Zebadiah, as usual," Gedera says. "I submit we take advantage of his tenuous situation. Take care of some things we've been putting off."

"Such as?" Zebadiah says.

"That's for this body and its committees to decide. We could suggest to Pilate a revolutionary leader is fomenting an overthrow for, say, removing the Roman votive shields from the palace."

"He does not take kindly to bribery," Zebadiah says.

"What are his options?"

The room disintegrates into a shouting match of factions, and Yussif wants in on it. But Shmuel stops him short. "Yussif!" he says, "Hold your tongue!"

"I have a seat and I will use my voice. This is absurd!"

Shmuel hustles him toward an exit and into the bet midrash. "Listen, I know what you mean. I know you have things you want to achieve, but you're new. No one knows you. You'll be shouted down."

"Then where do I start?"

"Pick your battles. What do you want to accomplish?"

If he only knew ... Yussif bites his tongue.

"Whatever you've come here for," Shmuel continues, "the key is to get yourself onto a committee committed to the same ends."

"What are the committees?"

"The entire range of Jewish interests. There's a committee on Ritual Purity and Sacrificial Inspection, very practical. Tithes and Treasury. Agriculture and Food Law. Education and Labor. Sabbath and Festival Observance. It depends what you came here for."

"I came to make a difference," Yussif says.

"Everyone says that at first."

"And then what happens?"

"I'm trying to help you, Yussif. You come from a prominent business family, and yet you chose to work among the common people in rural Galilee where there is no room for intellectuals like us. But at some point you decided to move on from your youthful posturing and—"

"It was not posturing!"

"Youthful idealism then. You decided to grow up."

"Don't insult me."

"Do you lean toward Hillel interpretations," Shmuel says, "due to contact with Nicodemus?"

"Did your time with him have the opposite effect on you?" Yussif senses he has struck a chord and that Shmuel cannot counter his insight. "None of the committees sound very interesting."

Shmuel shrugs. "There are short term assignments too. A Select Committee on Investigation of Civilian Deaths in the Maccabean Revolt. Another on Temple Renovation. Liturgical Reform. Reclamation of Beersheba at the Southern Border—"

"Beersheba?! Part of Edom, yes?"

Shmuel nods. "Stodgy old men hung up on a passage from the time of the Judges that describes the borders of Israel from north to south as 'From Dan to Beersheba.' They want to take it back, restore the original borders."

"I cannot think of anything more tiresome, or futile."

"I can," Shmuel says. "Preservation of Davidic Artifacts for the National Archive. Investigation into the Authorship of Job. Theorization of Fulfilled Late Babylonian-Exilic Prophecies. Historical Accuracy of the Books of Judith and Tobit—"

"Wait!" Yussif says. "What's the one about the Babylonian prophecies?"

"Eh, it's academic. A proposed list of prophecies from the time of Nebuchadnezzar the Second that may have been fulfilled through the reign of Antiochus Epiphanes, and which ones are yet to be fulfilled."

"That one."

"Really? You suddenly seem very sure."

"I am."

Chapter 42

OLD FRIENDS

The Road to Bethany

Judas is at a loss as the disciples follow Jesus all the way back to the fork in the road that leads to Bethany. When Jesus insisted they go another mile with the Romans' heavy gear, it really meant three miles, including the two miles back to where they'd left their own stuff. How did that make any sense?

Miraculously, nothing had been touched. He and his comrades nearly empty their canteens before loading up.

"I'm proud of you all," Jesus says. "I know how hard that was. You did well. Now, on to Bethany."

Later, when Bethany finally becomes visible in the distance, Judas rushes to catch up with Jesus near the front. "Rabbi?"

"Judas! How are you feeling?"

"Exhausted. I'm not used to life on the road, being a missionary—"

"Give it time. I'm tired too. But we're nearly there. Have you been to Bethany?"

"Yes, uh, actually. I wanted to ask you—when you're with your ima, I wondered if I might visit an old associate in town."

"Old?"

"Well, a former associate. He took me on as an apprentice after my father died."

"An important person …"

"Not more important than you, Rabbi! Don't get me wrong."

"I understand, Judas. By all means, go see him. But wait until after supper."

At the end of a long lane, Jesus pauses and the others stop. "Wait for it," he says.

"Jesus!" It's one of Lazarus's sisters, Mary, who has burst from a house in the distance. "You're here!"

Jesus smiles at the disciples. "I think we're in the right place."

She races to them. "At last! Oh! Come, come, all of you, this way!"

In the house, Lazarus's other sister, Martha, bustles about, tidying, dusting, sweeping, even adjusting the position of the furniture. Wiping a windowsill, she sees her sister leading Jesus and his followers toward the house. She squints. "Three, four, five, six—Adonai in heaven!"

Jesus swings open the door with a flourish and says, "Why is my dearest Martha hiding in the house?"

"My Lord!" Martha says, bowing. "Oh, Rabbi, please pardon the state of—"

Lazarus appears from his office. "What's the meaning of this?" he demands. "You barge in here unannounced—"

"Oh, hello, Lazarus," Jesus deadpans. "We were just passing through and, well, I thought we might crash here."

"The nerve!" Lazarus says.

The two old mates stand feet apart, staging a staring contest to see who smiles first. Lazarus loses. "It's been too long, my friend."

The men embrace as the disciples look relieved.

Martha says, "What can I get you? Water? Olives? Wine?"

"Something better than all of those," Jesus says.

"Such an ima's boy," Lazarus says.

Sister Mary says, "She went into the woods to pick berries."

"Alone?" Peter says.

Lazarus tells Jesus, "I try, but you know how she is."

"Impossible to hold down," Jesus says.

"Honestly," Mary says, "she's the only one in this household who knows which berries aren't poisonous and where to find the tastiest ones."

"She's had a lot of practice," Jesus says.

"Lazarus," Martha says, "go get her."

"It's fine," Jesus says, "not to worry. She'll return before dark. Let's all sit."

"Yes, yes," Martha says. "You must have had a long journey. Please …"

The Jerusalem Sanhedrin

Yussif enjoys meeting various committee members. Shmuel introduces him to Pharisee Zebadiah as the "son of Arnan."

"Ah, yes!" the portly man says. "Recently appointed. Congratulations. It was of note to see your name show up on the list out of nowhere."

"Well," Shmuel says, "I wouldn't say out of n—"

"Let's cut right to it," Zebadiah says. "Where did you get the money for your seat?"

"Zebadiah!" Shmuel says.

Yussif holds his head high. "My family owns a construction business in Jerusalem."

Zebadiah rolls his eyes and looks away. "Land ownership would be one thing, but construction? How vulgar."

Shmuel drags Yussif away, urgently whispering, "That was the chair of the Prophecy Fulfillment committee!"

"What's so vulgar about construction?"

"They see new buildings as a blight on the city's aesthetic."

They approach the Sadducee. "Gedera!" Shmuel says. "That was a marvelous speech on Pilate!"

"So," Gedera says, "you will support me?"

"Let's schedule a lunch with my colleague, Yanni. This is Yussif, son of Arnan. He has just—"

"I know Arnan," Gedera says. "Which rabbi sponsored your application?"

"Annas," Yussif says, "son of Seth."

"A fellow Sadducee," Gedera says. "I won't bother asking why he sponsored a new member from a rival party. I already know the answer."

"We are all sons of Israel," Shmuel says, "though we may disagree on particulars."

Gedera zeroes in on Yussif. "The next time you see your abba's old friend Annas, tell him I want to talk to him about his sons' booths. They keep buying up market stalls on the Mount of Olives before they're even listed for sale. I want to know who his contacts are. I may have to sing Caiaphas a song about Annas's son-in-law and a certain slave-beating incident. He'll know what I'm talking about, I assure you."

"You want me to threaten him?"

Shmuel intervenes again. "This way, Yussif. We have so many people to meet today! Gedera, let me know about lunch."

Gedera dismisses him with a wave.

"Speaking of lunch," Shmuel says, "let's eat. I'm exhausted."

"*I'm* exhausted."

Chapter 43

HOSPITALITY

Lazarus's home

Warmed at being back to familiar surroundings and precious memories, Jesus drifts to a window while munching roasted chickpeas. For the moment he is at peace, especially anticipating the reunion with his mother. That will thoroughly complete an arduous day in the best way he can imagine. Even the thought of it brings teaching to mind—something he's been eager to share with the disciples, the women, and now his old friends too.

The room is crowded with loved ones, but Lazarus, just like in childhood, is nearest. Jesus asks him how his vineyard is doing.

"It's been a dry summer," Lazarus says. "But we're managing."

"What's the going day rate for waterers and pruners?"

"Same as carpentry."

"A denarius. Hmm. That reminds me of a story."

The others, though they've been idly chatting with each other, turn their attention to him. He appreciates that they seem ever eager for a lesson, a parable, some teaching. But before he can even begin, everyone turns at a crash from the kitchen—everyone but Sister Mary who has settled in to listen to Jesus.

"Everything all right in there, Martha?" Lazarus says.

"I'm fine! Just, um, I've got it. Carry on!"

Lazarus nods at Jesus who is ready with a parable he wonders how many will comprehend. After all the annoying bickering about who will have what rank in the kingdom, Jesus is not optimistic, but he is eager to tell the story. And they do seem attentive.

"The kingdom of heaven," he begins, "is like the master of a house who went out early in the morning to hire laborers. After agreeing to pay them a denarius a day, he sent them into his vineyard."

Lazarus smiles. "You make that sound so simple."

"And going out about the third hour, he found others standing idle in the marketplace and said to them, 'You go into the vineyard too, and whatever is right I will give you.' So they went."

Jesus hesitates as Martha carries a precariously loaded tray into the room and begins handing cups of hot tea to each one, whispering, "Steeped with sage." The disciples look grateful.

"Going out again about the ninth hour," Jesus continues, "he did the same. And about the eleventh hour he went out and found others standing. He said to them, 'Why do you stand here idle all day?' They said, 'Because no one has hired us.' So he told them, 'You go into the vineyard too.'"

Jesus continues, aware that Martha stands at the edge of the group with her empty tray, clearly trying to get her sister's attention, staring intensely at her. But Mary seems spellbound. Martha huffs and rolls her eyes and rushes back to the kitchen.

"When evening came, the owner of the vineyard said to his foreman, 'Call the laborers and pay them their wages, beginning with the last, up to the first.'" Jesus hears clatter in the kitchen and smells sweet bread, hoping that doesn't distract his listeners. "So when those hired at the eleventh hour came, each of them received a denarius. Now when those hired first came, they thought they would receive more, but each of them also received a denarius. And when they got it, they grumbled to the master of the house, saying, 'These last worked only one hour, and you've made them equal to us who've been here all day in the scorching heat.'

"But he replied, 'Friend, I am doing you no wrong. Did you not agree with me for a denarius? Take what belongs to you and go. I choose to give this last worker the same. Am I not allowed to do what I choose with what belongs to me? Or do you begrudge my generosity?'"

Martha bustles in again with the fresh bread sliced and adorned with peach slices, blackberries, shaved almonds, and dusted with fine sugar. Jesus works to keep everyone's attention. "So, the last will be first, and the first last."

As Martha hands each person an embroidered napkin and a dessert, Peter says, "Whoa, whoa, whoa! Hold on!"

Judas says, "The ones who worked one hour got the full denarius? That's twelve times what was owed!"

"The owner of the vineyard is cheating himself!" Lazarus says.

"The kingdom of heaven is unjust?" Judas says.

"I get it," Big James says. "I'm happy to be last."

"Through earthly eyes," Jesus says, "I suppose it looks unfair. But I didn't say 'the kingdom of this world.' I said 'the kingdom of heaven.' That's where people are not measured by what they deserve."

Martha hands him an elaborate slice of bread. "Thank you," he says. "This looks delightful!"

"You're welcome, though it would have been better if I didn't have to do it all alone."

"Better?" Jesus says.

"Yes! More befitting of someone as important as you. It seems you didn't notice my sister left me to serve alone." Jesus is aware that the others are now looking up from their treats, appearing to eavesdrop. "From the moment you got here," Martha continues, "Mary hasn't done a thing to serve you. She's ignored everything I've been doing to make you all comfortable, and it's clear that on her own she's not going to notice how hard I'm working. Maybe if *you* told her to help me—"

Noticing Mary's pained expression, Jesus says, "Martha, Martha, please sit down, here with me."

"How can I? Only half my guests have been served!"

Jesus gently takes her arm and her demeanor changes. "We can discuss this another time," she says. "I'm sorry."

"I want others to hear this," Jesus says. "There's nothing to be embarrassed about. You've done a wonderful thing." She sits next to him, and he continues. "You are anxious and troubled about many things, and that is not for nothing. Hospitality will always matter, and I'm grateful for what you have done."

"It's what you deserve," she says. "And more."

"You mean well," he says, "but only one thing is truly necessary. The best way to serve me is to pay close attention to my words. That is the priority, and that is what your sister has chosen. It is a good portion, and it will not be taken from her."

"Taken?"

"Your food, Martha, the servings, they're wonderful. But they'll pass away with the rest of this world. My words will never pass away. Mary has chosen to feast on something of eternal value." He turns to the others. "I want you all to hear this clearly. I am not rebuking Martha. Acts of service are beautiful. Action is good. Martha, you were doing what you thought was expected of you, and what you do is valuable. And Mary probably could have helped, a little." Mary shrugs and nods, and Jesus chuckles. "But I don't want you distracted from being able to be present with me and the friends I have brought. I invite you all to something that is better—to sit at my feet, listen carefully to my words, and devour them as a meal more nourishing than actual food."

Jesus holds up his dessert with a smile. "That said, I definitely don't want to waste Martha's amazing food. So if you all got the lesson, let's thank her and eat!" As the others applaud, Jesus takes a bite and closes his eyes. "Divine!"

As everyone laughs, Andrew—one who has not yet been served—raises his hand. "I enjoy divine—"

Lazarus heads toward the kitchen. "I'll bring the rest." Peter joins him.

Jesus asks Martha, "What is that bright flavor in the bread?"

"I snuck in some mint and lemon in the dough."

"Brilliant."

Lazarus and Peter return. "All right," Lazarus says, "who didn't get any?"

Big James's hand shoots up.

"What?" Peter says. "You had one!"

The group roars as James wipes sugar from his chin.

Later, after a sumptuous meal, Jesus enjoys being in the middle of the revelry. He's still eager to see his mother, but meanwhile jokes are told and those who know how are playing makeshift instruments Lazarus has collected. Jesus' old friend quietly stops playing, rises, and discreetly moves to lean against a table, steadying himself, one hand on his back.

As Jesus sips his wine, he stops at his own undulating reflection in the liquid and is overcome with a sense of foreboding. He sets down his cup and quietly slips outside. A short walk from the house, he recognizes a familiar silhouette carrying a basket in the darkness. He breaks into a run toward her. She drops the basket and they embrace.

"My son," she says.

"Ima! Ah, you're really here!"

"*You're* really here."

"Yes," he says, "but there is a grave problem."

"What?" she says. "What's happened?"

"I just—I don't know what we're going to do. It could ruin the whole night." He adopts his most somber tone. "They've—run out of wine."

She thwacks him with her shawl. "Oh, whatever will we do? Ha!"

"Rabbi?" It's Judas, carrying his bag. "I don't mean to interrupt—"

"Not at all," Jesus says.

"You said after supper. Is now a good time?"

"Yes, and please give my best to your friend."

Judas nods and looks puzzled, probably wondering how he would go about that. Shyly he addresses Jesus' mother. "Nice to see you again, Woman. Shalom, shalom."

Chapter 44

ONLY HUMAN

Outside Lazarus's home

After Judas disappears into the night, Jesus' mother says, "Sounds like quite a party in there."

"It is. But let's not go in yet."

"All right," she says, sounding decisive. "Come with me to the well. Your hair needs washing."

Behind the house, she pours a bucket of water over his head as he asks, "How is your new life here?"

"It's not home, but I think we both know neither of us can ever go back to Nazareth."

"Do you miss it?" he says as she lathers his scalp.

"Nazareth is just a place. And after the way they treated you …"

"But Abba's tomb is there."

"My thoughts dwell in the land of the living."

"Laz is taking good care of you?"

"Too good. If it were up to him, I'd sit inside all day shaded from the sun and doted on by Martha like I'm the Queen of

Sheba. I had to put my foot down and insist he let me contribute, collecting seeds and berries."

"So I've heard."

She dries his hair.

"Your turn," he adds.

She removes her head covering. "I would really love it if you could make it so no one comes around that corner."

He laughs aloud, but when he reaches for the water bucket, he's choked with emotion.

"What is it?" she says.

He wipes his face. "Reminds me of when life was simple."

"It wasn't so simple," she says. "We struggled. Some nights your father and I had to decide which of us would eat."

"I know." He pours water over her hair. "It was important to learn the uncertainty of poverty. My followers are poor in another sense—their way of understanding, of listening, of faith. Destitute, I'm afraid."

"That bad?"

"They ask for earthly things—positions of prestige at my right and left hand in glory. They take offense when I show humility and deference to the powers of this world instead of, I don't know, turning Roman soldiers into pillars of salt."

"They're only human," she says. "What did you expect?"

"I'm human too, you know."

"Do I know? Darling, I changed you when you were an infant. Believe me, I am aware."

He laughs as he rinses her hair. "What grieves me is the—yes, very human—feeling that no one understands this, by no fault of their own. They're simply incapable. I speak the words of my Father in heaven. The religious leaders call it blasphemy and plot against me while some just generally take it the wrong way. My own followers say they agree but turn around and act in a way that makes it seem they've not absorbed a word I've said."

"What will it take for them to understand?" she says.

He dries her hair.

"Son?"

"Bitter."

"What?" she says.

"It's a bitter answer to a bitter question."

She puts her head covering back on. "You speak in parables."

"I do."

"Remember how your father taught you to cut a dovetail joint? He didn't tell you a story. He put his hands on yours, wrapped your fingers around the tools, and guided you."

"Cypress, oak, sycamore," Jesus says. "These obey the master's hand. But human hearts, that's another story."

"Well, it doesn't hurt to try—being direct, I mean."

"I tried that recently. I told them exactly what's going to happen. It didn't even register. The human desire to avoid difficult news sometimes makes one deaf."

"True," she says. "You'll figure it out. Let's go inside. I want to see how Simon is doing."

"For starters, he has a new name."

"Oh, really? Like Abram to Abraham?"

"Kind of."

Chapter 45

FAME AND INFAMY

Hadad's office

Judas enjoys a strange feeling of freedom and nostalgia as he quietly slips in to where he knows his former business partner will still be working even in the dark of night. It hasn't been that long since he left the man to follow Jesus, and he can't deny that this has been the most—how should he put it—intriguing season of his life. He's heard profundities and seen miracles that persuade him that Jesus is who he claims to be and who his other followers know him to be.

And yet the rabbi is so full of mystery and contradiction that Judas is relieved to have even a brief respite from the day to day with these strange new friends. Jesus embodies paradox. Leaders must be servants. To become rich you must become poor. The last shall be first. Love your enemies. Pray for them even. That is fascinating, revolutionary, and diametrically opposed to Judas's background and training, primarily under the man he's about to surprise.

Hadad had seen something in him that Judas was himself slow to recognize—the ability to quickly learn and adapt. He caught on to the vagaries of business and excelled at discovering and using whatever means were necessary to favor himself and Hadad and their interests, regardless the transaction. While their smooth duplicity often left him conflicted, that had proved a temporary malaise quickly forgotten in the rush of totaling up and splitting the profits.

Judas could not fault Hadad's work ethic—perhaps the only ethic the man employed. He was willing to do whatever it took to maximize his advantage, and his mantra was that a business either grows or soon dies. As Judas tiptoes in without the lock making a sound, he has to smile at what Hadad is up to even now—a scheme he had taught Judas his first day on the job. He's melting wax over a contract, which will allow him to fudge the date on it.

"Still using that old trick?" he says, and Hadad nearly jumps out of his skin.

"Hades and Styx! How did you get in here?"

"The key was still under the fennel plant. You know, it's advisable to change the locks and the hiding places after terminating an employee."

"I didn't terminate you. You quit! I thought I'd never see you again. Did everything fall apart?"

Not exactly, Judas thinks. *But …* He pulls up a chair. "We're just passing through."

Hadad raises a brow. "Make yourself at home."

Judas laughs. "Sorry. I should have knocked."

"Where is home for you these days?"

Judas shrugs. "We're nomadic, mostly camping. I'm still unused to it actually."

"Your rabbi has no home base?"

"Capernaum, I guess. If you can call any place we haunt a home. We're *strategically displaced* from Capernaum for the time being. Too much attention."

Hadad settles back. "I have heard both his fame and infamy are spreading. Shouldn't he be amassing an army as opposed to being run out of backwater towns in the north?"

Exactly, Judas thinks. "I'm newer than the others. My opinion doesn't count for much."

"He could learn from you," Hadad says. "He clearly does not understand the importance of perception in business, business of any kind."

How Judas has missed this man's insight. "His image among religious leaders is a problem. They're threatened by him."

"Not just religious leaders of his own sect," Hadad says. "I hear one of his followers was murdered by a high-ranking Roman. True?"

"That was a terrible, tragic accident. It was the praetor himself. He's been punished—demoted."

Hadad scoffs. "They kill one of our citizens and get a slap on the wrist. Imagine if we laid a finger on one of them. I mean, we're going to find out, because that has to happen soon, right?"

"I—assume?"

"Come on, Judas."

"Look, he *is* the Messiah, no question. He heals people, works miracles. His teaching is like nothing anyone has ever heard. You said it yourself."

"So why don't you seem convinced?"

Leave it to Hadad to cut to the heart of the matter.

"What I remember," Hadad continues, "is that he didn't take up a collection. That crowd was *enormous.* He had every ear, every heart, and therefore the strings of every purse. All he had to do was ask."

Judas tries to convince himself as well as Hadad. "That's what makes him great! No one can call him a charlatan or a con artist, which is more than I can say for myself."

"For needing to eat?"

Well, Judas thinks, *there is that.* "I admit I don't understand what we're doing or why we're doing it, or why we're not moving more quickly. I'm trying to learn. But in the meantime, hey, I'm not starving."

Hadad smiles. "You were skinny even when we ate like kings, how would I know?" He grows serious. "Do you have savings?"

"I try to be careful how I apportion out money, keeping some aside for a dry spell. But they're so frequent, I—"

"What do you mean *I*?"

"They put me in charge of finances."

"Did you learn nothing from me?"

"I've tried to forget," Judas says, trying to interpret Hadad's exaggerated appearance of having been wounded. "I'm sorry. I'm grateful for my apprenticeship. Now I'm trying to use what you taught me to help the group."

"Are you compensated for this special skill?"

"There's another who has exquisite skill with bookkeeping, but he won't go near it. He was a tax collector."

"Aah," Hadad says. "Guilty conscience."

"You're one to talk."

"If you're the only one qualified, and willing, you deserve a stipend for your specialized work, at a minimum. Like Solomon says, 'Woe to him who makes his neighbor serve him for nothing and does not give him his wages.'"

"That's not Solomon."

"Who cares who said it? The principle stands. You also know how to prudently invest. It's just good business to put a portion where it can earn interest."

"Jesus has a parable about that actually."

"In favor of interest?"

"Yes, very."

"Then you have the confidence to know you're doing exactly what he would want you to do!"

"I didn't come here for advice, Hadad."

"Why are you here, other than to sound confused and at turns holier than thou and embarrassed? You're angry, Judas."

Can't argue with that. "Yes. My understanding is shaken. I know nothing except that he is the one true Messiah, the future king of Israel who will sit on David's throne. And that he has called me."

"And called you for a purpose," Hadad says. "Until you figure out what, you can at least be sure there are enough resources to keep the mission going, so when he takes up that Davidic throne you speak of, you'll be his natural choice for Secretary of the Treasury."

Secretary of the Treasury! "I—wasn't thinking that far ahead."

"They gave you complete fiduciary responsibility. So stop waiting for permission to make the ministry better or to make adult decisions. They all need to grow up, you need to be paid, and he needs to lead. If you truly believe Jesus is the future king of the Jews, then help him act like it. That's what he's got you there for."

Chapter 46

EITHER/OR QUESTIONS

The Jerusalem Sanhedrin

Yussif can hardly believe the session is finally over. What an ordeal! He nods cordially to departing colleagues and looks forward to solitude, a comfortable chair, maybe even a nap. Shmuel and Yanni approach and the three move toward the exit.

"Quite a couple of days, eh, Rabbi?" Yanni says.

"Learn a lot?" Shmuel says.

Yussif sighs. "Mostly that I have a lot to learn."

"Everybody starts somewhere," Yanni says. "I'm not yet part of the seventy-two like you. You'll catch on." As Shmuel peels off, apparently distracted by someone, Yanni says, "Take heart. Tomorrow's session will not be as excruciating. Everyone needs to get home before Shabbat."

"Rabbi Yussif!" Shmuel calls out. "Over here! I never got the chance yesterday to introduce Lehad, son of Ethnan. He chairs the Select Committee on Reclamation of Beersheba and Southern Border Reform that I told you about."

Yussif forces himself to be cordial despite his exhaustion and the fact that this is a committee in which he has zero interest. "It's an honor to make your acquaintance, Rabbi."

"The honor may be all mine," Lehad says, "but we shall see by how you answer my famous either/or questions."

Yanni rolls his eyes, but Shmuel seems to gleefully egg on the man. "Yes, very famous indeed!"

Oh, for the love … Yussif thinks. "What are they?"

"Haddock or sea bream?"

What in the—? "Uh."

"Just go with your first instinct," Yanni says.

"Bream."

"Rope sandals or bridle leather?"

"Rope."

"Hillel or Shammai?"

"Why?" *Uh-oh, have I stepped in it?* "I sat at the feet of Rabban Nicodemus."

"The teacher of teachers!" Lehad crows. "Feared by all, including Shammai, and respected throughout the land. He has been away on a research trip for several weeks. Was he a guest instructor at your Hebrew school? You seem a little young for that."

"He visited Capernaum where I was interning."

"Why did you choose Capernaum?"

"To be among the Galileans, the common people, away from my family's home in the Upper City here."

"Very noble. I'm impressed. It calls to mind the story of Samuel going to Bethlehem to anoint one of the sons of Jesse to be the next king of Israel. They hadn't even thought David worth bringing in for Samuel to see. You never know what you'll find in the small, obscure places."

How long must I endure this? "Indeed," Yussif says, knowing he must strive to be polite. "Rabbi Shmuel tells me you're interested in redrawing the southern border to encompass the city of Beersheba."

"That's right. To honor God's original promise of the borders, north to south, 'From Dan to Beersheba.'"

Yanni says, "Might be difficult to attract much enthusiasm for such an agenda when we have so much going on with Rome, don't you think?"

"We have a strategy," Lehad says. "Beersheba may not seem like an urgent matter to many in the Sanhedrin, but we know how to get their attention. The assassination of Jesus of Nazareth."

Yussif recoils. *What?*

"I'm sorry?" Shmuel says.

"Surely," Lehad says, "you encountered him in Capernaum."

"Of course we have," Yussif says, "but—"

"The man is making enemies everywhere. A group in Tel-Dor sent a delegation to Jerusalem to lobby for his prosecution."

Shmuel says, "I had not heard that citizens were moving to prosecute."

Lehad nods. "They claim his actions led to the death of a man's daughter. Jesus makes Jerusalem nervous, and someone in Pilate's confidence is said to have been at an event in the Decapolis in which he broke bread with heathens."

"Rome is taking him seriously now?" Shmuel says.

"If we have him killed," Lehad says, "it will make a big splash and draw attention to our cause."

"Forgive me," Shmuel says, "but I'm surprised at how casually you speak of ending a life."

Yussif speaks up. "Aren't capital punishments allowed only on temple grounds? And when was the last time the Sanhedrin carried one out?"

"Blood on your hands," Yanni says, "doesn't always equate to wrongdoing."

"The blood of someone from Nazareth, no less," Lehad says. "The nation will practically thank us."

Lazarus's home

As the sun rises, Judas steals away from the others as they pack up and trade embraces, handshakes, and express farewells. As he gathers his belongings from an inner room of the house, he quickly retrieves the bag of coins from Joanna's gift and slips a handful into his own purse.

Outside he joins the others as Jesus tenderly bids goodbye to his mother.

PART 6

Battered

Chapter 47

THE ABOMINATION

Perean village inn

Sopping wet from head to toe, John is on a dead run in the darkness, Peter having commanded him—because of his renowned speed—to get back to the common room at their place of lodging. The entire retinue of Jesus, the disciples, and the two women had swum across the Jordan River from Jerusalem and are following as fast as they can, slowed by carrying one of their own—the biggest of all of them—who has been stoned nearly to death.

John barges through the door, desperate to clear the table so they can lay out the battered James and stanch his bleeding. He sweeps a long cotton placemat from under a mostly-lit nine-branch menorah, sending it crashing to the floor along with a small piece of parchment.

Jesus and Peter haul in the groaning James and gingerly stretch him out on the table while John tends to the wounds with the fabric of the placemat.

As the others tumble in, Zee brings up the rear, pulling Tamar through and locking and deadbolting the door. Ashen, they collapse into chairs.

"Everywhere we go," Matthew says, teeth chattering, "he—his teachings …"

"… he scares someone in power," Philip says, draping a blanket around Matthew.

Mary of Magdala wrings out her hair, appearing to try to catch her breath.

"We need kindling!" Nathanael says.

"We need to dry these clothes before we catch our death," Thaddeus says.

"That was terrifying," Andrew says. "How can we ever go back there?"

"Surely we'll have to," Tamar says.

"We should stay here for the time being," Zee says.

"We'll talk about that later," Peter says.

Little James puts a cup of water to James's lips while Judas sits staring. "What does it all mean?" he says.

Jesus wipes blood from a cut on James's hairline, then leans to reach the parchment John had noticed flutter to the floor. As he scans it, tears come to his eyes.

Seven days prior, Perean village inn

Jesus has Big James light the shamash candle from the flames in the fireplace and hand it to Peter who passes it to Thomas in the otherwise dark room. Jesus is moved by the man's deep grief as Thomas stares at the light and it dances on his face. Thomas recites a bracha: "Blessed are You, Lord our God, King of the universe, Who has given us life and sustained us and enabled us to reach this season."

Thomas passes the candle to Matthew who uses it to light the outermost side wick on the menorah.

Jesus says, "And so the Feast of Dedication begins."

They all applaud and quote in unison the ritual recitation of Hallel from the Psalms. They add, "Blessed be the name of the Lord from this time forth and forevermore! From the rising of the sun to its setting, the name of the Lord is to be praised! The Lord is high above all nations, and His glory above the heavens!"

Zee lights a torch and settles it into a wall sconce. He seems to notice Tamar watching and pressing her lips together. "What?" he says.

"I don't know," she whispers, approaching. "I sort of liked the atmosphere with just the candles."

"The menorah cannot do the work of lighting or warming," he says. "It's cold out and we need to see better for the story of why we're celebrating. Come on."

She joins him and the others as they gather around Jesus. The rabbi begins, "After Alexander, son of Philip the Macedonian, whom some have taken to calling Alexander the Great but whom we call Alexander—"

Everyone shouts, "The Worst!"

"—had defeated King Darius of the Persians and the Medes, he succeeded him as king. He fought many battles, conquered strongholds, and slaughtered the kings of the earth."

Andrew appears in an Alexander armor costume with gold laurels on his head and fights off John, Little James, and Thaddeus—all wearing paper crowns and wielding wooden swords. Everyone laughs when each dramatically falls dead.

Jesus continues, "He advanced to the ends of the earth and plundered many nations, gathering a strong army and ruling over countries, nations, and princes." Andrew raises his arms and puffs out his chest, exaggerating his victories. "Then," Jesus adds, "he fell sick and perceived that he was dying."

Andrew collapses and Nathanael catches him and sits him against the wall.

"So he summoned his most honored officers and divided his kingdom among them." Andrew summons Nathanael, Zee, and Judas—all in Macedonian costumes. "Then he died." Andrew keels over and the three officers rise. "From them came forth a sinful root, Antiochus Epiphanes." Zee pulls a red monster mask from within his costume and rises menacingly.

"Antiochus," Jesus carries on, "hated Israel and he hated God. He attacked Jerusalem on the Sabbath, knowing the Jews would not fight. He went into the temple and defiled it by slaughtering a pig on the altar, sprinkling its blood in the Holy of Holies, and poured the swine's broth onto the Torah scrolls, which were then shredded and burned—"

The others shout, "The Abomination of Desolation! Tremble, O earth, at the presence of the Lord, at the presence of the God of Jacob, Who turns the rock into a pool of water, the flint into a spring of water."

It's time for gift giving, so Peter gives his brother a hand-hammered calfskin belt to replace the sad rope he usually wears.

Mary gives Tamar a handwoven scarf.

"Matthew," John says, sitting next to him. "I got you something."

Matthew looks thrown. "That's—wait, I got something for you too."

"Well, lucky for both of us then!"

John produces a small, long box, and Matthew hands him a bag. "You go first," Matthew says.

"No, you."

Matthew appears to panic, so John says, "It's fine. We'll open at the same time."

"A new pen!" Matthew says.

John pulls a batch of crude pages out. "Ah!"

"I saw you were running low on parchment," Matthew says.

"And I noticed you've been using the same quill since—well, you know, the early days before—when you were still—"

Matthew seems so touched that he awkwardly reaches for a hug. "I'm just glad," John says, "that I'm not the only one writing it all down."

The next day

Thomas uses the shamash to light a second candle on the menorah, and Jesus continues speaking. "Antiochus set up pagan altars in every town in Israel and forced Jews to eat pig flesh to prove their conversion from Judaism. If they refused, they were executed. But God raised up a band of fighters led by Judah Maccabee, also known as—"

"The hammer!" everyone shouts.

Philip brandishes a wooden sword at Zee in his red monster mask. Zee is joined by Peter, also with a wooden sword, and Judas with a pitchfork. To show how outnumbered the Maccabees were, Zee, Peter, and Judas are backed up by the rest of the men in Greek togas and carrying wooden swords. The only remaining audience consists of the two women.

"For seven years," Jesus says, "the Maccabees revolted against the Greeks, just a handful of rebels against sixty-five thousand troops."

As the men play fight, Mary and Tamar cheer for the Maccabees.

"Until finally," Jesus says, "190 years ago this very week, they at last reclaimed Jerusalem, destroyed the statue of Zeus in the temple, and rededicated the altar." The Greeks fall as the Maccabees cheer. "There was just one problem," he continues. "They found only enough uncontaminated oil to light the temple menorah to burn for one day. But miraculously, it burned for eight nights! This gave them enough time to produce a new batch of pure oil. That is why we celebrate this Feast of Dedication for eight days."

The next day

Mary uses the shamash to light a third candle in the menorah as the disciples gather around Jesus and recite: "Precious in the sight of the Lord is the death of His saints. O, Lord, I am Your servant. I am Your servant, the son of Your maidservant. You have loosed my bonds. I will offer to You the sacrifice of thanksgiving and call on the name of the Lord."

Big James and Little James examine a bump on Peter's head from the mock battle between the Maccabees and the Greeks. "It really did leave a mark," Little James says.

Peter smiles. "You're stronger than you think, Matthew."

Mathew looks away, clearly embarrassed.

His heart heavy, Thomas listens in the flickering firelight as Nathanael and Andrew play stringed instruments and sing, and Little James harmonizes.

All recite: "It is better to take refuge in the Lord than to trust in man. It is better to take refuge in the Lord than to trust in princes."

Now the whole group sits at the table around Andrew and John, who are arm wrestling. Peter and James each root for their brothers while Matthew judges, watching closely. As Andrew slowly appears to take the lead, the group's cheers grow louder. Everyone looks shocked as Matthew says, "I formally declare Andrew the victor!"

"Sons of Jonah revenge!" Peter cries out, hugging Andrew.

Nathanael tells Jesus, "I can't believe Andrew won that."

Jesus says, "Even I didn't see that coming." Everyone laughs but John.

"I have an announcement," Jesus adds. "On the final day of the feast, we will make a pilgrimage to the Holy City where I will give a sermon—a teaching." He studies their faces. "What? Is that bad news?"

They seem to cover quickly. "No," Peter says. "It's great."

"Of course that's good," Thaddeus says.

"Yes," Andrew says. "We're excited."

"It will be wonderful!" Mary says.

Several others murmur their assent. Thomas, serious as a Roman edict but sounding neither accusatory nor angry, says, "Rabbi, it was not great or good or wonderful the last time you preached a sermon in front of religious leaders. I see no reason why your teachings will be acceptable to the ruling class of priests any time soon. We should be prepared."

Thomas stands and leaves the table. Peter rises to follow, but Jesus stops him.

"This has been a festival night I will never forget," Jesus says. "Thank you all."

Dawn

On day four of the Feast of Dedication, Matthew is one of four disciples waking in an upstairs room. Big James rubs his eyes as Andrew proudly shows off his new belt to John, who is munching an apple. "Hand-hammered!" Andrew says. "Real calf leather."

"What other kind would there be?" John says.

"I can't get over how thoughtful it was, and from Peter."

John says, "You're way too comfortable calling your brother by his new name."

"He slugs me if I don't."

"It's definitely an upgrade from that sad little string you used to have."

"Matthew, are you going to record that my brother gave me a handmade belt for the Feast of Dedication?"

Matthew considers this. "No," he says.

James says, "We need to think of the right gift for Thomas."

Matthew notices how somber everyone grows.

"He wants only one thing," John says. "And we can't give it to him. Anything we give him will just remind him he can't share it with her."

"But we can't *not* give him anything," Andrew says. "Even if it seems pathetic, it's the gesture."

"Something practical," James says. "He could use new sandals."

"He has nicer sandals than any of us!" John says.

"Except Matthew," James says.

"Thank you," Matthew says.

"But those," James says, "were made for standing and showing off. Not for walking the miles we log in a day."

"Yes," Matthew says, "I do have blisters. Oh, Thomas, yes—"

"He's hurting in so many other ways," Andrew says, "he doesn't even notice."

"Do we have enough money for a new pair?" John says, as everyone glances at Matthew.

The former tax collector shrugs and grabs the fabulous bag containing Joanna's donation. It feels lighter than usual. He riffles through it unable to hide his confusion.

"Matthew?" Andrew says.

"Is there another purse?" Matthew says.

The others shrug and look around. "Check with Judas," James says.

Moments later, Matthew finds Judas outside poring over a map. "We want to buy new shoes for Thomas, for his gift."

Judas looks surprised. "He has vegetable-tanned sandals imported from Cypress!"

"But they're not made for walking."

"Then he should trade them in. He could get three fully functional pairs with a barter like that."

"We set aside money for gifts," Matthew says.

"For gifts we can afford."

"Where is the other purse?"

"What are you talking about? There's only one. From Joanna."

"But there has to be another. I went through it and it contains only half of the shekels Joanna sent."

"Yes," Judas says. "We spent that on the inn. It's a lot of people and a lot of rooms. Some on food, and then the gifts."

"I've done the math and it doesn't add up. I know what the allotted amounts were."

"I don't know what to tell you," Judas says. "Do you want to take over keeping the purse? You sound like you think you could do it better."

"I'm not asking for your job. It's something I'd like to leave behind. But facts are facts. Numbers don't change just because I've directed my attention elsewhere."

"Maybe that's where you should keep your attention. Lives are at stake, Matthew."

"Lives?" *What in the world is he talking about?*

"Our people have been waiting thousands of years for this moment!"

"I'm aware—"

"We're on the knife's edge of history, Matthew. The Messiah is finally here, but we are so inefficient and moving so slowly that we might very well run out of funds before he even gets to spread his message!"

Matthew is not following this reasoning, yet Judas forges ahead. "We owe it to the entire nation of Israel to be more scrupulous with the money entrusted to us for his work. It's too important." And Judas walks off, leaving Matthew holding the bag.

Peter, John, Big James, Andrew, and Thomas emerge from the inn. "Let's head into town, Matthew," Peter says.

Matthew joins them as Peter pulls Thomas along at the front. James leans toward Matthew and whispers, "Did you get the money from Judas for the gift?"

"I think we're going to have to barter."

"Why? Judas being stingy?"

"I don't know."

Chapter 48

A RIDDLE?

The Jerusalem temple

Yussif has set up shop in the bet midrash with scrolls, tablets, ink wells, and quills scattered on the desk assigned to him. Just now he's ignoring them all and pacing the room. He forces himself back into his chair and begins to feverishly write. He's finding his rhythm when his father breezes in, clearly in high holiday spirits.

"My son! They told me I'd find you here. The servants are headed to the butcher to buy lamb shanks for tonight's Feast of Dedication. Are there any other cuts you'd like? Your ima is intent on fattening you up."

Yussif scribbles furiously. "No, thank you. Whatever you get will be feast enough."

His father pauses, seeming to study him. "Yussif, are things well here?"

"I just need to finish this thought."

"Who are you writing to?" Arnan hesitates again. "I don't mean to pry."

Yussif looks up abruptly. "If I asked you for bread, would you give me a stone?"

"What?"

"If I asked your servants going to market to bring back a fish, would you instruct them to bring a snake?"

"This is absurd."

"Answer the question."

"Never! You're my son!"

"'If you then, who are evil, know how to give good gifts to your children, how much more will your Father in heaven give good things to those who ask Him?'"

"'You who are evil'?" Arnan says. "Is this a riddle? Talk to me!"

"It's something I heard a rabbi teach. If you are seeking God, he said, 'Ask and it will be given to you, search and you will find, knock and the door will be opened for you.' God will not hide His messenger from us, if only we have eyes to see him!"

"Have you been getting enough sleep? Your eyes are red."

If he only knew. "I am plagued by thoughts too difficult to explain."

"Well, let's get you some help. Surely one of the priests can—"

"Don't give up on me, Abba."

"Don't *what?*"

"Please. Like the fragment from the sermon I just quoted, and as you yourself said, I'm your son and I'm asking you one thing—to not give up on me. No matter how things go for me in the Sanhedrin, trust me that I love God and will always be faithful."

Arnan grips Yussif's shoulders. "I've never doubted you," he says. "Even when I didn't understand you, when I disagreed with your decision to go into the north. I spoke harshly to you at that time, but …" He waxes emotional, his voice thick. "Deep in my heart I thought what you did was noble, and I secretly sometimes regret that I've always taken the path of least resistance in my life."

"You honor me beyond my deserving," Yussif says.

"You do deserve it."

"Stand with me?" Yussif says.

"Always," Arnan says. He backs toward the door. "It seems you have some very important writing to do. I'll leave you to it."

Chapter 49

ACHING

Bethany market

Peter shops with Matthew, Andrew, John, James, and Thomas, wondering how to distract their grieving friend so they can find him an appropriate holiday gift. Andrew nudges Peter and nods toward a booth several yards away where a young cobbler displays shoes and sandals. "Can you get Thomas away from us for a while?"

"Hey, Thomas," Peter says, "let's check out the apothecary booths. We're low on soap."

"That never seems to bother this group."

"That's why I need you. I don't know about the finer things." As they mosey to a fragrance booth, Peter adds, "Eden says I have no sense of smell or taste."

"Is that true?"

"No. She says I don't know what to call things or that I use the wrong words. I try to compliment her cooking by saying something is sweet, but it wasn't meant to be sweet. I just meant it was so good."

"Hmph," Thomas says, handing Peter a vendor's sample. "What would you say this is?"

Peter sniffs. "I don't know. Some kind of flower?"

"Herbaceous. Close enough." He holds it close to his own nose. "Cedar leaf and basil. Maybe a little lemon."

"So I wasn't close at all. You're just being nice."

Thomas keeps moving. "I thought we were supposed to be looking for soap."

Small talk isn't working, Peter decides. As they roam the booths, he says, "Thomas, how have you been feeling?"

"It's Feast time."

"You didn't answer my question."

Thomas stops and shrugs. "We're celebrating the Feast of Dedication. I'm supposed to feel grateful, I think."

"Who cares what you're *supposed* to feel? The Maccabees overthrew the Greeks so we could live full lives, not be wooden figures."

"Then I feel horrible," Thomas says, moving along again.

"Thank you."

"Thank you?" Thomas says.

"For the truth. That's always the best place to start."

"What I'm interested in is when it will end."

"Is there any time you don't feel awful?"

Thomas seems to weigh this. "When we have important work to do, that takes my mind off things. If I can just think about the task at hand, I'm okay. But apart from that, in the stillness, everything just—"

"Aches."

"You know?" Thomas says.

"I never met the person I lost."

Thomas stares at the ground and takes a deep breath. "Ramah told me about Eden's miscarriage. Women tell each other those kinds of things."

"Did she tell you how badly I took it?"

"She didn't have to. I was on the boat, remember? You weren't subtle."

Peter snorts. "I don't know the meaning of the word. You remember what Jesus said to me on the sea? That he allows trials because they prove the genuineness of our faith and strengthen us."

"At the cost of someone's life?"

"I wondered the same in the depths of my pain, and I assure you, that made things only worse."

"That doesn't make those questions wrong," Thomas says.

"No, it's not wrong to question, but it is wrong not to accept the answer."

"I just don't understand why he didn't help Ramah. We've seen the miracles he performs—walking on water, multiplying loaves and fish for thousands—manifesting powers no one has seen in the history of the world. Why couldn't he have stopped time right before she died? Or even bring her back?"

Peter has seen Jesus do that very thing, but he's forbidden to say so. "When I turn these things over in my mind," he says, "I come back to what God said through the prophet Isaiah: 'My thoughts are not your thoughts, neither are your ways My ways.' He can create a world where we have no freewill and nothing ever goes wrong, but that's clearly the future, not now."

"Don't throw scraps of prophets around, Peter. I know all the same words. Were they of any help to you?"

Peter is glad to see they've arrived at a soap vendor and doesn't have to answer. Thomas hands him a block of soap. "This one is for the women."

Peter sniffs it. "Cloves?"

"Nope. Lavender oil. And these two are for the guys."

"Okay, I've got this one—wet moss."

"Vetiver and basil."

"Maybe I'm a lost cause."

"Absolutely."

The Perean village inn

That night, Philip lights the fifth wick in the menorah and the entire group recites a psalm: "Not to us, O Lord, not to us, but to Your name give glory, for the sake of Your steadfast love and Your faithfulness! Why should the nations say, 'Where is their God'? Their God is in the heavens; He does all that He pleases."

As Andrew and Little James lead the others in singing and playing, Thomas opens his gift. The others make over him and his new sandals. Judas flashes a look of frustration and confusion at Matthew, who just shrugs.

Jesus answers a knock at the door. The innkeeper says, "Sorry to interrupt."

"Not at all."

The man hands him a piece of parchment. "Someone dropped this off for you today from the other side of the Jordan."

The innkeeper leaves, and Jesus peeks at the note. Peter notices his pained expression. Jesus crumples the note and tosses it into the fire. Peter rises and approaches him as he moves toward the stairs. "What happened?"

"Rabbi," John says, "are you all right?"

"It's word from Bethany," he says. "Laz is sick."

"Sick?" Peter says. "How sick?"

"Very."

"What?" John says. "We were just with him!"

"He would never let on something was wrong," Jesus says.

"Do you need to go see him?" Matthew says.

"Not now. This isn't the sickness that leads to death." Jesus turns to the rest. "My friends, I think I will retire for the night. You all please continue. Shalom, shalom."

As he makes his way up, the common room falls silent, save for the crackling of the fire. Peter says, "Why don't we, uh— Andrew, let's have another song. Little James, I can't get enough of that voice. Come, come."

Littles James says, "Let's bring the women in on this …."

"Yes!" Andrew says. "The Song of Miriam!"

"I need that!" Thaddeus says.

"Ladies, please do it," Zee says. "Bless us."

"Someone has to teach me!" Tamar says.

"Okay," Nathanael says, signaling Mary, "it goes like this …" She joins him, "I will sing to the Lord, for He has triumphed gloriously …"

Tamar repeats the line and they continue, teaching her by way of call and response.

The next day

The disciples and the women work outside making flour for bread. Some separate weeds from the wheat, others take the sheaves to the threshing floor. Still others beat it with stones before winnowing the chaff from the grains. Then it's milled into flour by hand.

"I have an idea," Judas announces. "What if we set up donation points in the various villages we visit?"

"Who would manage the funds?" Matthew says. "And how would they get them to us?"

"Everywhere we've gone," Judas says, "Jesus made a special connection with someone, sometimes even hundreds! We'd collect upon visitation."

"I don't get it," Nathanael says.

Judas says, "We appoint one person in each village who could tell others who believe in the message of our rabbi that they can support his work by gathering aid so he will be well-supported the next time he visits."

"How would you vet their character and trustworthiness?" Peter says.

"Ask for references, letters of recommendation."

"If Jesus were worried about funding," Philip says, "don't you think he would have set up something like this already?"

"If he had," Judas says, "we wouldn't be threshing and winnowing wheat ourselves. We could just buy flour at market."

"I, for one, am enjoying learning about how it's made," Matthew says.

"Manual labor feels good," Thaddeus says, "when you've been sitting around a lot, doesn't it, Matthew?"

Judas looks perturbed at losing their attention. "No one? Really?"

Mary says, "We've bought flour before, Judas, but this just isn't one of those times."

Little James says, "In the words of Qoheleth, the preacher, 'For everything there is a season, and time for every matter under heaven.' This is a time for making the flour ourselves."

Chapter 50

OBSTACLES

As the group sits in the shade of a cassia tree eating a light lunch, John makes the rounds with a pitcher of water, refilling everyone's cups. He reaches Judas last and sits with him. "I was thinking about your idea from earlier."

"You like it?"

"I had an idea of my own a few weeks back."

"About supporting the ministry?"

"Not directly. Actually, no, not even indirectly. My brother and I asked Jesus for something we wanted, based on our own understanding, our own ambitions. And I am telling you, he was not happy. In fact, he was heartbroken over how little we understood."

Judas nods. "I was there. But do you believe I'm suggesting this from a lack of understanding?"

"It is *your* idea."

"He doesn't want us to be creative or think critically using the gifts Adonai gave us to serve him?"

"I've been here since before he announced who he is, and there's still so much I don't understand."

"I'm not presuming," Judas says. "I'm seeking to understand. I want to reduce the strain, the uncertainty around resources, so we can get to work on building the kingdom *he* is here to build!"

"I don't question your intentions," John says.

"What do you think I should do?"

"Ask *him*."

Here's my chance, Judas decides, finding Jesus in a field. He appears to be watching a shepherd in the distance sitting in the pen gateway opposite his flock. Judas quietly approaches. As they watch, the shepherd rises and calls out to the sheep, "Fern! Mabe! Sunny!"

Jesus smiles. "He calls them by name. I have sheep and shepherds on my mind, Judas. Is something on yours?"

"All I want is to see your kingdom come."

"Well, that's quite a conversation starter. I want you to see that too."

"I want everyone to," Judas says, "and I want to remove any obstacles in the way of it."

"Obstacles?"

"Limitations. Barriers. Whatever your vision is, and I know it's beyond my wildest dreams, I want to make sure you're never held back by not having enough resources. You told us to be gentle as doves but also wise as serpents. Isn't this wisdom?"

"Has Joanna's donation run out?" Jesus says.

"No, but we're close. With the holiday celebrations and gift giving …"

Jesus turns his attention back to the sheep and seems deep in thought. "Hmm …"

"I was thinking," Judas says, "we could set up collection points in each of the villages we visit, so that—"

"You're right that my vision for the world is bigger than what you dream of. I want you to pay close attention to my sermon tomorrow—the events surrounding it and your own feelings."

Judas is bewildered and feels his prudent ideas have been met with resounding indifference.

Chapter 52

THE MESSAGE

Capernaum

Light-headed with excitement, Zebedee doesn't mind making this oil delivery run alone. He hefted the two vessels onto his cart by himself and can't wait to impress one of his most important clients. He rumbles through the streets and up to the gates of the synagogue, spotting his man at the top of the stairs. "Jairus!" he bellows. "The first pressing, a full day early! Ahead of schedule."

Jairus seems unmoved. In fact, grave. "Zebedee, come inside, quickly."

"I—but the oil—"

"Leave it for a moment. I'll have someone watch it. Please, it's urgent."

He trots up the stairs and follows Jairus to his office. The temple administrator closes the door and they sit. "Are my boys okay?" Zebedee says. "What is it?"

"Rabbi Yussif, who secured a seat in the Great Sanhedrin in Jerusalem, you remember him?"

"Of course."

"He's learned of a plot by a group of Pharisees who lead a select committee on the reclamation of Beersheba from Edom into Judea."

"What?"

"They want Jesus executed to bring attention to their cause."

"What does Jesus have to do with land boundaries?"

"He doesn't," Jairus says. "I'm familiar with these men from my time in Jerusalem, and I'm sure they barely know what he teaches. This is wholly political. Killing him would be purely for the benefit of their pet cause."

"On what grounds? I know of the edict issued from Jerusalem, but it was not a death sentence. Not anything close!"

"Torah contains passages prescribing the death penalty for both false prophecy and Sabbath breaking. All they need is an event. One misstep."

Zebedee shakes his head. "All kinds of people break Shabbat—"

"He's not all kinds of people, Zebedee. This situation is fraught with danger. Jesus is highly controversial."

"He's the Messiah!"

"But not the one they're looking for apparently. And anyway, this is not really about Jesus. They're obsessed with their agenda, and they're ignorant."

"Surely ignorance is no match for who Jesus is. That would never get in his way."

"I don't know, Zebedee."

"What do you mean you don't know?"

"We *must* get word to your sons of this imminent threat—it affects them as well as all of us."

"Can you dispatch a synagogue messenger?"

Jairus shakes his head. "Too risky. The Sanhedrin has eyes and ears everywhere, especially with Jesus' history here in Capernaum."

"Then who can we trust?" Zebedee says. He clearly sees Jairus's wheels turning. "What?"

Moments later, Zebedee is at home, throwing clothes into a small bag and telling Salome, "It will be only a few days, a week at most. Jairus is sending me with a letter of introduction to some of his colleagues in the maintenance department of the temple in Jerusalem."

"*The* temple?" she says.

"Would I be talking about another one? He endorses the quality of my oil and its suitability for use in the sacred rites."

"Zeb! This is unthinkable! The honor! Your oil? In *the* temple?"

"While I'm in Judea, I'll divert to find James and John and the others to get a message to Jesus."

"A message?"

He kisses her head as he moves toward the door. "Don't worry, my love. Trust Adonai."

"Please be careful," she says. "At least let me send some food for the boys!"

"There's no time!" he says. "Shalom, shalom, Salome!"

She watches from the door as he climbs into the cart. "Tell the boys I love them!"

Chapter 52

THE SERMON

Perean village inn, dawn

Jesus leads the others to bow and pray the Hallel Psalm in unison: "Save us, we pray, O Lord! O Adonai, we pray, give us success! Blessed is he who comes in the name of the Lord! We bless you from the house of Adonai. The Lord is God, He has made His light to shine upon us."

Jesus quietly adds, "Amen."

As most of the rest hoist their packs and prepare to leave, Peter notices John staring grimly at Thomas across the room. "What's wrong?" he asks him.

"The last time Jesus preached in public, it ended in tragedy, especially for Thomas."

Peter squeezes his shoulder. "Let's go."

Late in the morning, Peter instructs Judas to press coins into the palm of a ferryman who pilots them across the Jordan to a sweeping landscape. From there, they'll walk a little over fifteen miles to Jerusalem.

By the golden hour late that afternoon, Peter feels haggard, soggy from sweat, yet dry and dusty from the knees down. He knows the others—including Jesus—are in the same state, but physical discomfort is the least of their worries.

As they reach the temple courts and pass the livestock exchange area the Pharisees are supervising, Jesus stops to fondly pet the wool of one of the sheep. He eyes Peter and turns to the others. "Listen carefully," he says. "He who does not enter the sheepfold by the door but climbs in by another way, that man is a thief and a robber."

This is off to an interesting start, Peter thinks.

Jesus continues, "But he who enters by the door is the shepherd of the sheep. The sheep hear his voice, and he calls his own sheep by name and leads them out." The rabbi sits on the stone stairs as Peter and the others gather around him. "When he has brought out all his own, he goes before them, and the sheep follow him, for they know his voice."

Peter is distracted by the livestock Pharisees talking amongst themselves and pointing at Jesus. They drift near.

"They won't follow a stranger," Jesus continues, "but they will flee from him, for they do not know the voice of strangers."

"I'm, uh, not sure I follow," Nathanael says.

"This figure of speech you're using," Peter says, "could you say it more plainly?"

"We want to understand," Andrew says.

With the Pharisees now plainly listening as well, Jesus says, "This is important. I am the door of the sheep. All who came before me are thieves and robbers, but the sheep did not listen to them."

One Pharisee turns to another and whispers in his ear, whereupon he rushes away.

"I am the door," Jesus says. "If anyone enters by me, he will be saved and will go in and out and find pasture. The thief comes only to steal and kill and destroy."

The Pharisee returns with an elder cleric.

"I came that they may have life and have it abundantly. I am the good shepherd. The good shepherd lays down his life for the sheep. He who is a hired hand and not a shepherd, who does not own the sheep, sees the wolf coming and leaves the sheep and flees. And the wolf snatches them and scatters them."

Now shuffling toward Jesus are an elegantly dressed religious leader and a portly, more shabbily dressed one.

"He flees," Jesus continues, "because he is a hired hand and cares nothing for the sheep. I am the good shepherd. I know my own and my own know me, just as the Father knows me and I know the Father. And I lay down my life for the sheep."

Peter can tell the others notice the interlopers and their obvious angst.

"I have other sheep who are not of this fold," Jesus says. "I must bring them also, and they will listen to my voice."

"Other sheep not of this fold," the elder cleric says. "Are you referring to Gentiles?"

Judas shushes him and Peter is amused by the cleric's look of shock. People simply don't shush Pharisees.

"So there will be one flock," Jesus says, "one shepherd. For this reason the Father loves me, because I lay down my life that I may take it up again."

"That's not real," the well-dressed one says. "There is no resurrection." Peter decides he must be a Sadducee.

"At least not one that any mortal man could have authority to enact for himself," the portly one adds, "once perished."

"We have to do something!" Judas whispers to Peter.

"Just pay attention."

The elder leader says, "Someone has to go get Shammai immediately!"

"He's gone for the holiday," the big man says.

"How am I supposed to pay attention," Judas says, "with these men talking and insulting him?"

Matthew says, "Jesus didn't specify what to pay attention to."

Peter is thrilled when Jesus aims his gaze directly at the religious leaders. "No one takes it from me, but I lay it down of my own accord. I have authority to lay it down, and I have authority to take it up again. This charge I have received from my Father."

The disciples respond with questions, but so do the religious rulers, shouting over them. Judas confronts them. "Will you be quiet so we can listen to our rabbi?"

The elder says, "Those are not the teachings of any credible rabbi, but of an *insane* person!"

"Mark my words," Judas says, "you will regret saying that."

"Watch your mouth," a tall Pharisee says. "You're speaking to a member of the Great Sanhedrin."

"Judas," Peter hisses. "Get back here. You're missing all the details."

As the sun descends, the clerics huddle and Ozem, the elder, says, "I didn't see his face when I went to the Decapolis to investigate, but Jesus of Nazareth is the man who broke bread with the mass of Gentiles there."

Gedera the Sadducee says, "The heretic in Shammai's screed is said to be well-spoken and a remarkable teacher. These are the ravings of a madman."

"Or like someone demon-possessed," a Pharisee says.

"If possessed," Gedera says, "he must be removed from the temple! Unclean!"

Zebadiah says, "What does he mean by *my father*? Certainly he's not speaking in the manner of God through the prophet

Isaiah: 'But now, Adonai, You are our Father; we are the clay, and You are our potter.'"

"The *we* is Israel," Ozem says. "We are all God's children!"

"Then what *father* is he talking about?"

"Shammai reports," Gedera says, "he claims to be the Messiah."

"I was too late last time," Ozem says. "I won't be this ti—" But as he turns to confront Jesus, the man has led his followers toward Solomon's portico. The religious rulers rush to catch up to them. "You!" Ozem shouts. "You're Jesus of Nazareth, aren't you?"

"How long will you keep us in suspense?" Zebadiah says. "If you are the Christ, tell us plainly."

"I told you," Jesus says, "and you do not believe."

"When?" the clerics demand in unison.

"When did you tell us?"

"Blasphemer!"

Bystanders and scribes come running at this.

"The works that I do in my Father's name bear witness of me—"

"What do you mean *my father*?" Ozem says.

"—but you do not believe because you are not among my sheep."

"You utter this profanation amid the pillars of Solomon's porch?" Zebadiah says. "Have you no shame?"

"My sheep hear my voice and they know me. And they follow me."

"He said he's the Christ and that we did not believe!" Gedera says. "This blasphemy is enough for capital punishment, and we are on temple grounds!"

"Stones!" Zebadiah says. "We need stones!"

Peter grows frantic as the scribes gather stones and the disciples huddle behind Jesus.

"I give them eternal life," Jesus says, and they will never perish, and no one will snatch them out of my hand."

"No one can grant eternal life!" Gedera thunders. "Your desecration, your heresy, will be purged from this sacred place!"

"Rabbi," Peter says, "maybe we should—"

Jesus stretches out his arms as if protecting his flock. "My Father, who has given them to me, is greater than all, and no one is able to snatch them out of the Father's hand. I and the Father are one."

Zebadiah hurls a stone, which misses Jesus as he ducks. A stone from another direction strikes John. As more stones fly, Big James steps in front of Jesus. A rock blasts James in the head, knocking him to the ground.

Peter and the others rush to his aid as Jesus roars, "I have shown you many good works from the Father! For which of them do you stone me?"

"Good works?" Zebadiah says. "If you've done any, that's not why we're stoning you! It's for blasphemy, because you, being a man, make yourself God!"

"You call me a blasphemer because I said I am the Son of God?"

"He who utters such a thing," Zebadiah says, "shall be put to death according to the Law of Moses!"

"You know little of the Law of Moses."

"Guards!" a Pharisee calls out. "Someone call the temple guard!"

"Arrest him!" Ozem yells.

Zee takes up the position James had assumed and catches one of the thrown stones. He slams it to the ground and bares his teeth, appearing eager to fight.

John grabs Jesus' arm and tries to pull him away.

"If I am not doing the works of my Father," Jesus continues, "then do not believe me. But by my works you should understand that the Father is in me, and I am in the Father!"

The crowd attacks, and Peter joins Zee, Philip, and Little James to try to keep them back. Mary reaches toward Little James. Judas watches intently, and Thomas stands to the side, terror on his face. Andrew and Matthew yank Mary and Tamar away as stones ricochet off the columns and the mob fumes.

Somehow all break free and escape the temple, Peter and Jesus dragging a staggering James. Many of the rest are bleeding and limping, but all maintain a remarkable pace under the circumstances. Judas demands, "Why is Jesus running? Why can't he fight if he's—"

"Later, Judas!" John shouts.

"Off the road, everyone!" Zee says. "We can't take the roads!"

They peel off into the forest and continue running by the light of the moon. When they finally reach the Jordan, Peter decides there's no time to wait for a ferry and leads everyone into the water.

Chapter 53

THE NEWS

Perean village inn

Sopping wet from head to toe, John is on a dead run in the darkness, Peter having commanded him because of his renowned speed to get back to the common room at their place of lodging. The entire retinue of Jesus, the disciples, and the two women are following as fast as they can, slowed by carrying one of their own—the biggest of all of them—who has been stoned nearly to death.

John barges through the door, desperate to clear the table so they can lay out the battered James and stanch his bleeding. He sweeps a long cotton placemat from under the mostly lit nine-branch menorah, sending it crashing to the floor along with a small piece of parchment.

Jesus and Peter haul in the groaning James and gingerly lay him on the table while John tends to the wounds with the fabric of the placemat.

As the others tumble in, Zee brings up the rear. He pulls Tamar through, locking and deadbolting the door. Ashen, they collapse into chairs.

"Everywhere we go," Matthew says, teeth chattering, "he—his teachings …"

"He scares someone in power," Philip says, draping a blanket around Matthew.

Mary of Magdala wrings out her hair, appearing to try to catch her breath.

"We need kindling!" Nathanael says.

"We need to dry these clothes before we catch our death," Thaddeus says.

"That was terrifying," Andrew says. "How can we ever go back there?"

"Surely we'll have to," Tamar says.

"We should stay here for the time being," Zee says.

"We'll talk about that later," Peter says.

Little James puts a cup of water to James's lips while Judas sits staring. "What does it all mean?" he says.

Jesus wipes blood from a cut on James's hairline. He leans to reach the parchment John saw flutter to the floor. As Jesus scans it, tears come to his eyes.

Desperate to know what has so affected Jesus, Peter starts at the sounds of a conveyance shambling to a stop outside the door. He raises his arms to quiet everyone, and Zee peeks through a curtain. "It's Zebedee!"

John lunges for the door and quickly unlocks it as Mary approaches Jesus.

"Abba!" John says. "What's going on? What's happened?"

"You tell me!" Zebedee says. "You're soaked and bleeding!" He rushes to the table. "James!"

"I'm all right, Abba," James manages.

Jesus hands Mary the note and slumps into a chair. She reads and murmurs, "Lazarus is dead."

Thaddeus shushes everyone. "Mary! What?"

"Lazarus has died," she announces.

"How did this happen?" Little James says.

"Peter," Judas says, "you told us Rabbi said—"

"Master," Peter says, "you told us his sickness wouldn't lead to death."

Jesus wipes his tears. "We will go back into Judea."

"Rabbi," Peter says, "not two hours ago they tried to stone you there."

"*Stone?*" Zebedee says.

John points at James. "That's how this happened."

"You would go back to that?" Andrew says.

"It not safe," Zee says.

"Rabbi," Matthew says, "perhaps your friends would agree we should delay coming back and might appreciate it."

"Our friend has fallen asleep," Jesus says. "But I'll go and awaken him."

"Wait!" Nathanael says. "He's just asleep? Rabbi, what are you talking about? What did the note say?"

"If he's asleep," Judas says, "then he'll recover. There's no need for you to be at risk."

James slurs, "Asleep like that little girl?"

"James!" John says.

Mary says, "The note says *dead.*"

"Rabbi," Peter says, "tell us what you intend to do."

"Lazarus has died," Jesus says. "And for your sake I am glad that I was not there so that you may believe. You're about to be given firmer grounds on which to believe."

Thomas looks shaken to his core.

"Rabbi," Nathanael says, "you just said he was asleep. Are you feeling all right?"

Matthew says, "What does his death have to do with our belief?"

"Come with me," Jesus says, "and I'll show you. Everyone put on dry clothes. The sun will be up soon."

"I don't understand," Judas says.

Thomas speaks up, sounding firm. "If we're going back into Judea, it might as well be to the house of Lazarus—" He stares at Jesus. "—that we may die with him."

Mary searches Jesus' face, but he's not making eye contact with her. "John and Zee were not able to shield you from every stone," she says. "Where does it hurt?"

"Everywhere," he says. "Inside and out."

He finally meets her gaze. "I hurt inside too," she says. "Why?"

He sighs. "Because you've been listening." He heads upstairs.

With the help of his father, James rises from the table and stands, wincing. John asks if he's able to walk.

"I made it here, didn't I?"

"I mean on your own."

"Why did you yell at me a minute ago?"

"Because we're not supposed to talk ab—"

"Boys, boys," Zebedee says. "I need to talk to you about something."

"Is Ima all right?" John says. "Why did you come all the way down here without sending word?"

"We couldn't risk the dispatch being intercepted."

"*We?*" John says.

Zebedee gestures toward their wounds. "This happened to you in Jerusalem at the hands of whom?"

"Religious leaders," John says. "They tried to stone Jesus and arrest him."

"On what charge?"

"The usual," James says.

"Blasphemy," John says. "False prophecy."

"Premeditated?"

"No, they just overheard him teaching."

"Jairus received a letter from a source within the Sanhedrin. What just happened to all of you—it's about to get worse."

PART 7

Acquainted With Grief

Chapter 54

A TREASURE
FOR ALL TIME

A.D. 60, The mountains of La Sainte Baume, Gaul

She has never allowed an uninvited soul even close to the cave, and Etienna is not about to make an exception today. Though friends and clients tell her she could look more feminine, she nurtures her look as part of her armor. Whether it's someone with designs on the woman she has been hired to protect or just a lost wanderer, one glimpse of her wild red hair, wind- and sun-bronzed face, and the handmade monstrosity of her bow and arrows, and they suddenly head back to public paths.

Today Etienna has been testing her ability to patrol the mountain enclave foliage without making a sound as rain turns the terrain to mud. A carriage shambles to a stop on the road below. A hooded figure slowly emerges, bearing a rucksack and leaning on a cane. The figure pays the driver and waits until he pulls away. *Interesting,* Etienna thinks. *He wants no one to know where he's headed.* She pulls an arrow from her quiver and loads the bow as she slips into hiding.

She's guessing the figure is a man, but she can't tell whether it's his malady or his age that makes his trek up the leafy mountain so seemingly painstaking. He takes his time, deftly using his cane as a walking stick and securing his footing up the steep slopes. He seems to know exactly where he's going. Etienna is ready. He'll have to get past her to get to the cave, and that's not going to happen on her watch. Not today.

Etienna silently moves behind a large tree that stands sentry to a wide ledge leading to several cave entrances. She holds her breath as his laborious footfalls approach. Just as he appears, she steps out with her bow drawn, the arrowhead inches from his face.

"Drop the stick," she says. He obeys and raises his hands. "Who are you and how did you find this place?" He pulls back his hood. "Matthew!" She lowers the bow. "For heaven's sake, why the hood?"

"It's raining," he says in the precious tone he's used for decades.

"You should have sent word so we'd be prepared."

He looks puzzled. "I thought the point was that people aren't supposed to be able to find out where she is."

"Zee has people who sneak letters in and out. You know that."

"Etienna?" comes a voice from inside the cave. "Who is it? What's happening?"

"An impromptu guest, my lady," Etienna says, stepping aside as Mary of Magdala emerges.

At the sight of her dear old friend, Mary's eyes fill.

"I hope this isn't an inconvenient time," he says, and they rush to embrace. He steps back as if to take her in. "Still unusually pleasant to look at."

Mary scoffs. "I see your eyesight has started to go."

"All right," Etienna says, "inside, both of you. The others will never forgive me if you catch your death out here."

Inside, Matthew pulls off his outer garment and opens his pack.

"I can't believe you came all this way," Mary says, "with the danger, and at your age!"

"*Our* age," he says. "It was important." He pulls from the bag a huge leather folio bound with string. "Mary, I have finished it."

For real? "You—"

"I couldn't risk sending it by courier. I want you to read it, please, and give me your thoughts. I had to be here for that."

Weeping again, Mary cradles the priceless manuscript like an infant. "I can't believe it. Matthew, you've worked so hard for so long. It will be a treasure for all time."

"I'm here to see about that," he says. "It will outlive us. We know that much."

"I know I'm right," Mary says, also knowing she has made Matthew uncomfortable.

"Over by the fire, you two," Etienna says. "We've got to dry you off."

As they settle, Matthew says, "Before we say anything further, I'm afraid I have some bad news."

Mary feels her shoulders slump. "I've gotten used to that."

"This I could have sent word of," he says, "but I thought since I was coming, I would tell you in person."

She can tell he's having trouble telling her. "Who is it?" she says.

He swallows and whispers, "Little James."

Oh, no! The very news exhausts her. "How? Where?"

"Mary, you don't want to kn—"

"No, I want to know. I can handle it."

"Lower Egypt," he says. "King Hyrcanus had him run through with a spear."

She gasps. "What about Onya and the girls?"

"Mercifully, they were not there to see it."

"Thanks be to God."

"Zee's men are moving them to stay with Nympha and her husband at Colossae. Paul has been sending letters to the church there."

"They should be safe," Mary says. "I'll write to Onya. She loved him so much."

"What will you say to her?"

"That he's not suffering any more. He was in pain his entire life and so rarely complained."

Later, after a meager but delicious dinner, Mary says, "I'm going to stay up all night and read your manuscript. I want to relive it all. Even the hard parts."

Strangely, Matthew doesn't respond. Something seems off about him. "Is something wrong, Matthew? That's why you came, isn't it, so I'd read—"

"It is," he says, looking uneasy. "I just—something I noticed—"

"What?" She follows his gaze to her desk, strewn with fragments of parchment. "I write letters there."

"I apologize," he says. "I don't mean to pry, but I couldn't help but notice, those scraps don't look like letters."

"You read them?"

"No! No, I would never. They just struck me as odd."

"Matthew, just let me read your volume. Don't busy yourself with my scribblings."

"I'm sure they're more substantial than scribblings."

"Why are we talking about this?" she says, watching his wheels turn as if grinding a millstone.

"Parchment is expensive," he says. "You live far from merchants or civilization. No one in your position, or mine, wastes paper."

"It's true," she says. "I'm not wasteful."

"Mary, I value your thoughts and am eager to read them. Will you allow me?"

Mary catches Etienna's gaze as the young woman clears the table. Should she come clean with Matthew and admit what she has been trying to create with her quill?

"It's fine," he adds. "You know I'm here for you, now and always."

She peeks at Etienna again, whose look seems to encourage her. "I've been having dreams lately," she tells Matthew. "About some of the darker times."

"Dark?"

"In my life and his, and others among us. I've been writing them down so I don't forget, trying to assemble them into—I don't know—something just for me."

"I understand," he says. "I'm sorry to have pried. I would want you to share only what you feel comfortable sharing."

She studies him and turns her gaze to the desk and the parchment fragments. *Should she?* She softens and turns back to him. "Perhaps I can share it with you, my oldest friend. I'm eager to get to your account, but I'll read you some of my musings first if you wish."

Chapter 55

HOW LONG, O LORD?

Perean village inn, three decades prior

So this is how it's going to be, Peter decides. Had he known the extent of the danger when he first decided to follow Jesus, he still would have come. But it might have given him pause. Maybe this is why Jesus gave him a new name and nickname. Well, if he is to be The Rock, he'll be The Rock. He's happy to have Zee and Big James in his corner, especially with this decision to return to a scene of mayhem.

As the entire group assembles outside, Zee hacks away at the branches of a tree and James is tended to by his father, who touches up the bandage on his forehead.

Zee appears with two freshly fashioned walking sticks and hands one to James, who nods. Zee moves on to where Mary and Little James are filling canteens. "James," Zee says, "I made this for you. Might be stronger than your regular one." James looks surprised and touched. "For the journey today," Zee adds. "You fought bravely when they tried to arrest Jesus yesterday. Didn't even hesitate."

"No way were we going to let it happen," James says.

"What about me?" Peter says. "Do I get a walking stick?"

"Are you badly injured?" Zee says.

"Just joking."

"This isn't a day for jokes," Zee says.

"That remains to be seen," Mary says. "We'll either sit shiva or we won't."

Peter wonders what she thinks Jesus meant about Lazarus falling asleep.

As the group walks west toward Bethany, John speeds up to catch Thomas. "I was thinking about what you said."

"Thank you, by the way," Thomas says.

"For what?"

"The sandals. I barely noticed how uncomfortable the expensive ones were. I'm actually enjoying the walk today."

"That makes one of us," John says. "So what did you mean last night about going to Lazarus's?"

"I said what I said."

"That we may *die* with him?"

"If we go back into Judea and they kill us, like they tried to yesterday, then that is God's will. And if God's will is for us to die with Jesus, at least I won't have to feel anything anymore."

"That's what I thought you meant. In our faith, it's generally frowned on to wish for one's own death. In the final words of the last book of Moses, God says if it's between life and death, blessing and curse, we should choose life."

"I wonder what that means," Thomas says, "when one doesn't have the choice."

"I'm just saying you should hope to live."

"It's the nature of life itself, John. That's what everyone has been saying for weeks. Only time separates one from the other."

"We're in the middle of remarkably unusual circumstances."

"No, John, these aren't unusual circumstances. We have been forced to accept that death is a part of life."

Farther back, Peter approaches Big James. "How are you feeling?"

"I'll manage. Peter, listen, last night my mind was clouded from being hit in the head. Did I say something about Jairus's daughter?"

"Keep your voice low."

"So I *did*. Maybe it doesn't matter now. Lazarus is dead. Jesus said he will wake him, and we both know what that means."

"Well, we know what that *can* mean."

"Jesus said he is glad he wasn't there to prevent Lazarus's death," James says. "And that whatever's about to happen is his will, which means we have no reason to fear."

"You make it sound so simple."

"Pain has a way of flattening things," James says.

Elsewhere in the group following Jesus, Judas asks Nathanael, "What was it like before I got here?"

"Quieter."

"You mean I talk too much?"

"Sometimes," Nathanael says. "But I meant we were relatively unknown. There was no fame or infamy. No one had even tried to stone us yet. But that wasn't all your fault."

"Well, if it's not me, has something gone wrong?"

"Uh, don't you think so, Judas? Lazarus is dead."

"That's what I mean! We're on the way to our third shiva in three months."

"And?"

"He's the Messiah. Shouldn't we be winning, not constantly losing? Stumbling around in sackcloth and ashes all the time hardly looks like glory."

"Only Jesus knows what true glory looks like," Nathanael says.

"It certainly can't be this."

Near the back of the line, Mary walks with Little James who is clearly in pain, his limp aggravated by yesterday's violence. He says, "'We'll sit shiva or we won't,' you said. But weren't you the one who read the note that Lazarus was dead?"

"Yes. But then there's what Jesus said after I read it."

"'Asleep. Awaken.' Are you familiar with the Song of David, 'How long, O Lord?'?"

"I've heard the first few lines," she says. "I don't have that one memorized."

"I won't tell you how to live your life," James says, winking, "but that's a good one to commit to memory."

"Aren't they all?"

"It starts with these big questions: 'How long, O Lord? Will You forget me forever? How long will You hide Your face from me?'"

"Been there," Mary says.

"And yet," he says, "it ends with acceptance and even praise. 'But I have trusted in Your steadfast love; my heart shall rejoice in Your salvation. I will sing to the Lord because He has dealt bountifully with me.'"

"Done that," she says, "although not very prettily."

"But in the middle, there's this line: 'Consider and answer me, O Lord my God; light up my eyes, lest I sleep the sleep of death.' Sleep and death, sometimes they're used interchangeably."

"Does that answer your question about why I said we'll sit shiva or we won't?"

"Before we went out on our missions, I asked Jesus about the irony of how I would be given the power to heal others and still bear the burden of this limp."

"What did he say?"

"He explained some of it, and it was beautiful, but that doesn't mean I'm not still in pain. The pangs were already steadily getting worse before what happened yesterday. I think what I'm getting at is that if Jesus is going to waken Lazarus from sleep, won't it bring up questions even bigger than what I've wrestled with?"

"Of course it will, and we'll deal with them then. There's no use agonizing about it now."

They walk on in silence until James says, "Is all this what you expected?"

"James, I wouldn't wish on anyone what I went through, but being lost to myself all those years means that I never expected anything other than darkness. Constant shadows, screeches in the night, strange voices. Even the daylight felt dark with only rare moments when flecks of light would come through. Now it's flipped. Ever since he called my name, everything has been light, more or less, with occasional bits of darkness that hurt just as much as before, only now they're the exception. I've had so much practice with grief, with loss, with unanswerable questions. So now I'm grateful for the light. I'm not special, James. Please understand. This is not an enviable perspective. It has been gained only by torment."

"I wish my own torment would grant me the same level of acceptance and wisdom you've found," he says.

"I have a long way to go. And you *have* grown. I've known you and Thaddeus the longest, ever since that first Shabbat in my tiny apartment when I had no idea what I was doing."

"Thaddeus and I barely did either. None of us could have dreamed where all this was headed."

"We still can't," she says.

Chapter 56

DO YOU
BELIEVE THIS?

Lazarus's home

Jesus' mother reels, her heart aching at the shocking loss of her son's best friend. She sits holding her namesake, the deceased Lazarus's sister. A half dozen others, wearing garments that have been torn, sit shiva behind windows draped in black velvet curtains. Plates of boiled eggs here and there remain largely untouched.

Lazarus's other sister, Martha, stands alone at a window. *These poor dears,* Mother Mary thinks.

A man in black arrives and Martha hastens to welcome him. "Arnan!" she says. "How is your son?"

"Yussif is fine, Martha. May Adonai comfort you, together with all mourners of Zion and Jerusalem. This earth is a worse place without Lazarus. He was taken from us far too soon."

Mother Mary rises and approaches, and Martha introduces Arnan as an old business partner of her brother's from

Jerusalem. "The golden age of construction in the holy city has ended with Lazarus's death," he says. "Truly there was no greater ironsmith in all the land."

"He was like family to me," Mother Mary says, "and a beloved friend of my son."

Mary feels the sharp look from Martha upon her reference to Jesus. That she knows Jesus has heard and has yet to arrive is a sensitive subject. Fortunately, this visitor seems oblivious. "Beloved by all," he says.

A door opens behind them. Mary turns.

"Hello, Jabez," Arnan says.

Martha whispers to Mary, "Our family lawyer."

"Is everything in order?" Arnan says.

"As you would expect from Lazarus. Martha, you and your sister will be well taken care of. His property, assets, and all of the money will pass directly to you, with a special clause that the resources be used in part to include the ongoing care of one Mary of Nazareth, daughter of Joachim."

Mother Mary can barely breathe. With Joseph in heaven, Jesus not long for this world, and his siblings only modestly employed, she resigned herself to a meager existence. "Lazarus never said anything," she manages.

"Why should I be surprised," Arnan says, "that Lazarus was friends with someone from Nazareth?"

"He was never elitist," Jabez says.

"We grew up there," Martha says.

Arnan coughs and reddens. "I apologize. I meant no disrespect."

"Martha," Jabez says, "most of the money is in the bank, but there is some in the safe in his office."

"Can we do this later?" she says.

"Certainly," he says, handing her a key. "If you need anything in the short term ... Oh, as I was arriving, Naphtali told me to tell you there's a group approaching to see Lazarus."

"How many?" she says.

"Over ten, coming from the Jordan. He said to tell you, 'He's coming.'"

Martha hands the key to her sister and rushes out the door.

It hasn't been that long since Jesus chided Martha about her priorities, yet both the sting of having disappointed him and the refreshment of her spirit from his counsel have faded in the wake of her devastating loss. She can't deny she's put out with him, Messiah or not. Years before he was revealed as the chosen one of God, everyone knew him as her brother's closest friend. That hadn't seemed to change the last time he was here. *So where has he been?* A true friend would have come immediately.

Now she's running through the streets of the city toward the gates, hoping to intercept him and his followers on the road. Just outside the gates, there they are on the horizon, with Jesus leading the way. She knows he sees her because he stops the whole procession. She slows to a walk, gathering her thoughts until she's face to face with him. She's still not sure what she's going to say until it erupts from her. "Lord, if you had been here, my brother would not have died!"

"Martha ..."

"I'm trying not to be angry that you didn't come sooner, Lord. I'm just—"

"Confused."

She nods.

"And devastated," he adds. "I understand."

"But even now I know that whatever you ask of God, He will give you."

"My child ..."

"Won't He? Whatever it is to give us hope or relief, I know you can—"

"Your brother will rise again."

"I know he will, with all of us, in the resurrection at the end of the age. That's a long time to wait."

"That's not the resurrection I'm talking about. I *am* the life that overcomes death."

Martha sees that even the disciples are wide-eyed at this, and John has pulled out his leather booklet and pen. "I don't understand," she says.

"I am the resurrection and the life. Whoever believes in me, even if he dies, he will live, and everyone who lives and believes in me shall never die." Jesus pauses. "Do you believe this?"

"I believe you're the Christ, the Son of God, who is coming into the world. So even what I don't understand, I believe."

"Now that I am here, physical death does not interrupt our eternal life."

What is he saying? "I believe you're the Christ. That I know."

"It's all you need for now. Quickly, go get your sister."

She runs back through the gates.

"Master," Peter says, "should we—"

"We'll wait here."

"Forgive me, Rabbi," Matthew says, "but are we supposed to understand everything you're saying?"

Peter says, "I admit I'm wondering the same thing."

Jesus looks sad. "I suppose not yet."

Thomas hangs back. John approaches. But before he can say anything, Thomas says, "I don't trust my hearing. And I'm too afraid to confirm what I thought I just heard."

Back at her home, Martha finds her sister calmed by Jesus' mother. "He is here," Martha says, "and is calling for you."

"Me? Now? He's here?"

"Just outside the city gates."

"Who are they talking about?" Arnan asks Jabez as young Mary hurries toward the door.

A Sadducee enters, and as she passes him, he says, "Sister of Lazarus, may Adonai comfort you, together with all mourners of Zion and Jerus—" But she's gone.

"I guess," Jabez says, "she's gone to the tomb to weep there."

"She ought not to be alone then," Arnan says, and they all file out to follow.

Jesus' mother knows the young Mary is not headed to Lazarus's tomb. They follow her through the city gates to where Jesus stands before his followers on the road.

Young Mary falls at his feet. "Lord, if you had been here, my brother would not have died! We sent word! Why didn't you come?"

Mother Mary catches Jesus' eye, which seems to choke him up.

"Why did you wait?" young Mary says. "Why?"

Jesus seems to address everyone. "I will show you why. Where have you laid him?"

Martha says, "Lord, come and see."

Jesus sees his mother in the crowd and ponders how his own impending demise will affect her. And his disciples. Tears pour as he wraps his arms around his mother, Martha, and young Mary and walks with them toward the tomb. They pass Thomas who seems to sleepwalk.

Arnan asks Jabez, "Who was this man to Lazarus? Is he family?"

Jabez shakes his head. "I've never seen him."

Andrew leans into Peter. "I've never seen him like this. What did he mean by 'I'll show you why'? Show who?"

Nathanael joins them. "He said Lazarus wouldn't die from his sickness. What is happening?"

Peter tries to shush them both, but Andrew says, "He's healed countless sick people and opened the eyes of the blind! Couldn't he have kept Lazarus from dying?"

"Just stay calm, okay?" Peter says.

"He's *weeping!*" Andrew says.

"And what are you going to do about it?" Peter says.

Nathanael asks, "Is he mad at us?"

"Stop asking questions, both of you!" Peter says. "We'll just watch."

Peter notices that Thomas has stopped and shares a fearful look with John, who goes back to help Tamar keep the man moving. "Come on, brother," he says.

Chapter 57

THE END
OF SHIVA

Lazarus's tomb

Jesus is aware of the huge crowd behind him as his mother and Lazarus's sisters lead him to a cave sealed by a massive stone set in a trenched slot. All his disciples are present, along with James and John's father Zebedee, Mary Magdalene, Tamar, friends and associates of Lazarus's family, professional mourners, and numerous passersby and clerics, including a Sadducee.

Jesus wipes his tears and says simply, "Take away the stone."

Some behind him gasp, others murmur, but no one moves.

"Was I unclear?"

"Lord," Martha says, "by this time there will be an odor. He has been dead for four days."

"Martha, surely you know that is a minor matter. Did I not tell you that if you believed, you would see the glory of God? Your priority in this moment is faith." He turns to the others. "I say to you again, remove the stone!"

Zee, Peter, Andrew, and Zebedee gather on one side of the stone. Zee supervises and leads the effort, counting to three and urging all to use their legs. Jesus takes his mother's hand as a mourner cries out in fear and others recoil. Matthew ducks behind Philip and peeks around him.

The four grunt and groan and slowly get the stone rolling. When the dark, gaping maw of the cave comes into view, they cover their noses and mouths and retreat to join the crowd. No one moves or speaks.

Jesus exhales and looks to the sky. "Father," he says, "I thank You that You have heard me. I know that You always do, but I said this on account of the people here, that they may believe that You sent me."

"*Sent?!*" the Sadducee shouts.

"What is Jesus doing?" Thomas says.

"He told us last night," Mary Magdalene says. "You don't remember?"

Little James says, "He's doing this so that we and many others would believe in him."

"We already believe in him," John says.

"Not everyone for everything," Mary says.

Jesus steps toward the tomb. "Lazarus! Come out!"

Footfalls on gravel sound from inside and a figure slowly appears, wrapped in strips of linen that fall with each halting step.

A woman screams. Others flee.

Young Mary collapses, sobbing, "Lazar—Laz—"

"Well," Jesus says, suppressing a grin, "unbind him. Get him out of that wrapping."

Martha and Jesus' mother rush to Lazarus, freeing his face and legs. He appears to try to focus. "Martha?" he says, sounding parched.

"Yes, brother, I'm here!"

"What happened?"

"You're—you're back!"

Jesus cups Lazarus's face in his hands.

"Jesus? Am I dreaming?"

"No dream," Jesus says. "You just woke up."

"I was asleep?"

Jesus nods, overcome, and presses his forehead to Lazarus's. "The land of the living, my brother."

"Thank you."

"I'm sorry it had to be this way. But also not, because there is a high plan in all of it."

"I trust you," Lazarus says, looking down. "Um, I know you like to keep me humble, but I am naked under this wrapping."

"And you could use a bath."

"But I'm starving."

"Don't be dramatic," Jesus says. "It's been only four days."

"Four!"

Mother Mary smiles. "Longest nap of your life."

People run to spread the news, and when one passes the Sadducee he shouts, "It's real! The stories of Jesus of Nazareth are true!"

The Sadducee's eyes bulge. "Of Nazareth? I have to go back to Jerusalem!"

"What is it?" Arnan says.

"Jesus of Nazareth!"

"You know who that is?" Jabez says.

"The name sounds familiar," Arnan says.

"I have to go back, right now!"

As he runs off, Arnan calls after him, "You can't leave now! We need to find out what just happened!"

"I think it's clear what just happened," Jabez says.

"But *how*?"

Mourners try to approach Jesus, but Peter, Zee, and Zebedee block their way. "Please, everyone," Peter says, "go back to your homes. There's no longer a shiva."

Big James asks Jesus, "Why aren't you telling people not to share this? Why did you do this in front of so many?"

"It's time, James. You'll understand."

Meanwhile, Judas exults, "This is everything! Don't you see? This will bring everyone together. Now no one can deny him!"

But Thomas has collapsed onto all fours, gasping. John and Tamar rush to him. "It's all right," John says. "Let's get you some water."

Nathanael gives John a canteen. Thomas swats it away. Jesus approaches and Thomas demands, "What have you done?"

"Thomas, please. Come. We'll talk."

"When? Soon? I'm tired of all this *soon* talk."

"Thomas," John says, "don't. Not here."

"Yes, right here! Rabbi, look me in the eye."

"I am. I always will."

"That's not an answer! Why Lazarus and not Ramah? Why not your own cousin? This is sick!"

Arnan and Jabez approach, but Peter intercepts them. "Sorry to interrupt," Arnan says, "but we need to speak with Jesus immediately."

"Our rabbi has things to attend to," Peter says.

Jesus kneels until he's face to face with Thomas. "I don't expect you to understand now. I don't. What the Father allows, what I allow, in order to bring about His will and grow the faith of His people—it can be crushing. For you, and yes, even for me."

Thomas lowers his head. "It's too much. I don't understand."

"I know," Jesus says through fresh tears. "And that hurts my heart. But please stay with me. You will understand in time." He kisses the top of Thomas's head and stands to face Arnan.

"What you did just now made a Sadducee very upset," Yussif's father says.

"Someone I'm happy to upset right now."

Jabez says, "He already left for Jerusalem. I know his kind. He's going to make trouble."

"I imagine he is."

"You really don't care?"

"I do," Jesus says, turning back toward the house. "It's why I did this. But I need to go be with our friend now."

Chapter 58

WHAT A DAY

Lazarus's home

Martha has nothing to compare this to. She can barely form the words, even in her mind, to accommodate the reality of it. It was one thing when Jesus chided her for being too busy about *things* when she should have been focused on him alone. She had thought that's what she was doing, fussing over him and his followers. But as usual, he kindly, lovingly set her straight.

And then, after so horribly losing her precious brother far ahead of his time, she'd lost patience with the Messiah himself! Imagine! She had even confronted him, demanded to know why he'd been so long in coming—knowing Lazarus was near death.

Well, the master had showed her why, hadn't he?

Now, as she and her sister attend to their brother in the bathing room, all she feels is gratitude and wonder. Who has ever seen someone resurrected? She cannot fathom it.

Lazarus, for whom she'd sat shiva for four days, stands in the alabaster tub in his underclothes while she and her sister

Mary scrub and rinse him and help him dress. Mary asks, "Is your strength coming back?"

"More and more each minute," he says, beginning to sound normal.

"What about the old aches?" Martha says. He's always been such a hard worker.

"The click in your knee?" Mary says.

Lazarus extends his leg. *Click!* "Still there," he says.

"Wouldn't be you without it," Martha says.

"What was it like?" Mary says.

"I told you. A deep sleep."

"You didn't see Ima or Abba?" Mary says. "Or Uncle Lamech with his creepy one eye?"

"Mary!" Martha says.

"It terrified me when I was little!" she says. "Lazarus, you called him Cyclops!"

"Abba never liked that," he says. "He considered the old Greek poets pagan."

"I wonder if he'll have both eyes in the resurrection," Mary says.

Lazarus looks past his sisters. "If only there were someone we could ask …"

Martha turns. "Rabbi!"

"How are you feeling, my friend?" Jesus says.

"He still has the click in his knee," Mary says.

Jesus shrugs, smirking. Lazarus says, "Yes, we're grateful, but we do have ideas for next time."

"The Father grants me only one miracle per person," Jesus says, and they all laugh. "Ladies, if I may, could I have a moment alone with Lazarus?"

Mary chuckles. "What are we going to say, no?"

The sisters move to the main room where shiva remnants, boiled eggs and cups, are strewn about. Martha plops down in a chair as Mary pours herself a cup of wine and leans against the wall. "I almost just said out loud, 'What a day.'"

"Yeah," Martha says. "That wouldn't quite cover it." Her sister seems to be studying her. "Mary, why are you looking at me like that?"

"You're just sitting."

"And?"

"Look at this place. Total disarray. You're not busying yourself cleaning it up."

Martha can only smile. "Give me a sip of that," she says.

Mary hands her the cup. "I wish there were some way we could repay him."

Repay him? Martha thinks. "What do you give someone who can raise the dead? Or feed thousands with a handful of bread and fish? What could he possibly need?"

"Well, of course he doesn't *need* anything. Maybe that's the whole point."

In the other room, Lazarus sits next to the window by Jesus, wondering how one is expected to respond to a miracle.

"Feeling better?" Jesus says.

"Understatement."

"You certainly look better."

I should hope so, Lazarus thinks, laughing. "Thank you? I should think I would look very refreshed after a four-day nap."

This appears to sober Jesus. "Mm," he says. "Four days of sleep …"

"But it wasn't really. I know that."

Jesus sits staring out the window, and Lazarus has to ask. "Why'd you do it?"

"I should have anticipated you'd have questions."

"I'm serious. Why me?"

Jesus looks pained, perhaps burdened. "It's not so much about *who* as *when*. I'm glad it was you, of course, but ..."

"I don't understand."

"I'm out of time, Laz. This was the last."

"The last what?"

"Public sign."

"No more miracles?"

"Not this side of—"

"This side of wh—"

"I have a confession," Jesus says.

"But you've done no wrong."

"Not a confession of sin. Something to acknowledge that you don't know."

Lazarus can't imagine anything he doesn't know about a friend he's cherished all his life. "Certainly there's no depth to that," he says.

"When you fell ill near the end of the Feast, your sisters sent word to our lodgings in Perea."

"The Feast of Dedication? Today was the last day by my counting."

"We got the letter on the fifth day."

"I was gone by sundown on the fourth day. Probably while the messenger was on his way to you."

"Even so, I didn't come right away. I had something to do, a sermon to preach, in Jerusalem."

Jerusalem? "In the temple? How'd that go?"

"Well," Jesus says lightly, "besides the attempted stoning, I thought it was above average."

"Stoning! So I guess you're not holding back anymore."

"No. I can't. The time has come. What they tried yesterday they will soon succeed in doing."

"The stoning or the arresting?"

"You will see."

"Hold on, no," Lazarus says. "Don't do that."

"Lazarus, please, just listen. The waiting, the four days your sisters grieved and suffered, I need you to know it was not out of cruelty—"

"I would never think that of you!"

"—but so the glory of my Father might be revealed to all in what happened today. It was painful for me to watch those of you who suffered through this. Even more painful that it was necessary for those who witnessed it, especially my own followers. But there are those for whom this will set off a series of events."

"Hasn't it been that way with the religious leaders since the beginning? They don't like it or understand it."

"This is different," Jesus says. "They now have firmer grounds for punishment. They're men. They must save face."

"You've become undeniable."

"They can't have that. And my followers will not understand. I have told them three times, and it is as if they're incapable of hearing."

"I feel incapable of hearing it myself," Lazarus says.

"Even after what happened today?"

"I'm human!"

"So am I!" Jesus says.

Lazarus is startled. "But you are the Son of God."

"That too."

"So I don't understand."

"Most won't," Jesus says. "To be frustrated is human, and I'm frustrated with my students for constantly missing the point—for forgetting what I have done. I'm angry at how the religious leaders have twisted faith into a craven theater of pretense. And I dread what is to come—the cup I must drink to fulfill the Father's will."

"You're scaring me."

"You've been to the grave and you're afraid?"

"For you. I love you! I don't want to see you suffer."

"The Son of Man must suffer many things."

"That doesn't mean I have to like it," Lazarus says.

"The prophet Isaiah gave you plenty of warning."

Lazarus searches his memory. "Yes, yes, 'He was despised and rejected by men. A man of sorrows acquainted with grief.' Those were words on a scroll. Now that I know they're about you, flesh and blood, it's another story."

"A story nearing its end," Jesus says.

Agitated voices outside make Lazarus peer into the moonlight. Thomas paces behind the house, followed by John who appears to be trying to placate him. The rest of the disciples and the women aren't far behind. "Do you need to go down?" Lazarus says.

Jesus rises and closes the curtain but shakes his head. "I will talk to them all at length during the Passover. Nothing will be left unsaid. The heartbroken one cannot accept my love or my words tonight. His brothers will carry him. Come, let's get you something to eat."

Chapter 59

SHATTERED

Out back of Lazarus's home

Judas feels alone, despite that he's among the rest of the disciples and the women and just as concerned for Thomas as they are. The man is still suffering, and just when his awful grief might have seemed about to abate—at least a bit—Jesus proves he can raise someone from the dead. No wonder Thomas has been plunged back into abject mourning and now rages with fury.

Thomas grabs a clay pitcher and raises it over his head. "Thomas, don't!" John yells, but too late. Thomas hurls it at the well where it smashes to bits.

"We'll have to replace that," Matthew says, and Judas can only shake his head. Leave it to Matthew.

"Yeah, Matthew?" Thomas rails. "Why? Because when Lazarus loses something, he deserves to have it restored? But when other people lose things, they just—"

"Because it's the polite thing to do," Matthew says.

Nathanael adds, "The polite thing would be to not break the jar in the first place."

"I'm done with polite," Thomas says. "I'm done with all of it."

"You don't mean that," Andrew says.

"Then tell me what I mean!"

"You're hurting," Peter says. "We get it."

"No, you don't! If you did, you'd be as offended as I am!"

Philip steps in. "There's no use putting suffering on a scale, Thomas."

Judas agrees and feels desperate to be the peacemaker. "What happened today should make us all more united than ever. We need to set aside our personal grievances and prepare for things to change, in a big way."

Judas startles when Thomas flashes him a blazing look. He's grateful when John steps between them. "He doesn't mean you, Thomas," John says. "He didn't say that. Don't worry. Just still yourself." He pulls Thomas off to the side.

Feeling the need to defend himself, Judas says, "I hate what he's going through. I do. But think about what happened today. Dozens of mourners saw what happened with their own eyes. The religious leaders will be forced to admit who Jesus truly is, and they'll work *with* him now to unify us against our oppressors. This is one of the greatest days in the history of our people!"

"I agree," Big James says. "We just need to be sensitive around Thomas."

Zee looks unconvinced. "The Jerusalem religious leaders don't like people more powerful than they are, Judas."

"Right," Philip says. "I'm not sure this moment means what you think it does."

Judas is sure he's right. "If they don't like it, Jesus can snuff them out like a lamp, with a single word."

"That's something I'm still wondering about," Matthew says. "Why didn't Jesus speak healing from a distance, the way he did for Gaius's servant?"

"He wanted us there," Tamar says, "to see the stone rolled away and to see Lazarus walk out of the tomb in burial strips."

"He also wanted us to participate," Thaddeus says. "He could have moved the stone and unwrapped Laz with a word too."

"He told us last night, Matthew," Little James says, "'that you might believe.'"

"It certainly worked for me!" Judas says.

"If Jerusalem hears this and believes," Big James says, "could this be the beginning of the army?"

Now you're talking, Judas thinks.

"When has Jesus said anything about an army?" Mary says. "Ever."

"He threw away my dagger," Zee says.

"I'm sorry," Judas says, "but some of you are overthinking this. Look, the time for restraint has passed."

"But he asked nothing more of us than to come with him and observe," Tamar says. "Why are we discussing anything beyond that?"

"Because," Big James says, "we could lose Thomas over this."

Peter says, "He said yesterday that no one and nothing could snatch us from his hand."

"Well," Judas says, "he said that of what he called his true sheep, those who hear his voice and believe him. Maybe Thomas isn't one of the true sheep."

"How dare you!" Mary says.

"Has the devil gotten into you?" Andrew asks.

"Take it back," Nathanael says.

Peter says, "Everyone, please …"

"I said take it back!" Nathanael says.

"Please," Mary says, "do not dishonor Jesus by acting this way."

"She's right," Peter says. "The hour is late. A lot has happened in the past two days. Let's rest."

"I'm sorry," Judas says. "Truly. I love Thomas. I'm just excited about the poss—"

Little James cries out, knees buckling as he twists, clutching his walking stick to keep from going down. Thaddeus and Mary leap to his aid, holding him up. "It's all right," he says. "I'm fine." But another spasm hits him.

"From the fight yesterday?" Andrew says.

"His pain was getting worse before that," Thaddeus says.

"The pangs come in waves," Mary says.

"Thomas has a point," Big James says. "Why does everyone else get healed, but not James?"

"I don't want to talk about me tonight," James says, wincing. "I think we should do as Peter said and get some rest."

"How can you?" Nathanael says. "In this condition?"

"That's between me and God. As should be most of the things people have been arguing about tonight."

"We want you to be okay," Andrew says.

"Thank you," James says, agony written all over him. "But standing around watching won't do anything about it."

"The sisters have prepared the same rooms we stayed in last time," Mary says.

"And they won't sleep until we do," Tamar says. "It's disrespectful to keep them up late like this."

"She's right," Zee says. "I'm going. Come on."

Nathanael nods toward James. "But what about him?"

"I'll stay with him until this passes," Thaddeus says.

"I just need a few minutes," James says.

"Peter and I can collect John and Thomas," Andrew says. "Adonai in heaven knows it will take all three of us."

Matthew asks James if he's sure he'll be all right. Mary assures Matthew that she and Thaddeus will take care of him.

As Judas and the rest make their way back inside, Mary and Thaddeus cradle James, who says, "Mary, you got your answer. We won't sit shiva."

She nods. "Not tonight. But I still feel grief."

"I feel it too," Thaddeus says.

"I think," James says, "it's because Judas is right. This was the biggest public sign yet."

Mary says, "We no longer have to wonder about when *soon* will be."

Chapter 60

THE MAGDALENE'S MUSINGS

The mountain cave of La Sainte Baume, thirty years hence
Though infirm himself now, Matthew finds it jarring to see his old friend as an elderly, albeit still beautiful, woman. He can barely contain his excitement over the prospect of hearing what Mary's been writing, especially knowing from experience how demanding the task can be. She appears nervous as she gathers the fragments of her notes and seems to be arranging them in order.

"The more I read the songs of David," she says, "the more I felt I needed to express to Jesus one of my own. Just please know that whatever this is going to be, it is not finished."

The wind outside moans and haunts and reaches inside the cave just enough to make the flames of the lamps and torches dance. Matthew says, "You so rarely let people into your mind, but when you did, I was always grateful."

At last she settles, clears her throat, and reads: "Darkness is not the absence of light. That would be too simple. It's more uncontrollable and sinister—not a place, but a void. I was there once. More than once. And even though I couldn't see or hear you, you were there, waiting. Because the darkness is not dark to you. At least, not always."

How Matthew misses the master!

"You wept," she continues, "not because your friend was dead, but because you soon would be, and because we couldn't understand or didn't want to, or both. The coming darkness was too deep for us to grasp, but then so was the light. One had to come before the other. It was always that way with you. It still is.

"Tears fell from your eyes, and then from ours, before every light in the world went out and time itself wanted to die with you. I go back to that place sometimes, or rather it comes back to me uninvited—the night that seemed eternal until it wasn't. Bitter, and then sweet, but somehow the bitterness remained in the sweet and has never gone away.

"You told us that's how it would be. Not with words but with how you lived—the man of sorrows acquainted with grief. That grief wasn't what we wanted to see, so we tried to look away, and in so doing fulfilled your very essence, one from whom people hide their faces.

"But soon we couldn't hide from it any more than we could stop the sun from setting. Or rising. I remember you wishing there could be another way, and looking back, I do too. I still don't know why it has to be this way, the bitter often mingled with the sweet. Maybe I never will. At least not this side of—"

Lazarus's home, thirty years prior
The resurrected man sits alone in the candlelight, wondering, wondering, his own putrid burial linens in his hands.

Shmuel's bedroom, Jerusalem
The Pharisee awakes to an urgent knock at his door. It's bizarre, lifechanging news from Bethany.

Shammai's home, Jerusalem
A Sadducee pounds on the door until the Great Sanhedrin leader appears in his nightgown, candle in hand. It's news from Bethany that will change everything.

Lazarus's home
Young Mary enters her brother's office, unlocks the safe, and pockets an extravagant 300 denarii—a year's wages for a typical working man.

Upstairs, Peter finishes cleaning and redressing Big James's head wound and helps him into bed. Across the room Little James struggles to find a comfortable position. Zee snuffs out all the candles.

In another room, Thomas lies on his mat, gazing at the sundial he gave his beloved Ramah. It's all he can do to keep from smashing it into a thousand pieces. But he tucks it into a cotton pouch and blows out his candle.

In the women's guestroom, as Tamar settles in her bed, Mary Magdalene goes to the window to douse the candle. Outside she sees Jesus come upon the pitcher Thomas broke against the well. He fits two of the shards together, running a finger along the sharp edges. He looks deep in thought. Mary continues to watch as he heads in the direction of Lazarus's tomb.

PART 8

The Time Has Come

Chapter 61

SPOTLESS

Jerusalem, 1004 B.C.

Fulfilling as it is to return from conquering a foe, King David is eager to be out of the glare of public adulation and reach the palace where Abigail and his four-year-old son Daniel await. He stops just before coming within view of the city gates to change into royal finery and mount a resplendent and garishly adorned white stallion.

He and his trailing entourage are soon welcomed by his subjects, who line the path to the city with their own cloaks and wraps. And as he enters the gates, flower petals rain down, cheers erupt, and music announces his arrival. He returns the waves of palm branches, smiling and raising a fist.

To God be the glory, he thinks, while also realizing that the populace needs this—needs to see him, the embodiment of the blessing of the Lord in victory. He's happy to give them their due but will be happier still behind closed doors in his own citadel.

As David breezes into the palace, Daniel runs into his arms. "My boy!" David says, scooping him up. "I'm home at last!"

He sets the boy down with a kiss as his wife approaches and they embrace. "Is it over?" Abigail says.

"The Ammonites are defeated!"

Abigail gasps and leads her young son in clapping.

"And not a moment too soon," David adds. "It's almost Passover. Has the lamb been selected?"

"Inspected and approved by the Levites this morning."

"Have the rights been performed?"

"They didn't say. I can—"

"No, I will do it. Daniel, come with me."

Outside a few moments later, David holds a blanket as he and the little boy wait in the courtyard. A servant appears with a lamb on a rope.

"Ah, here it is," David says. "Exactly one year old. Spotless. Passover is six days away, so today we anoint his feet."

"Why, Abba?"

"Because he's going to live with us in our house for five days. We have to mark him as special and keep him clean. Understand?" David spreads the blanket for the animal and rubs oil onto its ankles and feet.

"Clean?" Daniel says.

"Yes, because he will be what we call the paschal lamb, the one offered as a sacrifice to atone for our sins. The oil smells good, right?"

Daniel nods as David gathers up the lamb in the blanket and they head back inside. He quotes for his son from the Torah: "'It is the sacrifice of the Lord's Passover, for He passed over the houses of the people of Israel in Egypt, when He struck the Egyptians but spared our houses.'"

That night the family of three and the lamb settle by the fireplace. Abigail serves a plate of matzah. "Even the royal family," David says, "eats unleavened bread during Passover."

As she hands Daniel a cracker, Abigail says, "When God redeemed our people and set us free in Egypt through Moses, our ancestors had to leave so fast that there was no time to let their bread rise. So they took their dough before the yeast was added and carried it on their shoulders in kneading bowls bound in cloaks."

"And," David says, "God commanded us never to forget. I have one more Passover story to tell you, one that goes all the way back to that very day when they left with no time to let the bread rise." He produces a long, thin box and hands it to Daniel. The boy eagerly opens it to find a donkey bridle ....

Chapter 62

SPOOKED

Jerusalem

Jesse has formed an unlikely bond with Veronica as they share unique histories. Both suffered long seasons of physical ailments that left them hopeless until they were healed. As the temple courts swarm with pilgrims in town for Passover and undoubtably to see Jesus, Jesse and Veronica debate the celebrated Sanhedrin leader Gedera at the top of the stairs. The Sadducee had demanded to know of anyone who could prove the rumors about the blasphemous rogue preacher and so-called miracle worker.

As the crowd around them multiplies, Jesse says, "The word has spread that he raised a man four days dead at Bethany, and there were over a hundred witnesses."

"They witnessed only the man walking out of the tomb," Gedera says. "They did not see him go in, which means it could have been staged."

"Why would so many people have come to sit shiva if the man was not actually dead?"

"He has orchestrated more elaborate spectacles in the past!" Gedera says.

"I was bleeding for twelve years," Veronica says, "and my faith in him healed me. That's no illusion."

"Who can corroborate the facts of your supposed previous condition?" Gedera says.

"Are we really getting into this?" Jesse says.

"Where is Jesus now?" Gedera says, dismissively. "Will he show up for the Feast?"

"I doubt he would miss Passover," Veronica says.

"Unless he has something to hide," Gedera says, and the crowd protests. "The coward won't show his face," he adds.

"How can you call him a coward," Jesse says, "when not a week ago he stood up to you and the others when you tried to stone and arrest him?"

"We do not take blasphemy lightly. The law commands we put to death false prophets. You would have us shrink from our duty?"

"I know what happened to me," Veronica says.

"And *I* know what happened to me," Jesse says.

Veronica says, "He's the Christ, and instead of embracing his power, you feel threatened by it because he'll be your authority when he is king."

"Insolent witch!" Gedera says. "You will recant your statement!"

"Or what?" Jesse says. "You'll stone her too?"

Someone from the crowd shouts, "Tell us more about Jesus!"

Viewing all this from the balcony of the governor's mansion, Pontius Pilate tells Cohortes Urbana Atticus, "If I understood any of this it would be remarkable, wouldn't it? Jews from every corner of the known world. I could do without the endless slaughtering of lambs, the shrieking, and the blood—"

"You've read the story," Atticus says. "What's to understand?"

"I guess *care* is what I meant," Pilate says. "If I cared, it really would be remarkable."

"Tell yourself whatever you like, Pontius, but I'll bet if I look in your library there will be a piece of flat bread."

"Stop it. You know I've eaten it all." Atticus snorts, and Pilate continues. "Why has Tiberius not sent more troops? He knows the scope of this pilgrimage. The population doubles and doubles again."

"It's not just the numbers," Atticus says. "It's the fervor. Maybe he's testing whether you can go a week without incident. I don't know."

"A test I intend to pass, with your help. Oh, Atticus! Have you heard about the ghost? Everyone is talking about the Ghost of Bethany." He reads Atticus's look and presses, "It's true then?"

"So what if it is? A raising of the dead. A corpse one minute, fully restored the next."

"These people's superstitious madness knows no end," Pilate says.

"So you don't believe it?"

"Of course not. But Jews have rallied around lesser phenomena before, with lethal consequences."

"Now you're thinking clearly," Atticus says. "It doesn't matter if it's true. It matters only that they think it is."

"What concerns me," Pilate says, "is that it concerns Caiaphas. I don't know if he believes it or not, but I can tell he's spooked."

"He probably doesn't believe it. But he's spooked that the people do." When Pilate falls silent and appears alarmed himself, Atticus adds, "You'll be fine. You just need to know whether the arrival of a Jewish sorcerer is a good thing or very bad for them."

Chapter 63

THE PURCHASE

A Bethany apothecary

Lazarus's sister Mary is on a mission. *What,* she wonders, *can I give the person who has lavished on me the greatest gift of all?* Her brother's best friend, her own lifelong chum, has been revealed as the Messiah, Son of the most high God. And it was proven to her in no uncertain terms when he resurrected Lazarus. No price is too great, no present too lavish. Others may think her out of her mind, and many already do, but neither will anything stop her from following her heart.

Mary tells the proprietor of the shop that she's looking for something *very* special, knowing full well she is vastly understating her wishes. The woman shows her an array of essential oils. She knows this won't even begin to fill the bill, especially with three hundred denarii in four small bags, but she politely listens as the pitch comes.

"This one is called 'Cove,'" the woman says. "Three parts myrrh, two parts cassia. Lovely for burning to purify a house. Ten denarii." Mary gives it a sniff and shakes her head. "And this," the woman continues, "is 'Cleopatra.' Four parts cypress, one part myrtle, in rose oil. Very good for the skin and hair. Fifteen denarii. Top shelf."

"Not top shelf enough," Mary says.

"Excuse me?"

It's time to put her cards on the table. "I want to see your oils that aren't for sale. I know you have them. I've been to dinners with very wealthy people."

"Oh, ma'am, I bring those out for only my most loyal, and liquid, customers."

She's about to learn how liquid Mary is. Mary plops a velvet purse of coins onto a table and empties it. The perfumer runs her fingers through the coins. "Wait here," she says.

She returns with a small silk-wrapped bundle. "Derived from a rare flowering honeysuckle varietal in the mountains of Nepal, used to anoint kings in China and India, protected in a premium alabaster vessel for temperature control—pure spikenard."

The woman unveils the long-necked jar, which takes Mary's breath. The container alone would cost more than she's ever paid for a fragrance. The perfumer theatrically pulls on a velvet glove, carefully uncorks the jar, and reverently dips in a sample stick. She keeps her gloved hand below the stick as she holds it to Mary's nose.

Impressed, no, overwhelmed, Mary feels her brows involuntarily raise.

"How many ounces would you like?"

"The whole jar."

The perfumer laughs. "Oh my, you are charming, dear. But truly, what do you think? One and a half ounces?"

"I said the whole jar." Mary sets two more velvet bags onto the table.

The perfumer seems at a loss for words. "I—it's not possible. This jar would cost more than half a year's wages, and I need the supply to satisfy the demands of my wealthiest clientele. It would take several months to obtain another jar. It's—"

"You need to listen," Mary says. "This is for the most important king the world has ever known." She produces the fourth and last bag of coins. "Three hundred denarii." Mary wraps the jar in the silk. "Take the rest of the year off."

Chapter 64

A POX

The Great Sanhedrin, Jerusalem

Yussif imagined for years what it might be like to be a member of this august body, but not once did he envision a day like this one. Resolved to keep his personal feelings under wraps as long as possible, now he fears he cannot stay silent. What it will mean for him and his future he cannot say. But this controversy is bigger than he is. In fact, it's superior to all assembled. What they decide to do about Jesus will determine the very legitimacy of their calling and purpose. If they're not all about the prophesied Messiah, for what reason do they exist?

With the High Priest, Caiaphas himself, in the head seat, the Sadducee Gedera has the floor. All about Yussif sit anxious colleagues from all religious factions. The very air feels wrought with apprehension. Yussif can only puzzle over where his colleague and old friend Shmuel stands on the issue. He's sensed turmoil in the man's mind, not unlike his own.

Gedera says, "Whether by sorcery or necromancy or other dark arts, we can no longer deny that these so-called signs have been escalating in performances, each more outlandish and hysteria-producing than the one before."

This, Yussif decides, *is beyond the pale.* He bolts to his feet, caution tossed to the wind. "We say they are just performances, but what about the resurrection of one Lazarus of Bethany?"

The great Shammai weighs in. "There is no proof, but rumors like these are exactly why this rogue is such a pox on this institution!"

Yussif recognizes Shammai's counterpart, Hillel's secretary, a man named Dunash, who says, "Has no one in this room considered the implications if the man were indeed brought back from death?"

"That's what we're doing right now!" Gedera says.

"No!" Yussif says. "We're strategizing how to maintain the status quo and hoping these signs cannot be real."

The heavyset Pharisee Zebadiah calls out, "On this issue, I am with Gedera. Jesus of Nazareth is not Elijah the Tishbite! Only Elijah can raise people from the dead."

"What if he *is* Elijah?" Yussif says. "Honored Nicodemus encountered him in Capernaum and observed that—"

"Sit down, Yussif!" Shammai thunders. "Nicodemus is still away, but I'm certain he would agree that you do not know what you say."

But Yussif will not sit. "My own father went to sit shiva for Lazarus and witnessed the miracle!"

That renders the room silent, and even Shammai's eyes go wide and his nostrils flare.

Shmuel stands. "Everyone, please! Listen! The possibly false teachings—"

"*Possibly?!*" Shammai shouts.

"—of Jesus of Nazareth and his purported signs are the very reason I came to study in Jerusalem in the first place. I have the most complete record of his words and deeds. This matter of Elijah, it bears investigating."

Shouts erupt from all over the council, but Shmuel continues even more loudly. "I will go to Bethany and ask him myself if he claims to be Elijah!"

"We don't have any more questions, Shmuel," Zebadiah says. "The man claimed to be God during the Feast of Dedication!"

"If we let him go on like this," Gedera says, "everyone will believe in him. I'm seeing it firsthand even now. And the Romans will want to prevent a revolt. Pilate will come and take away our positions here and destroy our entire nation!"

The room becomes a cacophony again as Shmuel appeals to their leader. "High Priest Caiaphas, may I go?"

Caiaphas stands and the room quiets, everyone else now sitting. "Gedera," he says, "you know nothing at all. I have been given a prophecy from God, and I believe it is about this issue exactly. The prophecy is that a man will die for the people so that our nation will not perish. Jesus may be that man. We will hand him over ourselves before there is an uprising. Rome will not destroy us. They will be grateful."

"The only answer," Zebadiah says, "is immediate arrest and execution, as Caiaphas has said."

"I did not say immediately! We are not legally allowed to execute anyone, with the exception of a ritual stoning within the temple courts. If Jesus' death is to be public, and a spectacle, it must be carried out by Rome. If we move too quickly, they won't recognize the favor we've done them."

Over murmurs of agreement, Gedera says, "But how?"

Caiaphas says, "Herod Antipas and his court will be arriving in Jerusalem for the Feast soon and will attend the annual state dinner with Pilate's administration. I'll see to it that the topic is brought up."

"King Herod is pathetic," Shammai says, "and we ought not be endorsing his attendance at that dinner tomorrow."

"Making sure our voice is heard there, Shammai, is not the same as endorsing him. I will make sure a letter is waiting at Herod's compound here in the city when he arrives. This meeting is adjourned."

Caiaphas swiftly exits toward his chambers as the council explodes in shouted questions.

Shmuel grabs Yussif and pulls him out of the chamber and into his office, where he shuts the door and says, "This is no longer about God to them, Yussif."

"You're just now noticing?"

"I suspected some of them to be utterly devoid of conscience, goodwill, or true devotion to Torah, but this proves it beyond all doubt."

"What are you going to do?"

"You say your father was at Bethany for the—"

"Yes. He was a close friend of Lazarus—is, I should say."

"Could he arrange a meeting with Jesus?" Shmuel says. "I've observed the man, confronted him, even prayed with him. But I've never conversed openly with him without an agenda."

"You don't have an agenda now?"

"If it's true he has power over life and death—"

"It surely must be," Yussif says. "My father is a rational man, not given to sensationalism."

"Then I simply want to know what his intentions are. After all, we want the same things, don't we, to uphold the faith and honor God's Law?"

"I wonder if it's as simple as that."

"I'm not suggesting any of this is simple. But we in the Sanhedrin have been only reactionary toward Jesus. Perhaps we have all, myself included, been too quick to take offense at his words. I had not considered the sum of his teaching and deeds as worthy of a fair and openminded inquiry."

"The Sanhedrin is well beyond that," Yussif says.

"Your father could at least get us to Lazarus, right?"

"That much I know, yes."

"Then let's go to him immediately."

Chapter 65

THE THANK YOU

Capernaum

Gaius doesn't himself patrol anymore, but he justifies an occasional stroll to observe and supervise, making sure his troops are on the job. *Yeah, that's it,* he tells himself. *Managing by walking around.*

In truth, however, he wants and needs to connect with new friends. There's no one among his own people he can tell of his radical change of mind and heart after what Jesus did for him. He finds his way to Peter's home where Eden, Salome, the mother of two of Jesus' disciples, and Jairus, the temple administrator, load luggage onto a cart. "That time of year again," Gaius says.

"Praetor!" Eden says with a smile.

"It's Gaius, please."

"Gaius," she says.

"Your Passover always makes my job a little easier. The town nearly empties."

"I would imagine so," Jairus says with a twinkle. "Will you miss us?"

Gaius laughs, but the fact is, he will miss them. Yet he plays it off. "It's not like we get to just take the week off. Who is it who stays behind?"

"The elderly," Jairus says. "Those with child, the infirm, their caretakers."

"Makes sense."

"Bu they still observe the Seder meal."

"Yes, Seder," Gaius says. "I'm aware."

"You can expect to see an uptick in demand at market for apples, walnuts, and cinnamon for the charoset."

"Apples, walnuts, cinnamon—"

"You gonna make your own?" Jairus says.

"Not this year," Gaius says, turning to Eden. "You'll be with your husband for the holiday?"

"That's the plan."

"And so that means you'll also see—"

"Yes, hopefully. I can't imagine not."

Gaius suddenly finds himself trying to suppress tears. "It's strange. I wish I could go with you all."

"You could," Eden says.

"No, it would cause trouble, and I have my family to think of. My full family, thanks to him. Please send word to Jesus of my gratitude and love."

"I will."

"And tell Peter I said shalom, shalom. Make sure you say it twice."

"Wouldn't do it any other way," she says.

"Time to get going, everybody!" Jairus says.

Eden says, "They will all be so pleased to hear from you, Gaius. Especially Jesus. Sure you don't want to come?"

"Thank you for passing the messages along. I won't hold you up."

"Are we late?" Shula calls out as she and Barnaby scamper to the wagon.

"Almost!" Jairus says. "You have the Praetor of Capernaum to thank. If he hadn't stopped to chat, you might have missed your ride. We still have to pick up Michal and my kids."

"I hope he enjoys his week off!" Barnaby says.

"Our first Passover pilgrimage," Shula says as she climbs aboard. "I've never seen the holy temple. Can you believe that?"

Chapter 66

THE BURIAL

Lazarus's home

Judas slips out of bed just before dawn and tiptoes into a side room where he silently transfers a few coins from the group's purse to his own and adjusts the numbers in his ledger.

A clanging outside startles him and he ducks, then peers out. Thomas emerges from a small shed carrying a shovel in one hand and something Judas can't make out in the other. Thomas heads toward the woods.

Judas quietly leaves the house, taking great pains to close the door without a sound, and follows Thomas from a distance. He slips behind a tree when Thomas stops in a clearing and digs a hole. Into it he drops the sundial he purchased for Ramah, stares at it for a moment, then covers it with dirt. He stands there, seemingly in reverence, before heading stone-faced back toward the house.

Judas stays out of sight but can't take his eyes off the new mound of dirt. That sundial was brand new and never used ....

Herod's Jerusalem compound, morning
Joanna would have once considered this a high privilege, something to one day tell her grandchildren about—arriving in a lavish caravan of carriages with a gaggle of courtiers, the king, his wife, her own husband Chuza, Cassandra—until she discovered the affair between Cassandra and Chuza. Now the pomp and circumstance are lost on her, and she'd rather be anywhere else.

"I have never seen the city so crowded for Passover," the king says.

"I'm telling you," his wife says, "it's because of all the rumors about that magician from Nazareth."

"Some place for a magician to come from," Chuza says. "Who'd he learn his tricks from, a goat?"

"He'll be coming for the Feast, yes?" Cassandra says, not even trying to hide her gaze at Joanna's husband.

"I hope so!" Herod says as a servant hands Chuza a scroll. "I've been hoping to meet him for a long time. He sounds so entertaining."

"Your honor," Chuza says, "this is from High Priest Caiaphas. Apparently it's urgent."

Herod scans the scroll, frowns, and mutters, "Caiaphas."

Chapter 67

GLORY

Lazarus's home

As much as he misses Eden and can't wait for her to join them for the Feast, Peter loves times like this with Jesus, Jesus' friends, all the rest of the disciples, Jesus' mother, Tamar, and Mary Magdalene. Even Zebedee is along, enjoying a sumptuous evening meal prepared, as usual, by Martha. The only person missing is Martha's sister Mary, who is, Martha says, "who knows where?" And yet Martha, busy and bustling as always, seems to have had a change of heart. She says this without a hint of resentment or rancor and has cheerfully prepared the meal with the help of Magdalene, Tamar, and Mother Mary.

Peter can't get over casually dining with a resurrected man, but here they sit, and with the Messiah himself. Peter anticipates that Jesus will engage in some teaching, as he usually does when so many are reclined with him at table. It feels bizarre to engage in normal conversation at such a time as this, but Peter is curious. "Six days to go, Lazarus," he says. "Have you selected your lamb?"

"Yes, he's out back. Still need to perform the rites and bring him in." He turns to Jesus. "Whenever you're here, I seem to neglect all my duties."

"You're not neglectful," Jesus says. "We have to soak up our time together."

At a knock at the door, Lazarus asks Martha if they're expecting someone. She rises. "No one knows where Mary is, but she wouldn't knock."

As she heads to the door, Peter says, "We should be careful who we let in these days."

Martha peeks through the curtains. "It's Arnan!"

"Oh, bring him in!" Lazarus says. "He can take Mary's seat until she gets back."

"Oh, he has two others with him."

Peter quickly looks to Lazarus, wondering if this is wise.

"Arnan is trustworthy," Lazarus says.

"Of course," Jesus says.

As Martha welcomes them in, she says, "Much better circumstances than the last time you came to my door."

"Pardon the interruption," Arnan says. "I've brought with me a member of the Sanhedrin—"

"Shmuel," Jesus says.

The man looks startled. "You—remember me?"

"Of course I do."

Other disciples look as surprised as Peter. These two have history?

"I am relieved," Arnan says, "that I have not made a terrible mistake in bringing him here. Also with us is a newcomer to the Sanhedrin, this is—"

"Yussif," Tamar says.

What's this?

Andrew says to Jesus, "He's the one who warned us in Jotapata that people were looking for you."

Shmuel looks surprised again. "That was me! I was looking for you."

Uh-oh.

Jesus smiles. "Well, you've found me. And congratulations to both of you for your appointments—Capernaum's finest. Will you join us?"

As the disciples scramble to make room, Judas leans in to Peter. "This is a tremendous opportunity for a strategic alliance."

Peter isn't so sure. "We'll see."

The three men settle, and Arnan says, "Rabbi, we have reason to believe danger lies in wait for you at the highest levels of temple leadership."

"I never would have expected that," Jesus says, to the obvious shock of the visitors. "I am joking," he adds. "Go on."

"Jesus of Nazareth," Shmuel says, "your situation has become a matter of life and death."

"It always has been."

Lazarus says, "They tried to stone him in the temple courts!"

"What we mean," Yussif says, "is that your fame has now gone beyond fame, not just in numbers, but also in debate." He nods toward Lazarus. "Lately because of him."

"I'm sorry," Lazarus says. "I'll try not to die next time."

"No," Jesus says. "It's all part of the plan."

"Your ruin?" Shmuel says. "That's part of your plan? Because that's where this is headed."

"Is that what you've come to tell me?" Jesus says.

"You've called yourself the Son of Man."

"Here we go again," Peter says.

"I'm not here to contest that or take offense this time," Shmuel says. "I'm open."

"I can tell," Jesus says. "I can see it in your eyes."

"If you are who you say you are, what is your plan? The entire city of Jerusalem is awaiting your arrival for Passover, some with open arms, others with daggers. Do you have an army we don't know about? If you are more than a rabbi, you will have more than just Rome to overthrow, but also many religious leaders. They will not join you in your quest."

"Perhaps," Judas says, "you can help them do so. This is the week."

Peter notices that Jesus ignores Judas. "What would you like to see, Rabbi Shmuel," he says. "Regardless of who it is, what is *your* hope for a Messiah?"

"To usher in a new Davidic kingdom that drives out our oppressors and restores justice and glory for Israel."

Peter can see Judas agrees and is into this.

"Glory," Jesus says.

"Yes," Shmuel says. "On a glorious throne. With prosperity for all, a new golden age with Israel as a light to the nations, revealing God to the peoples of the world."

"And you—what will *you* do in that day?"

Shmuel looks thrown. "Worship? Serve, I hope. How could I possibly know until that day comes?"

"I will tell you," Jesus says. "When the Son of Man comes in his glory, and all the angels with him, then he will sit on his glorious throne. Before him will be gathered all the nations, and he will separate people one from another as a shepherd separates the sheep from the goats. And he will place the sheep on his right but the goats on the left. Then the king will say to those on his right, 'Come, you who are blessed by my Father, inherit the kingdom prepared for you from the foundation of the world. For I was hungry and you gave me food. I was thirsty and you gave me drink. I was a stranger and you welcomed me. I was naked and you clothed me. I was sick and you visited me. I was in prison and you came to me.'

"Then the righteous will answer him, saying, 'Lord, when did we do these things for you?' And the king will answer them, 'Truly, I say to you, as you did it to one of the least of these my brothers, you did it to me.'"

Everyone looks surprised and Peter notices Shmuel shift uncomfortably.

Jesus continues, "Then he will say to those on his left, 'Depart from me, for I was hungry and you gave me no food. I was thirsty and you gave me no drink. I was a stranger and you did not welcome me, naked and you did not clothe me, sick and in prison and you did not visit me.'

"Then they will also answer, saying, 'Lord, when did we see you hungry or thirsty or a stranger or naked or sick or in prison and did not minister to you?'

"Then he will answer them, saying, 'Truly, I say to you, as you did not do it to one of the least of these, you did not do it to me.'"

After a long, conspicuous pause, Shmuel says, "This is a hard teaching."

Jesus says, "I do not know how to make it less so."

"The Son of Man," Shmuel says, "the Messiah is identified with the lowest of all people? The hungry and poor, the stranger?"

"I've been teaching this ever since my opening sentence on the mount."

Matthew nods.

Shmuel says, "But what of all the Torah requirements and traditions upheld by our forefathers?"

"The prophet Micah distilled things to their essence," Jesus says, "and you overlooked it. 'He has told you, O man, what is good; and what does the Lord require of you but to do justice and—'"

"'—to love kindness, and to walk humbly with your God?'" Shmuel finishes. "Yes, but how do you harmonize that with the conclusion of Qoheleth in the Ketuvim? 'The end of the matter; all has been heard. Fear God and keep His commandments, for this is the whole duty of man.'"

Jesus answers, "A new commandment I give to you, that you love one another, just as I have loved you." His gaze seems to take in Peter and all the others. "By this all people will know that you are my disciples, if you have love for one another."

Shmuel says, "And what of the temple, the sacrifices, the law, the feasts? Are not keeping these how the nations will know we are God's people?"

"The temple, the sacrifices, the law, the feasts—all are fulfilled in me."

"You would *do away* with them?"

"I said *fulfilled,* not done away with."

"I don't understand the difference."

"The law can do only so much, but now that I am here—"

The door opens and all turn to see sister Mary, teary-eyed and trembling, bearing a beautiful alabaster jar. Martha rushes to her. "Are you all right? Where have you been?"

Shmuel turns back to Jesus. "You were saying …"

But young Mary approaches Jesus and kneels at his feet.

"What's going on?" Shmuel says. "Who is this?"

"My sister Mary," Lazarus says.

Mary presses the bottle onto the floor, snapping the neck and releasing the extravagant fragrance.

"Mary!" Martha says.

"That's spikenard!" Judas says, gasping.

"Mary," Lazarus says, "What are you doing?"

Seemingly oblivious to everyone, Mary anoints Jesus' feet, emptying the jar, the aroma permeating the entire room.

"You're letting your sister touch his feet!" Shmuel says. "That's degrading!"

"Have you heard nothing the teacher has said?" Lazarus asks.

Mary removes her head covering, which appears to horrify Shmuel. "All right!" he says. "This is enough. Jesus …"

She begins to dry his feet with her own hair.

"Once again, Shmuel," Jesus says, "there is no law in Torah commanding a woman to cover her hair. That's just a tradition."

"Are you *commending* her? Excusing her?"

"Shmuel," Yussif says, "we don't know this family. It's not our pl—"

Mary, weeping, says, "Blessed are you, king of the universe, for you have done all things well …"

"Yussif, Arnan," Shmuel says, "we need to leave."

"Rabbi Shmuel," Arnan says, "I understand, but we need to—"

"She's performing an inappropriate act openly, without shame, and he's allowing it while being called God. We can't be found out to have witnessed this and done nothing!"

"An open investigation, you said. Let's see what he says."

Judas picks up the alabaster jar and seems to unravel. "Pure nard. Of the highest quality. This—we could have sold this for more than two hundred denarii …"

"What troubles you, Judas?" Jesus says.

"Why was this ointment not sold for hundreds of denarii?"

"You just told the story," Shmuel says, "about how caring for the poor is akin to caring for the Messiah."

"Yes," Judas says. "We could have given it to the poor. It's so wasteful! Where did you get the money for this, Mary?"

"Leave her alone," Jesus says. "She has done a beautiful thing to me. For you will always have the poor with you, and whenever you want, you can do good for them. But you will not always have me."

Shmuel looks disgusted and Mother Mary heartbroken.

Jesus continues, "She has done what she could. She has anointed my body beforehand for burial."

"*Burial?!*" Nathanael says.

Judas says, "What are you—"

Peter shushes him. "Let him finish!"

"And believe me," Jesus says, "wherever the gospel is proclaimed in the whole world, what she has done will be told in memory of her."

Shmuel leaps to his feet. "What your follower has said is right. This act was wasteful, immodest, and contradicts everything you said before about the poor and lowly."

"He said," Lazarus says, "we'll always have them with us."

"The very notion that such a disgrace would be proclaimed throughout the world as part of your gospel, when instead it should be reproached, rebuked, and condemned—it's—I can't—I can't be in the same room as this abomination."

"Sounds like a personal problem," Andrew says.

"I wanted to believe!" Shmuel says, rushing to the door. "I came here to give you a chance, and you've ruined it."

"Sorry I couldn't help you," Jesus says, and Peter hears the compassion in his tone.

Shmuel leaves and slams the door.

As Arnan and Yussif sit looking aghast, Judas says, "Rabbi, that is not a man we want to upset if we are looking to unite our people."

Jesus ignores him and looks to Yussif, brows raised.

"'For burial'?" Yussif says.

The room goes deathly quiet save for young Mary's weeping. Peter feels the same heavy sense of loss and sorrow he believes the others are suffering. All sit motionless except for Thomas who slugs down the rest of his wine and clunks his cup loudly on the table.

Judas heads outside to clear his head. Shmuel, standing by a cart, appears to brood as he waits for his fellow travelers. "You! Where are you going?"

"I-I don't know," Judas says.

"You're the one who asked why the nard wasn't sold and given to the poor."

"I'm not sure I should be talking you," Judas says.

"I think you're the only one in that room with any sense."

"It doesn't take a lot of sense. I was just pointing out the facts. If the parable he told was true, then everyone should have seen how incongruous the waste was, and there should have been more dissent."

"What are you going to do?"

"I'm not like you. I believe he *is* the one. I spoke up because I care about all of us getting this right. And we have an opportunity with the Passover coming up to unite over a million of our people against our oppressors. This is too important for us to be divided."

"I agree with you. Our people should be united."

The door opens as Lazarus sees Yussif and Arnan out.

"I'd better go," Judas says.

"May I speak to you again?"

Judas waves him off.

At the door, Arnan says, "Apologies again for the outburst. If I had known, I wouldn't have—"

"No, Jesus wanted to talk with him. He was glad you came. Shmuel made his choice."

"I want you to know," Yussif says, "that I do not share his indignation. Please."

"I know," Lazarus says. "Good luck on the ride back. It could be awkward."

Chapter 68

KING?

State dinner, Jerusalem banquet hall, evening

Joanna knows her place and determines to remain silent unless directly addressed as she and her philandering husband Chuza dine with King Herod, his wife Herodias, the preternaturally youngish Governor Pontius Pilate and his wife Claudia, and even Cassandra, Chuza's paramour. Again she is struck by how heady an event with such visible celebrities would have seemed to her not that long ago.

The king appears to begrudgingly nibble at the unleavened bread, while the governor seems to indulge himself with it. "Pontius," Herod says, "show some solidarity with me in enjoying the finer things, and stop pretending you enjoy our food."

Pilate scoffs. "I don't know why you hate being Jewish so much. I like this bread."

Joanna reaches for a matzah, and her husband's rolled eyes are not lost on her.

"I do not, however," Pilate adds, "enjoy accommodating these unprecedented crowds."

"Tell me about it," the king says. "I can't believe we made it here without running over someone."

"Not that you would have noticed if we had," Pilate says.

"You do know why there are so many here this year, right?" Herod says. "Lots of times people find excuses for not coming. Their ima is not feeling well, or their horse is about to give birth, or they have rolled an ankle and the journey is too long. But this year …"

"This year what?" Pilate says with a smirk.

"You're telling me you really don't know?"

"I want to hear you say it," the governor says.

Herod glances at his wife. "There's some kind of—miracle worker who—"

"Say his name," Pilate says.

"Jesus of Nazareth," the governor's wife says.

He shoots her a look. "Hades and Styx, Claudia! He was almost there."

"Nazareth," Herod mutters. "No one important or significant has ever come from there."

"The very fact that Claudia and I know his name suggests otherwise."

"Well," the king says, "no one *inherently* important. I admit I am curious about the perception others have of him."

Pilate guffaws. "I would imagine so, seeing as how the words *new king* have reached even my house."

"*What* words?" Herodias says.

"You heard *king* specifically?" Herod says.

"I'm sure it was just a joke," Pilate says. "But what about this issue of the man from Bethany, the one they say he raised from the dead?"

Herod offers a dismissive wave. "I've received assurance from the High Priest that the claims are being investigated.

According to Caiaphas—who is not given to overstatement—if the raising of Lazarus is confirmed, the masses here will rise and you'll be looking at an insurrection on the scale of the Maccabees."

Pilate says, "Didn't you just say he was only a curiosity to you, and before that no one of import? Now you're referencing the Maccabees? What am I looking at here?"

Herod says, "Caiaphas's words. Not mine."

"If Lazarus is all this comes down to," Pilate says, "then you all are woefully unskilled in the art of cunning. Puerile."

"So if I'm childish," the king says, "what would your move be?"

"If you want to delegitimize Jesus by proving that Lazarus is still dead, make sure he's still dead."

"He means kill Lazarus," Herodias tells her husband.

Leave it to Herodias, Joanna thinks, *to state the obvious.*

"I know what he means, dear," Herod says. "I'll pass your idea along, Governor."

"Hold on," Pilate's wife says. "If Jesus did raise Lazarus, and Caiaphas has Lazarus killed, why wouldn't Jesus resurrect him again?"

"Well now," Pilate says, lifting his ornate wine goblet, "that would really be something, wouldn't it?"

Joanna wonders why Jesus raised Lazarus and not his own cousin. She excuses herself and takes her goblet out to a balcony overlooking Jerusalem, alive with the buzz of pilgrims sitting around their little fires.

Presently, the governor's wife joins her. "They come on foot hundreds of miles to an overcrowded city with unsatisfactory lodging options," Claudia says. "Do you believe in anything so much? I wonder what it would be like to have that kind of belief."

Joanna studies the woman. "We Jews believe things."

"What if it cost you something dear? Would you believe then?"

It already has cost Joanna, but she wants to keep the conversation going. "I don't understand," she says.

Pilate's wife seems to shake herself out of whatever dark place her question came from. "I'm so sorry. It's Joanna, right? I'm Claudia."

"I know. Thank you."

"Joanna, I can't imagine how you must have felt in there."

What is she implying? What does she know? "How I felt?"

"Chuza and Cassandra."

"Oh …" Joanna is relieved that's all it is.

"The gall," Claudia says. "Bringing her here under the guise of—what? That you needed a travel companion? Disgusting."

"Well, the truth is, you're picking up on something I've already dealt with. We don't sleep in the same bed anymore."

"Neither do Pontius and I."

"Oh?"

"Nothing scandalous. He says I thrash too much lately."

"Do you?"

"How would I know? I think he's just having trouble sleeping."

Joanna hesitates. "So is he taking Jesus seriously?"

"He's trying not to. Or, better said, he's hoping not to."

"Why not?"

Claudia clearly has something on her mind and seems to be debating whether to say it. "Maybe it's the wine or that I haven't spoken with an intelligent woman in a while, but look, it's no secret Pontius's assignment was as much about his father's influence as his own qualifications. And perhaps some of his actions have been an attempt to compensate for that. Either way, his rebuke from Tiberius will be his last."

"I see."

"I suppose he hopes the tension in the air is about something other than the Nazarene."

"I have a bad feeling about it," Joanna says.

"So," Claudia says, "either we both have poor intuition or something serious is about to happen."

Joanna sips her drink. "What can someone like me ever do? I feel like a prop in their theater of power. Decoration."

"I think we could be more than that." Claudia gestures to the pilgrims. "If we believed in something as much as they do ..."

Chapter 69

MISSING

Lazarus's home, dawn

John wakes to find Thomas's mat empty. "Nathanael!"

Nathanael rolls over on his own cot. "What?"

"Thomas is gone."

They rush downstairs where John finds Mary Magdalene making breakfast. "Where's Jesus?" he asks her.

"He left early with Zee and Matthew. He told Lazarus to stay back and lie low for a while. Said the rest of us should meet him on the Mount of Olives at midday, ready to travel."

"Have you seen anyone else leave the house?"

"No, what is it?"

"Thomas is missing!"

The three of them rush outside, calling for Thomas, only to find him behind the house, slumped against the well, two empty bottles at his feet. "Thomas!" John shouts, but as they approach, he heaves. "Oh," John says. "My brother. I'm sorry."

Nathanael draws a bucket of water. Mary says, "I'll look for a silphium plant."

As Nathanael and John try to get Thomas to drink from the bucket, he rolls over, ghastly pale, and vomits again.

Big James, Zebedee, and Peter come running out of the house, and John realizes they fear the worst. "He's drunk," he says.

"Thank heaven," Zebedee says.

"I wouldn't," Peter says. "He's a wreck."

"I don't want to be here anymore," Thomas slurs.

John shushes him. "You're going to be okay."

"I don't want to follow."

"You don't mean that," John says, holding the bucket to his mouth. "Here, drink this."

"John," Peter says, "don't shove the bucket into his face."

"You do it then."

"Shalom?" a pleasant call comes from the front of the house.

"It's Eden!" Peter says. "They're here."

John goes into panic mode. "Quickly, get him inside. James, help Peter! No one else can see him like this!" Peter, James, and Nathanael pull Thomas up and set his arms over their shoulders. "Take him in through the back. Abba and I will go."

He and Zebedee hurry around to the front where Eden and Salome approach the house with their traveling gear. Much as he tries to act normal, Eden says, "What is it, John? What happened? Where's Peter?"

"Peter's fine. Jesus is fine."

Zebedee hugs his wife, but she says, "Are the boys okay?"

"Everything is fine," Zebedee says. "They will be out shortly. Thomas got sick is all. They're tending to him."

It's clear to John that Eden is having none of this. "Sick?" she says.

Salome also glares at him, and he feels cornered. He sighs. "Thomas is wrestling with questions. Some that Peter struggled with around the time of the feeding of the masses. I'm tempted to say he's handling it worse than Peter did."

Chapter 70

ONE DAY
AT A TIME

Mount of Olives

Matthew grows more curious by the hour. Just when he thought he was beginning to somewhat understand what Jesus is all about, the rabbi speaks more circumspectly. Everything sounds like a parable. But having witnessed the latest miracle, the most spectacular and undeniable of all, his faith is rock solid. Secure. He doesn't know what all this somber death talk is about, but he feels privileged to be invited along with Jesus and Zee now.

From the top of the mount, Jesus points to Bethpage. "You two go into that village and immediately you will find a donkey tied and a colt with her, on which no one has ever sat. Untie them and bring them to me."

Is he serious? Matthew wonders. "You want us to steal livestock?"

"Mm. Borrow."

"What are the terms of the loan?"

"If anyone asks you, 'Why are you untying it?' you'll say this: 'The Lord has need of it.'"

Matthew blinks. "You want to borrow a burro?"

For some reason, this makes even the normally stoic Zee appear to suppress a smile. Jesus laughs. "What?" Matthew says.

"Nothing," Zee says. "Let's go."

As the two set out down the hill toward town, Atticus emerges from the tree line, pulls his hood over his face, and follows from a distance.

Jesus looks to heaven. *We're really doing this, aren't We?*

He turns at footsteps. It's his mother. "You left your bag in your room," she says.

"On purpose. I knew you would know I needed it. This day has been so long in the making."

"Generations," she says.

"And since Joseph is not here to see the moment, I thought it only fitting that you bring it. It represents him, so it's a way all three of us can be together today."

She hands him the bag. "What you said yesterday about the perfume—that she was preparing your body for burial. Do you know how hard that is for a mother to hear?"

"I can't shield you from this anymore, Ima. I'm sorry. It might be better if you stay back with Lazarus. Perhaps that would be the more loving thing for me to have you do."

"One day at a time," she says. "But I want to enter the city with you."

Bethpage

Matthew walks the streets of this tiny Jerusalem suburb, he and Zee scanning everywhere. He sees a horse, an ox, some sheep, vendors—a donkey! "There!" he says, but someone mounts it and rides off. "'On which no one has ever sat,'" he reminds himself.

At last, in a residential neighborhood, he spies a donkey tied to a pole outside an upper middleclass home. Next to it stands a young colt.

"This must be it," Zee says, as they approach and begin untying it from its mother.

As they work, a laborer emerges from the house and starts feeding the chickens, his back to them. He hums as he works. Suddenly he turns, looking startled. "Who are you?"

Matthew feels guilty, exposed, standing there with the colt at the end of a rope.

"You're taking my master's colt?"

Matthew hesitates. "The Lord has need of it," he says, a little too loudly.

"Our master," Zee says.

"Now, hold on," the laborer says. "I don't know what kind of an arrangement you made—"

"Has anyone ever sat on this colt?" Matthew says.

"What?"

"Please," Zee says. "Just answer."

"Uh, no—no one. Born ten weeks ago. But what is this all about?"

"The Lord has need of this," Zee says.

The laborer looks shocked. "Are you followers of the Nazarene who raised Lazarus?"

"Do you know the prophets?" Zee says. "Especially the ones after the exile?"

The laborer nods.

"From Zechariah," Zee says, "'Rejoice greatly, O daughter of Zion. Shout aloud, O daughter of Jerusalem! Behold, your king is coming to you—righteous and having salvation is he, humble and mounted on a donkey, on a colt, the foal of a donkey.'"

"*This* colt?" the laborer says. "Today?"

Zee and Matthew nod and the laborer whispers urgently through his tears, "What are you waiting for?"

As soon as Matthew and Zee are out of site, the laborer mounts his master's horse and gallops full speed the mile to Jerusalem. He skids to a stop before a mass of pilgrims and shouts, "He's coming! He's on his way! Jesus is finally here!" He dismounts and runs up the steps into the temple courts. "Jesus of Nazareth is on his way to Jerusalem! Entering at the eastern gates!"

The crowds erupt as Veronica and Jesse rush to the laborer. "You're certain?" she says.

"His followers assured me. He will enter the city soon."

Jesse says, "I wonder if my brother is with them?"

"Only one way to find out!" she says, and they join the masses rushing past the resplendent columns in waves.

Chapter 71

HOSANNA!

Jerusalem

Joanna and Chuza have been assigned their own carriage, now stuck in the mass of pedestrian traffic running and shouting, pouring past them in the other direction. Joanna finds this strangely thrilling, besides that it offers respite from her having to speak to her husband. How long, she wonders, must she be forced to endure his ironically blatant duplicity?

Of course he knows she's onto him. And by parading his mistress around in public, even in her presence, he's seems to be daring her to speak up, speak out, do anything. It's as if he believes she would never give up her life of privilege, would never embarrass or expose him. If the king himself can dump his wife to marry his brother's wife, who's going to call out one of his top aides for living as he pleases?

"This infernal chaos!" Chuza rants. "Why can no one control these people?" He pokes his head out the window. "Driver! Press forward!"

Does he mean to actually run these people over? As the pilgrims stream by, even pressing up against the carriage, Chuza huffs and curses. From the multitude Joanna hears the name of Jesus. They must know something she doesn't! She has come so close to casting her lot entirely with the man she has come to believe, as do his many followers and apparently all these pilgrims, is the Messiah. Is now the time?

She surreptitiously places a hand on the door, her pulse thundering, her breath coming in gasps. She's going to do it, actually do it. She takes a deep breath and gives her husband a final look. He's clearly oblivious to her, nothing new, focused on the throngs and his own inconvenience. She shoves open the door. "Goodbye, Chuza," she says and leaps out to disappear into the crowd.

Despite the din, she can hear him. "What are you doing, Joanna? Joanna! Come back here! Are you crazy?"

Come back? Are you serious? She doesn't even hesitate, let alone turn. Joanna's grin makes her cheekbones ache as she's swept along.

Yussif hears the commotion and summons his father Arnan to the front door of their home to see what it's all about. Children climb palm trees, cut branches, and toss them down to the crowd. As the hordes rush past, grabbing the palm fronds and waving them, a woman shouts, "Hosanna! Hosanna to the Son of David!" and others join in, roaring the phrase.

"I know her!" Yussif says. "That's Veronica, the woman Jesus healed!"

They rush down the stairs and join the mêlée.

The Mount of Olives

Jesus's mother is overcome with sorrow, knowing what all this portends. The disciples will be here shortly, along with dear friends Tamar, Mary of Magdala, Zebedee, Salome, Eden, Jairus's family, even Barnaby and Shula. Drawing close to her son, they open his rucksack and pull out the fabled box. And here come Zee and Matthew with the colt of a donkey.

Tears welling, Mary puts a hand to Jesus' cheek.

The governor's mansion, Jerusalem
Claudia stands at the railing of her balcony, thrilled at what she's seeing. Pontius joins her, clearly annoyed but also, she senses, fearful. He stalks back inside. She continues to take it all in, her heart filling.

Jerusalem street
Joanna finds a vendor who normally sells the best palm branches to servants who use them to fan their masters. He's being nearly overrun by the crowds eager to buy. Suddenly feeling magnanimous, she wants everyone to have at least one, maybe more. "All of it!" she says, thrusting him a handful of coins. "I'll take the whole supply!"

She gathers up a bound sheaf of palms and quickly unbinds them, handing them to excited Jews in every direction.

Rabbi Shmuel tries to push his way through a crowd that would normally part for a Pharisee. He's resolute, eager to see what Jesus will do or say if indeed he's really coming. The man is risking his life, that's for sure. Shmuel has to give him that. But he's likely to get what he's asking for.

An exquisitely dressed woman laden with a sheaf of palms is handing them out and thrusts one into his face. He accepts it reflexively before dropping it to the ground, disgusted. Celebrate this crazy man? Not a chance.

Residence of the High Priest
Caiaphas peers out a high window, the chants reaching him from the streets. "Hosanna! Hosanna to the Son of David!"

This fool, he thinks, *this blasphemer is playing right into our hands!*

The Mount of Olives

Mother Mary is warmed by the arrival of the disciples, despite the pain she knows is coming. The brothers Jesus nicknamed the Sons of Thunder bring up the rear, virtually carrying the bedraggled Thomas, poor man. He's really been through it, the way Simon Peter has, and the way she must also suffer.

While Zee and Matthew carefully remove the colt's bridle, she opens the box. Some have heard and know the story behind the historic bridle. All fall silent as her son seems to look each of them in the face, one at a time. Mary sees expressions of expectation, pride, uncertainty, joy, fear, indifference, hope. And love.

"The time has come," Jesus tells them. "I must do the will of my Father in heaven. I know you all have a lot of questions, and there will be a time for those. But for now, will you come with me?"

Leave it to Peter to answer for them all. "Lord," he says, "where else would we go? You alone have the words of eternal life."

Mary sees sadness, perhaps finality, in Jesus' smile.

"No matter what happens this week," he says, "no matter what you see or think or feel or do, I want you to know that in this world I have loved you as my own. And I will love you to the end."

Jesus gently slides the ancient bit into the mouth of the colt and lifts the leather reins over its neck. As he mounts the tiny animal, Mary notes the clamor in the distance—cheering, singing, shouting, and shofar blasts. Her beloved son lightly presses his heels into the beast's sides, and despite that it's never been ridden before, it merely steps forward as if somehow knowing its role.

In contrast with the noise below, all Mary hears on the Mount are the colt's gentle steps and the spring breeze. Some of those who love Jesus hold hands as they follow, and all seem filled with anxiety, anticipation, and faith. Mary knows they have no idea what they're getting into, though they are well aware of the danger.

As the Holy City rises majestically on the horizon, she resolves to remember every detail, and just as she did at the birth of this singular man-child, ponder these things in her heart.

Acknowledgments

Thanks to:
My assistant, Sarah Helus
My agent, Alex Field
My editor, Leilani Squires
Carlton Garborg and Michelle Winger at BroadStreet
And my very life, Dianna